CANOES IN WINTER

Beneath the Surface

Bob Guelker

Copyright © 2016 by Bob Guelker

All rights reserved. No part of this publication may be reproduced, distributed, or transmitted in any form or by any means, including photocopying, recording, or other electronic or mechanical methods, without the prior written permission of the publisher, except in the case of brief quotations embodied in critical reviews and certain other noncommercial uses permitted by copyright law. For permission requests, write to the publisher at the address below.

Printed in the United States of America
ISBN 978-0-9977457-0-2

Five Pines Publishing
16910 County 13
Nevis, MN 56467
Cover Art by: Amelia Woltjer
Cover Design by: Eled Cernik

Cataloging-in-Publication data:

Names: Guelker, Bob, author.
Title: Canoes in winter : beneath the surface / Bob Guelker.
Description: Nevis, MN: 5 Pines Publishing, 2016.
Identifiers: ISBN 978-0- 9977457-0- 2 (pbk.) |
978-0- 9977457-1- 9 (e-book)
Subjects: Canoeing--Fiction. | Love stories. | Rodeos--Fiction. | Horses--Fiction. |BISAC FICTION / Romance / Contemporary. |LCSH Post-traumatic stress disorder--Fiction. | Sexual abuse--Fiction. Adultery--Fiction.

Classification: LCC PS3607.U445 C36 2016| DDC 813.6--dc23

DEDICATION

To the children–may you never have to keep adult secrets.

ACKNOWLEDGEMENTS

So many people have influenced this book, it will be impossible to list them all. Most important to me are those who not only walked this journey of writing with me, they often carried me. A special thanks to my son, Todd, and his wife Kara. Your unconditional, unflinching love may be the only thing I know for sure.

Heartfelt thanks for all of your encouragement and support to my fellow Nevis-ites Teresa and Jim, Barb and Dave, "The Gang" and this entire northern Minnesota community—natives, transplants and visitors alike—whose hearts and arms are always wide open.

And a special thank you to: my cover artist and fellow Nevis-ite Amelia Woltjer, who perfectly captured for me the serenity and beauty of the river in winter; Julia Willson, my editor, whose expertise in language and keen eye for story development helped turn me into an actual story teller instead of just another typist; and Julie Anne Eason, who produced this final product, built the book's beautiful website, and coached me through the maze of marketing options. Without you three truly professional and perpetually patient partners in my corner, *Canoes in Winter* could never had made it off my computer hard drive and into the hands of the readers.

CONTENTS

Acknowledgements v

Chapter 1: More Time Than Most Bears 1

Chapter 2: Midwifery 33

Chapter 3: Without Saying Goodbye 47

Chapter 4: Carpets and Curtains 59

Chapter 5: Like the Other Married Women 67

Chapter 6: Sam's Damn Rules 97

Chapter 7: Pop Smiles 113

Chapter 8: A Three-Pack of Condoms 121

Chapter 9: The Fire Ring 135

Chapter 10: Elvis and Roy 167

Chapter 11: Robert 201

Chapter 12: SIDAS WAPBO 211

Chapter 13: Canoed All Night 225

Chapter 14: Please Forgive Me 243

CHAPTER 1

MORE TIME THAN MOST BEARS

Sam Ryan is giving God one hell of an unholy earful. One of his most eloquent speeches, Sam thinks, since landing on Earth 53 years ago, considering he doesn't even believe in God, at least in the form most folks do.

"I would rather that barbarians had sold my grandchildren into slavery, that my underwear model wife (if I had one and if she wore any) had run off with a car full of Jehovah's Witnesses, and that my four-time world championship hunting dog (again, if I had one) had decided to go live with two spinster widows and their seventeen cats and eleven yapper dogs, rather than discover THIS—that someone has beaten me, most assuredly guided by Your not-so-divine intervention to my top-secret, personal morel mushroom Shangri-La!"

Even as a child, Sam couldn't wrap his brain around a God who would banish un-baptized babies from the Amazon to an eternal, hellish limbo. And wouldn't immediately strike down those followers who rape, pillage, and kill in His name. And wouldn't intervene when a little kid was gettin' it up the you-know-what.

"And another thing, God!" Sam admonishes, thrusting his middle finger to the heavens, "I'd rather have a well-rotted mouse fall out of my drinking faucet and my septic tank cave in, my pickup truck blow its engine, or fall out of my deer stand thirteen feet up a tree and land on the business end of an arrow all in one day. So take that!"

He sucks in a breath. "You got nothin' better to do up there than mess with me?"

Sam furrows his brow into a frown and shakes his head in disgust. He is certain that the interloper who kidnapped his precious fungi is one of those hairy, patchouli-doused hippies from the organic store in Park Rapids. His neighbor, Maureen, had mentioned that the tall guy from the organic store had put the word out he'd take all the fresh morels he could get and pay $20 a pound cash (then probably turn around and sell them for $50). The guy who's got a staple in one eyebrow, several rings and pins in both ears, and dreadlocks, and who in defiance of the health inspector never wears shoes or a hairnet in the store.

That offer the year before had incited greed, thievery, trespassing, noise, and littering all over the northern Minnesota hills that Sam calls home, and where he wanders as freely and unobtrusively as the breeze, deer, butterflies, and hummingbirds.

Anyone around Stone Creek who knows of, or cares even a whit about, morel mushrooms knows Sam Ryan is the area's preeminent expert on not just morel mushrooms but most subjects of the natural world. He doesn't fit the ungroomed "Jackpine Savage" look one might expect from a guy who jokes that he spends more time in the woods than most bears do. Nor does he resemble in any fashion the serious, self-absorbed academic who dresses in tweed and rubber boots, wears a necklace of binoculars, and smokes a long, curved pipe.

Sam's a little bit better than average-looking with his dark hair and short beard and green eyes, and is a lot more social than your typical middle-aged man living alone in the woods. He stands 5'11" and has slightly broader shoulders than most of his contemporaries. Not too much of a pot belly yet, although he's recently begun that journey from a 34-inch waist to 36-inch. Sam blames that on his 205 pounds' "natural shifting", even though he eats fairly well (for a bachelor who's unattached and intends to stay that way) and is more active than an average fifty-three-year-old guy.

The year before, during the hippie store-induced, greed-driven craze, amateur morel hunters had attempted to ply Sam with alcohol so he'd give up his spots. Three women offered Sam the chance to blindfold them and tie them up, and they wouldn't even have to leave his house. Others followed his truck around the hills and attempted to track him through the woods, but he gave them the slip by circling back and speeding away to one of his other secret mushroom lairs.

Yes, much of the hills is public land, and anyone is legally entitled to pick morels from it. But one particular morel mushroom larcenist—although technically picking them on a public, forty-acre, county-owned plot—must have trespassed, because the area is landlocked, surrounded by private lands. Sam can't imagine that any of his neighbors invited a hairy, smelly hippie to clomp through their woods barefoot.

He gives away at least five times more morel mushrooms than he keeps for himself. But he has always guarded his best spots like a foreign spy conceals his identity. It's not that Sam's being hoggish about morels. There are enough for everybody. That is, if they want to take the time and effort to find the better spots.

The thing is, Sam simply likes to be undistracted in nature, whether gathering mushrooms or berries, hunting, tapping maple trees for sap, cutting firewood, canoeing, walking, skiing, or cruising trails in his electric golf cart. Noise belongs in the city, the Stone Creek school lunchroom, and even his school bus, but absolutely not in Sam's woods or on the Fox River.

God forbid an army of morel pickers should form tie-dyed ranks strung out at arm's length like cops looking for a murder weapon—their bandana-adorned dogs barking and grubby kids whining—and march through his woods wearing headphones with their cell phones ringing. That's exactly what Sam saw last year in one of his public spots. He'd wanted to puke.

With Sam's Zen-like focus, uncanny knowledge of the woods, and rabid determination, it's like child's play for him to follow the alien's progress through the best picking he would've had in six years. The morel stalks left from the invasion, clusters of tan circles tight to the ground, half an inch to just over an inch in diameter, glow like neon signs in Sam's unerring scan of the woods floor. Dead, upturned leaves where the thief's toes had dug depressions into the ground are as obvious as mortar craters in a World War I battlefield.

Sam feels the soil between his fingers and smells it like a criminal investigator. Because the upturned soil hasn't begun to dry, he guesses the thief is less than half an hour ahead of him and is traveling slowly. It takes a while to slice off that many morels; he must have hundreds. He ignores the scant few that the son of a bitch had missed—obviously getting sloppy or tired from carrying such a heavy bag, or maybe just bored—and remains hot on the trail, hunched over like a cave man, his mind focused on his target like a laser-guided missile.

Suddenly, he spies the only thing in the woods that could possibly throw him off his mission. It's an immense deer antler that had been shed in a gooseberry thicket not two steps to his left. It was bleached white by the winter elements, so now it practically glows. Despite the fact that he's been tracking a thief, Sam should have noticed it from a hundred feet away.

He instantly recognizes the antler as the right one from an immense buck he'd seen only eight yards from his bow stand last autumn. A buck whose ribs he could have easily parted with an arrow. A buck he'd decided to spare because he cared nothing about trophy kills, and whose steaks would've been too tough and gamey to fill the freezer. The antler has five regular points plus an extra tine dropping from the main beam, about halfway between the tip and the base. He kneels down and runs his fingers over the cool smoothness of the huge antler.

Four decades of spending more time in the woods than most bears has taught Sam that the antler's counterpart will undoubtedly be nearby. A big buck's first antler will drop on its own. Then, with the sensation of imbalance on its skull (especially one of this proportion), the buck would purposely knock off the second antler on a tree or some brush, or even use the ground, often within a few yards.

Sometimes the shed antlers would be lying together touching, as if placed upon a coffee table, posed with a candle in their midst and surrounded by fresh balsam boughs.

Sam holds his ground and scans three hundred sixty degrees. There's hardly any cover in the woods this time of the year. No second antler is to be seen. Having forgotten about his morels and their thief, he takes note of the gooseberry tangle's location and begins circling, his counter-clockwise path spiraling further and further away. His search widens by fifty feet on each pass.

After fifteen minutes of fruitless searching, Sam's far from the gooseberry tangle. He has lost track and wandered to just sixty yards from where the forest ends at the rim of the old abandoned county gravel pit, over one hundred yards from where he'd found the antler.

Sam's perplexed and frustrated. Adding two and two together, he concludes that the thief—and the thief's God—has ruined his day, his spring, maybe even his entire life! The hairy hippie has assuredly pilfered the other shed antler (undoubtedly to sell), which had obviously been left for Sam right where the buck knew he'd find them both during morel season.

Sam retraces his steps back to where he'd found the antler and resumes tracking the thief. He sniffs the air in short, rapid inhalations, his head tilted back a little and eyes squinted, like a mother bear checking for unseen danger to her cubs. Except Sam is checking for the powerfully annoying stench of patchouli. He knows that shit lingers, sometimes for hours after a human air freshener's left the township.

For an expert woodsman like Sam, the trail is ridiculously easy to follow. He'd determined that the thief was a single barefoot interloper. At first, he mistook the footprints for a bear's (well, that's his secret). But the larcenist's trail is in fact leading toward the abandoned county gravel pit, close to where Sam had ceased his search for the other antler.

The closer he moves toward the gravel pit, the more morels he finds that the thief has left behind. The pilferer even stepped on half a dozen and squished them, like when Sam was a little kid and he'd run through the cow yard, not caring where his feet landed.

Sam's on a sacred mission and doesn't bother to pick any more mushrooms. It pains him to leave them behind, their caps reaching skyward as if begging to be harvested. To walk past the morels, ignoring their pleas to go home with only him is like when the prettiest cheerleader in high school he'd lusted over for years to no avail asked him for a ride home after practice, and he was already late for cleaning the barn.

First things first, though. He needs to find the thief and demand to know how the hell he got in here.

Thirty yards from the pit, the thief had quit picking altogether. His tracks—depressed leaves and last year's grass bent over, which would have been indiscernible to anyone but Sam or a pack of bloodhounds—meander to the right toward Sam's woods trail. Within forty feet of himself, he can see at least fifty morels, all freshly new and prime, the stems still light tan and half the diameter of the cap, the caps' ridges outlining the indentations tight and firm and still that coveted youngish gray-brown hue. Not a one in sight has even hinted it is thinking about becoming the overripe spongy dark umber that in only a few days will make them unpalatable and left in the woods.

There has to be half a grocery bag full here in Sam's sight, and only God knows how many more there are just out of sight.

Sam lets out a quiet sigh. He has been defeated, and by a rank (no pun intended) amateur. He decides to pick what is left behind, knowing they won't taste nearly as good and that it'll be a drudgery putting them up to dry. They don't even really feel like *his* morel mushrooms. It's like the neighbors giving him a deer they had gut-shot and didn't have a tag for. Tainted leftovers, giveaways unappreciated by some thoughtless amateur, who as Sam stands and bemoans this fate, is no doubt at that very moment calling a horde of other hippies, giving them and their dogs and kids in headphones directions to his previously virgin stash.

Sam feels like he placed second in a dog fight—hiding under the porch, licking his wounds, whimpering. He picks a joyless dozen morels and is about to crawl on his hands and knees to the next cluster a couple yards away, when he hears muffled sounds coming from the gravel pit. It sounds like a horse grunting then violently shaking itself from head to tail.

His first thought is *That fucker picked so damn many of my friggin' morels, he needs a goddamn horse to drag 'em all out...*

Ready to charge and pounce if need be, Sam tilts his head back and again sniffs the air. He doesn't smell the thief or his horse, but he knows the son of a bitch is just out of sight in the bottom of the gravel pit. And he's about to be busted by the land's most dedicated servant. Some things are sacred, in a non-sectarian manner, Sam assures himself. But just in case this has to turn into fisticuffs,

Sam will gladly plant a fist square into the thief's nose in the name of the morels, not some imaginary god.

Sam doesn't move a muscle after he hears the horse. He knows two things for certain about horses. (Karen, his second wife, had horses, and they too often seemed to enjoy unceremoniously depositing him in the dirt.) Because horses are several notches down on the food chain, Sam's well aware that they're unbelievably adept at detecting the most frightening creatures on Earth, such as a doe calmly nibbling browse while her fawn suckles.

Also, when a horse has stumbled into such a heart-stopping scene, if a person's stupid enough to be atop said horse in the first place, they might as well pull the rip cord of their parachute, because they're about to be launched. If they aren't atop the damn horse, but instead somewhere within a stone's throw of the hairy dynamite keg, chances are ninety-nine percent that the insane beast will run around nuts and eventually trample the person. Or at least drag the tree it's tied to, which has now been uprooted, right over top of them, shredding their clothes and relieving them of valuable skin.

Sam scans the woods between himself and the edge of the gravel pit to locate a route by which he can approach the rim without being heard or seen. He wants to get a better look before deciding his next move. Stooping over as far as he can and bending at the knees like a soldier on patrol behind enemy lines, he places each foot on the forest floor as if on egg shells, testing the twigs underneath that might betray him.

Fifteen yards from the rim, Sam stoops even lower to set the antler and the plastic bag with his pitiful dearth of mushrooms onto the ground. But first he inspects the resting place like a person would inspect a bowl of chicken noodle soup at a roadside greasy spoon for a gnat or a hair or a tiny chunk of meat. He allows the antler's weight to settle onto the forest floor an ounce at a time, like it's a bomb that will explode if the mercury switch is jostled off-kilter a hair's width. The bag rustles and the horse snorts one semi-serious blow.

Seven yards from the rim, Sam still can't see into the bottom of the gravel pit without standing up. He knows from having driven past the pit dozens of times, in his golf cart or on his tractor, that the embankment is near-vertical where he's approaching it.

He worries that the horse might already have steadied its wide-eyed and suspicious gaze in his direction. A blue jay flies overhead and screams. Sam has often heard the noisy birds warn their flockmates about other animals or his presence. If the horse understands blue jay talk, Sam's busted. He listens, but there's only silence beyond the rim's edge.

Sam sinks to his knees and leans forward on all fours. At the first careful shuffle with his right knee, he feels something cool and moist squish beneath it, sincerely hoping it isn't deer shit. He lifts his knee, assuming the posture of a dog anointing a fire hydrant, and looks back. A morel. He hadn't noticed it, was too busy looking for twigs that could betray him. More morels. A cluster of four beauties squarely under his torso. He scans ahead along his intended path, where many more morels lie. Avoiding them all will be impossible. He'll pick them best he can, breaking them off with his fingers, and place them into his baseball hat.

The horse shakes again and blows half-heartedly. Sam knows enough about horses to determine that the beast is relaxed and probably has its eyes only half open.

"Stupid horse," Sam mutters under his breath. Doesn't even realize there's an alien of hideous proportions that could haunt the horse with ghastly nightmares for the rest of its hay-eating, shit-steaming life, creeping up on it less than a hundred feet away.

Three yards from the rim, Sam begins a slow rise up to his knees. He can see the horse's back now, its hair matted in a square from a saddle blanket. Its head hangs relaxed, and is still out of Sam's sight. The horse has a long line hooked to its halter, and is tied to a spindly volunteer jack pine. The beast could easily pull it out by its roots if, say, a chickadee flew by or a painted turtle crawled past and startled it awake to run blind and crazy for its life.

Sam returns to all fours, scrunching his body lower yet, and crawls two more yards. Now he's in plain sight of the horse, who's still oblivious. He can't see the morel thief, who must be somewhere between him and the horse, probably at the base of the steep slope. He needs to get all the way to the edge and peer over it to get a look at his nemesis.

So he drops to his belly. It's only another yard. A murder of a dozen crows flies overhead, harassing a red-tailed hawk at the top of their raspy voices. His rustling hidden by the din, Sam slithers like a salamander on hot tar the last three feet to the edge of the rim.

Slowly, painfully, imperceptibly to even a deer that might be looking his way, Sam rises to his elbows and extends his neck to peer over the edge. Into his view, where the slope begins to rise out of the flat gravel pit bottom, appear a saddle and a saddle blanket tossed over a rock. A bridle is looped over the saddle horn. Next to the saddle are two large cloth bags that appear to be pillowcases, stuffed full and lumpy and tied with twine.

"Son of a bitch!" Sam mutters under his breath.

He rises up another couple inches. In front of the saddle, a clothes heap sits on a rock the size of a bushel basket. Sam can make out a shirt and blue jeans, a sock on the ground, and a few other articles of clothing he can't identify. Well-polished brown riding boots stand next to each other beside the rock.

The naked, hairy hippie has to be on the edge of the slope, probably sound asleep in the warm sunlight, sapped of energy by his arduous larceny (and who knows whatever he smoked). Sam sniffs the air again and detects the pungent odor of horse. And something else. Something sweet and perfumey that isn't patchouli.

Not that anything about Sam needs to see a hairy naked man-hippie. He thinks for a moment he might just back away so he doesn't have to blot that hideous picture out of his mind. Still, he props his front half another couple inches off the ground.

Coming slowly into view at the bottom of the slope: toes, feet, and bare legs. But they aren't hairy, as he expected.

Sam does a double take and shakes his head in surprise and disbelief.

Toenails painted bright red.

Sam raises himself further.

It *is* a woman! And buck naked!

Yes, definitely a female. She has all the right parts in all the right places (from what he can remember). A long, blonde ponytail flowing out the back of a baseball hat. No tan lines. Her legs slightly splayed apart. Sunbathing?

Oh my, God, Sam whispers to himself as he gazes skyward with his hands folded in prayer. *I think I owe You an apology...*

He drops flat onto the ground and she disappears from view. But the horse looks up and fixes its pea-brained gaze on Sam's exact location. He holds his breath and avoids eye contact with the beast.

It's been almost five years since Sam has seen a naked woman, so naturally he's curious about whether they've changed much.

He hears a rustling down on the blanket. The horse, bending its neck, switches its gaze to where the sound is coming from, then lets its head droop back into oblivious relaxation. Sam props himself up onto his elbows again. The sunbather has turned over onto her front side. She has a dimple at the top of each butt cheek—each really nice and firm butt cheek.

But who the hell is she? Sam wonders. Not his neighbor Maureen—she's blonde but with medium-length hair. And stocky. Not Joan, Maureen's life partner—she has dark hair and is built like Maureen.

His curiosity satisfied, Sam desires a graceful and clandestine exit from this predicament. First of all, he wants to avoid embarrassing the woman. How would he explain creeping up on her like that, like a common pervert? Or is his primary concern being branded as a Peeping Tom, which is not on his life's list of accomplishments, even if the temptation is less than seventy-five feet away and innocently oblivious?" And naked. And put together correctly, possibly even remarkably, at least from what he's seen so far.

But it's not his fault he stumbled upon her like that. He was just minding his own business, picking morel mushrooms like he had for six springs. It's a free world, county land where anyone can go.

Wait, no they can't! She probably trespassed to get to the state land. She needs to be sternly and in no uncertain terms advised of her crime.

Sam slumps his forehead onto his folded arms and considers his only option. He needs to retreat far back into the woods. He doesn't think it would be possible to slither backward as quietly. Plus, the stupid horse probably has his number and is biding its time for maximum dramatic effect. Back up on his elbows, he takes another look. *Yup, a naked woman.*

For a clean getaway, Sam will have to retreat all the way back to where the skid trail begins, then proceed down his woods trail toward the gravel pit while making a whole lot of racket—knocking over little, dead trees and whistling loudly like an idiot—approaching the gravel pit in a zig-zag path, giving her a chance to get dressed as if no one on Earth were the wiser about her nude sunbathing and his accidentally discovering her…and taking a second look.

He would go to all that trouble to save her obvious embarrassment only because he absolutely needs to find out who the hell stole his precious morel mushrooms. Then he'll try to make a deal with her so she won't blab his favorite hot spot to others all over the county.

All sorts of bribes roll through his brain like a tsunami flooding a tropical island. If it takes several cases of homemade wild grape wine and what's left of his venison sausage, so be it. If he has to toss in six months of fresh eggs, she's got 'em. Hell, she can have the damn chickens, and he'll pay for the feed and clean the coop! If he has to buy her morels at $20 a pound to get her to keep quiet, he'll sell his canoe to cover it. If she wants retail for them ($50), there goes the little Ford tractor.

Sam screws his body to the right into a tight arc, his face two inches from the grass. Strangely, the grass straw six inches in front of him begins to move like it's parting. Something alive is on the ground and moving toward him. He freezes and considers the possibilities—a frog or toad shuffling along, a wayward mouse or mole, a striped gopher—nothing to worry about. He congratulates himself for being so damn stealthy that he'd snuck up on whatever wild animal it is. He sees more movement. It's hard for Sam to focus his five-decades-old eyes on anything that close to him, just six inches away.

Into slow focus appears a goddamn snake, as big around as the handle of a baseball bat! It raises its head silently, slowly, as if it's taking aim at the bridge of Sam's nose. It looks like a cobra, its head flattened wide, and its tongue flicking in and out. It sways menacingly.

To say that Sam has never really cared for snakes, even those as harmless as this hognose, would be like saying it doesn't really matter to a colony of paper wasps if you smack a broom into their nest.

He'd touched only one snake in his entire fifty-three years. A garter snake, as harmless to humans as any newborn kitten, had gotten into his frog bait bucket when he'd taken his kids fishing for smallmouth bass on the river bank near his childhood home. In retrospect, he suspected that his son Matt had become bored with fishing, found the snake, and put it into the frog bucket for safekeeping.

When Sam had opened the lid and absently felt around for a frog to bait his hook, but got a handful of snake instead, he fainted dead away. His kids, Matt (age 3) and Ellen (age 7), had had to splash river water in his face to wake him up.

The snake hisses.

"AAAIIIEEE!!" Sam screams like a woman, so hard that his voice cracks.

He leaps to his feet, too paralyzed to step back. Thankfully, the snake slides down a hole in the ground between Sam's feet rather than up his pant leg.

The woman, naked except for a baseball hat, also leaps to her feet and faces Sam. Their eyes meet. Even scared shitless, Sam's looking a lot of other places, too, and she catches him eyeing her up and down. He was correct—everything's right where he remembered and, in what most men would agree, excellent proportions. Her eyes big as saucers and mouth agape, she snatches the blanket from the ground and covers herself.

The horse rears up on its hind legs and squeals like a pack of wolves is at its throat, flanks, tail, and underbelly all at once. The woman's attention shifts spastically back and forth, from wide-eyed Sam to the frantic horse, as she fumbles with the blanket to wrap it around her like a giant bath towel.

The tree that the horse is tied to tips against the weight of the unhinged beast. Half its roots suddenly become exposed in the loose sand. The horse lunges one more time and falls over backward, grunting, with all four hooves flailing in the air, and the spindly tree is pulled out by the roots. The horse bolts with the jack pine twenty feet behind it, in hot pursuit (or so the horse believes).

The woman looks at Sam again, then over her shoulder at the runaway horse, unsure which problem to address first.

"Sparky!" she screams. "Whoa! It's alright. Whoa, girl!"

To Sam's surprise, the horse—which Sam figured nobody would ever see again, at least not in this county—stops and looks back at the woman, immediately reaching its head down for a clump of spring-fresh, green grass.

The woman turns her attention back to Sam, who's still frozen in his tracks, speechless with his mouth half open like he had just opened the bathroom door and his grandma was sitting there with her underwear around her ankles.

He moves his lips, trying to find an apology behind them when suddenly, at the precipice of the gravel pit rim, a rock the size of a medicine ball dislodges itself from right under Sam. It instantly rolls down the steep bank, hell-bent for the woman fifty feet away, and quickly gathering speed.

She dodges to her right. The boulder hits a smaller rock and deflects, changing course. As if possessed by a demon, the big rock copies her dodge to the side. It gains more speed on its new collision course for the woman. She hops to the left a yard. The rock somehow follows her. She has about a second and a half to get out of the way. She rips off her blanket and lets it fly behind her, stooping forward and waiting for the last moment to dive away and save herself.

Things are happening pretty fast, but this is a moment Sam hopes will become frozen in his brain forever—as long as she doesn't get hurt. After all, a pretty woman wearing only a baseball hat is hunched over only 50 feet away, swaying back and forth, like a wrestler awaiting an opponent's lunge.

But he doesn't get to enjoy her naked athleticism for long. Suddenly, the ground disappears under him. Without the boulder as support, the precipice gives way. In an instant, Sam flips helplessly down the embankment head over heels, following the boulder, with the naked woman in his path.

The big rock glances off an embedded rock five feet in front of her, taking a sharp left and rolling harmlessly toward the gravel pit floor. Sam's head hits the embedded rock, then he flips one last time and lands on his heels, dazed. His knees buckle and he rolls onto his side, right into the woman's naked legs. She can't get out of the way, and falls forward on top of him.

She smells wonderful and feels warm. Even in his delirium, Sam realizes that something about her is vaguely familiar.

She scrambles to her knees and backpedals toward the blanket that had landed on the ground behind her. She covers herself as best she can while shuffling backward, one arm and hand above, the other hand down there. Their eyes meet again. Hers wide in horror, his half-conscious slits filled with sand and tears.

As she reaches back for the blanket, they blurt out simultaneously, "It's you!"

The nude sunbathing morel thief is Sally Hunter, the new receptionist at the insurance office in Park Rapids where Sam bought his homeowner and truck policies.

There are so many places Sam could be looking (and saving in the un-mushy part of his brain) for the next few seconds. He's wondering what else of Sally's feminine charm might be revealed when she bends to pick up the blanket.

But a trickle of gravel sliding down the embankment onto him catches his attention. He fears another rock has given way to gravity, and he is about to get a second lump on his skull. But he is helpless as a freshly-hatched baby robin. No rock coming at him. Just something about four feet long, olive green, with the diameter of a baseball bat.

"Oh shit…" Sam mumbles.

His arms and legs go dead and his brain loses its blood supply, thankfully before the snake rolls into him.

When Sam comes to, Sally's dressed, cuddling the snake and talking to it like it's her brand new puppy. She bends down to show him the snake, which is coiled loosely in her hands. And he's out again like a street light shot by a BB gun.

When Sam awakens for the second time, Sally's kneeling over him, carefully brushing the sand and gravel off his face while inspecting the lump on the top of his head. The horse, apparently satisfied that Sam has been rendered harmless, has pulled the jack pine back to her master and is curiously sniffing Sam's shoes.

With a grin, Sally says, "I'll give you a 9.8. Would've been a 10 if you'd nailed the landin.'"

Sam sits up and feels the top of his head, where he is already sporting the customary goose egg. He inspects his fingers. Not surprisingly, there's fresh blood on them. He feels dampness on his lower back and quickly reaches around to feel it. It isn't blood after all. His plastic bottle of wild grape wine had broken open during his ungraceful trip down the embankment. The purple trickle of 14% alcohol is heading for his ass crack. He arches his shoulders back and lets the pack slide off.

"Shit," Sam mumbles. He points up to the rim where he'd just made his grand entrance. In his best Pee-wee Herman imitation, he says, "I meant to do that!"

Sally seems preoccupied, looking closely at Sam's head wound. "Yeah, and I'm Miss Yvonne. You're gonna need a couple of stitches, maybe three."

She pulls a wad of tissue from her shirt pocket and carefully presses it against the wound. "From work and your address, I knew you lived out in this part of the county somewhere, but didn't put two and two together that you're my sister's neighbor. She's been *strongly* suggestin' there was a guy in her neighborhood I should meet. But I don't think she planned on us meetin' quite like this."

"How'd you do in Verndale?" Sam asks.

"You remember I told you about that race? Ya, Sparky here and I cashed. I didn't run Dakota, my faster horse. She got cut up on a fence." She points to Sparky, who's resumed dragging the jack pine behind herself, from one clump of grass to the next. "Sparky's not really a gamer, but she's a good girl.

"And yes—the wine worked! Thanks for bringin' it. It was wonderful, and…thanks for askin' about the race. I can't believe you remembered."

Sam replies, "It was only three weeks ago. I'm not *that* old. Might be a little clumsy though. Sorry 'bout that."

If Sally's angry or embarrassed about him catching her wearing only a hat, she isn't letting on.

He reaches up and takes over applying pressure on the knot. "You did a good job on the morels. I just wanted to find out who got into my hot spot. And there you were, you know…sunbathin.'"

"You aren't gonna believe this, I'm sure," she says, "but I've never done anything like that before, except in a tannin' booth. It was my new boots. Had to take 'em off before my walk, not quite broken in. And the warm ground felt so good on my feet. Then when I decided to take a nap…aaah, the warmth…I wanted it all over me. So peaceful out here. Seemed like a good idea at the time."

Sam smiles. "I think it was a wonderful idea, even if it cost me a gallon of blood and a patch of my scalp the size of Delaware—plus a sizable slice of my pride."

"You aren't gonna believe this either," Sally says with a grin. "I still have that second bottle of wine you gave me, right here in the saddle bag. But I forgot to bring a corkscrew."

"Well, I never go anywhere without one," Sam confesses. "One time I had two cases of wine with me on a trip to the cities and my truck broke down. No corkscrew. Lesson learned." He reaches for his pack.

They sit side by side on the blanket. He offers Sally the first sip. She drinks and sighs, then wipes her lips with the back of her hand.

"Whew, who ya don't meet when you're sunbathing after picking a boat load of morels, AND he has a corkscrew with?"

"*My* morels," he corrects with a wink.

"Hey, Maureen said her neighbor wasn't gonna be back for a couple more weeks," Sally offers in defense. "She told me about her neighbor picking morels somewhere back here and swore me to secrecy if I found any. Hope you don't mind."

"No, I had no idea how fun and *interesting* sharin' my morels could be. So Maureen's your sister, huh? Funny, I got a similar tip from Maureen about a young lady I should meet."

They pass the bottle back and forth again and shake their heads at the coincidence.

"I guess it must be since about the time you went out west that I've been comin' out to Joan and Maureen's on weekends, stayin' with 'em," Sally says. "I load my two horses. Leave home Friday before my husband gets home from his lumberyard job in Grand Forks. Then I go back during the week, because his dad lives with us. Pop's a sweetheart."

"Yeah," Sam agrees. "I met him at Maureen's. I really like Pop. We hit it right off. Come to think of it, he told me he had someone I should meet. Whole lotta matchmakers around here."

Sam had taken an immediate shine to Sally the first time he paid his bill about three weeks before. What red-blooded man wouldn't be attracted to her? She was young, pretty, and outgoing. Her personality reminded him a little of his own. (Sam could also talk to anybody like they were an old friend; he'd been told a hundred times that he should've been a salesman, a therapist, or a priest.)

Of course, it occurred to him that she was very young, probably in her mid-thirties (but not quite young enough to be his daughter), which would make her fair game if he was so inclined (and she was, too). Even if she were attracted to older men for more than fatherly advice and fixing things around the house, she undoubtedly already had one such geezer back in the barn. And she undoubtedly adored the old fogey, who probably didn't realize he was the luckiest old asshole on Earth, maybe even in the whole universe.

It was out of the question, whatever her taste in men, that someone as young and pretty and personable as her wouldn't already be attached. Besides, Sam had no plans to be anything but a casual and harmless friend to any woman ever again. But when he encountered a really attractive woman like Sally, it was still fun to take a trip down Walter Mitty Lane.

How could anyone not notice?, Sam thought that day in the insurance office. An attractive Nordic look about her, a tick or two taller than average (maybe 5'8"), trim just right, curves in the right places, eyes blue like a clear midday sky. Blonde—maybe tinted a bit, but who cares? A head-turner for sure. He definitely remembered her most alluring feature: that smile, beautiful white teeth and full lips…easy, radiant, and wholeheartedly sincere.

Sam had seen that memorable smile three times before today (yes, he'd counted), and he remembered every beautiful millimeter of it. The day before he was planning to drive to Boise for his grandson's birth, he'd stopped in to pay his car insurance. Sally had been a pleasant surprise behind the reception desk.

Her blonde hair had hung between her shoulder blades, a beautiful contrast with her black pantsuit. She'd been sniffling from a cold. Sitting across from her while writing out a check, Sam had teased that his homemade wild grape wine was good for anything that ails a person.

Sally, dabbing at her nose with a tissue, smiled. "I'll try anything once, maybe even twice," she joked.

"I'll bring you two bottles then," Sam promised, wondering if she believed him.

He'd left the insurance agency feeling certain she thought it was annoying that some old fart was so senile, he was flirting with the likes of her. Maybe he was. Maybe he wasn't. Sam wasn't sure what his intentions were. But there was something about Sally that seemed more than just another pretty, friendly face.

And that afternoon, she smiled even bigger and brighter when he returned to the office with two bottles of wine in a plastic grocery bag (smile number two).

"Could be a long cold," Sam said. "One bottle might not be enough to get you through." He set the bag on her desk and the bottles clinked lightly.

Sally's hands reached into the bag. "I didn't...I didn't really expect...You made a special trip back to town for this, didn't you?"

Sam wondered if he had indeed overstepped his bounds. She covered her mouth with a hand. Her eyes were wide and she shook her head in disbelief, her blonde hair dancing behind her shoulders. And out it came again, that gorgeous smile (number three).

"Naw," Sam lied. "Forgot a couple of things for my trip. Gettin' old, you know..."

Over the previous five years, if a woman had seemed interested in Sam in any way, shape, or form, he'd toss out something self-deprecating to make certain she stayed at bay. It had become habit. How stupid, he thought. Sally was just being nice. He needn't have fended her off with the "getting old" line.

"Just get well soon," he replied. "And let me know if you like it, okay, when I get back. Gonna be gone for a month or so."

I'm the worst dirty old man in the world, Sam thought. *Who the hell else on this planet would drive forty-five miles round trip just to see the smile of a pretty woman who was two-thirds his age?*

"I hope this stuff is miraculous," Sally said as she glanced down into the paper bag.

He stopped and looked back.

She pointed to a framed photo on her desk. "I've got a barrel race this weekend in Verndale."

She turned the photo around so Sam could see it. Sally on a horse, rounding a barrel, the horse low and digging, its torso bent, dirt flying. Sally was leaning so far forward her face almost touching the horse's mane, her ponytail flowing in a golden arc from under her black cowgirl hat.

"It'll work," Sam guaranteed with a small smile, as he turned again to leave.

Karen used to ride like that, he thought.

All these eager matchmakers and not a word about a husband in the picture, not from Maureen or Pop. Yes, Sam had glanced at Sally's left hand the day he'd brought her the wine. There had been no wedding ring. There is no ring today, either.

Sam thinks *Here we go again* and *It's time to run like hell*. Except, he doesn't even know if he can walk. He has his rules about married women.

Rule Number One: Don't talk about the problems with your schmuck of a husband to me. I'm not one of your girlfriends. We must just be buddies, even if you're screwin' me behind his back. I'm outta here unless you agree never to talk about Dipshit ever again. It must be kept platonic and with no expectations even if sex is involved.

Rule Number Two: If the married woman I'm screwin' asks me to do anything husbandly with her or for her, we're done. Period.

That one gets tricky because of the sex, and Sam knows getting slapped or even kicked in the nuts is the likely outcome.

Rule Number Three: Don't bother threatening to tell your husband about us; I've already got him on speed dial.

This rule is a safety net, like wearing two parachutes when you jump out of an airplane. Sam had to threaten to invoke Rule Number Three once (admittedly a bluff) but never actually ratted out anyone's wife.

He'd postulated the rules while drunk at his campfire one night, after the first year he moved to his house outside Stone Creek, when a married woman had threatened to tell her husband about him if Sam didn't keep screwing her. He made the first two rules for future reference, and skipped right to number three with that woman. Thank God it worked.

In fact, Sam's been so careful about which women he keeps company with since that married woman nearly six years ago, he's never had to consider dusting off the rules…until Sally.

"It's a long story," Sally confides. She instinctively brushes a small piece of hair that had escaped from her ponytail and tucks it behind her ear.

"Aren't they all?" Sam rolls his eyes. "I got a couple of stories myself…"

"I don't want to bore you with the details…" she replies, "lots of stuff goin' on with me and my husband. Not good, but we'll work it out. I'm glad I ran into you today. Actually, you ran into me, right? It's nice to put a face on the half-Renaissance Man and half-Jackpine Savage that Joan and Maureen have described. So, how many babies have you delivered?"

"Just three," Sam answers with a shrug, as if it happened all the time. "That reminds me, I need to get another O.B. kit from your sister. Used the last one on my grandson in Boise a couple weeks ago."

She laughs. "You're serious, aren't you?"

"Hey, it's my own fault. Years ago as a firefighter and emergency medical technician, I really wanted to help deliver a baby. I guess I forgot to take that wish back. It took a while, but I've made three deliveries in a little over two years. Two girls and a boy. I'm on a roll. Trust me, I'm not goin' anywhere there might be a pregnant woman, at least not without an O.B. kit."

"What do you charge?" Sally asks playfully. "If you're cheaper than Maureen, Bill and I should have you deliver ours!"

Of course Sam doesn't know anything about the Hunters' situation, but it's common knowledge that a baby never fixes any marriage that can't be fixed otherwise. Although sometimes a couple can be miserable with each other and go on forever "for the sake of the kids", who can tell at a very early age (even three or four) that their folks ain't the Cleavers.

Nudging Sam from his reverie, she asks, "Are we closer to Joan and Maureen's than to your house?"

"Yep, their place is closer."

"How about you ride back with me then. We'll get Maureen to look at your noggin. Sparky here really is a good girl. She won't mind you ridin' behind me."

She notices Sam closing his eyes for a second when she mentions her horse's name.

"What is it? You don't wanna ride?"

Sam lies, "No. It's nothing. Just rememberin' the last time I got my head stitched up. Novocain doesn't work on a scalp."

He hasn't brought along a jacket. Neither had Sally. The sun has made its way behind the treetops and they are in the shade, down in the bottom of the gravel pit. The spring air is cooling quickly and sinking.

Sam suddenly realizes how tired he is, still recuperating from Boise and the long drive home. "Yeah, I'll ride with you. Thanks."

"Can you shimmy up on that big rock?" Sally points to a flat-topped boulder a couple feet high.

He scrambles up onto the rock and watches Sally expertly saddle Sparky and slip the bridle on. Her left foot in the left stirrup, she swings her right leg over and settles into the saddle in one fluid motion. She nudges Sparky sideways to stand next to the rock where Sam is waiting.

He leans and reaches in front of Sally, grabs the saddle horn with one hand, swings his leg over and settles in behind her on Sparky's rump. Sam doesn't know how to hang on, other than the obvious. He puts his arms lightly around Sally's waist and tries not to hold on too tight. Her belly is flat—not too soft, not too hard. He waits for her to nudge Sparky into a walk, but instead she says, "Shoot! I almost forgot!"

Without explanation, she points to the valley rim, swings her leg over Sparky's head, and slides from the saddle onto the ground, leaving Sam alone atop the horse. Sally hurries to the uprooted jack pine.

"It's gotta be here somewhere..." She peers down the route where Sparky dragged the jack pine to the far edge of the pit and back, and follows it at a fast walk. "Just hang on, Sam. Don't go anywhere."

Sam and Sparky watch silently. The horse's ears perk up, as if she's expecting a surprise. Sam prays that the horse isn't planning to run after her master.

Half a football field away, Sally points to the grass in front of her and shouts, "There it is! I put it in the little tree I tied Sparky to." She bends over and picks up a giant shed deer antler. Pointing to the rim, she hollers, "Found it up there, back in the woods a ways!"

Since tumbling into the gravel pit, Sam hadn't given a thought to the antler he found...or to his hat or the pathetic few morels he'd left up there.

Sam informs her, "The other antler, that one's mate—it's up there." He swings a leg over Sparky's rump and slides off the horse, grimacing as his head pounds when he thumps to the ground.

"No, no!" Sally orders. "Wait here..."

"And my hat," Sam adds. "And a few morels in a bag and my hat..."

Sally's already scrambling up the slope. The view of her backside is, well, *interesting* to Sam, in spite of needing stitches in his head. He thinks, *Sally Hunter looks just as good in her clothes as she does without 'em, maybe even better.*

Sam is not normally a pervert, at least not out loud. He respects women. After all, his mother was a woman (may she rest in peace), as are his three sisters. He couldn't help but keep his eyes glued to Sally in her blue jeans, bent over, scrambling on all fours up to the top of the gravel pit.

"Careful," he shouts at Sally's backside, just in case she looks back and catches him staring.

She gathers his antler, hat, and bag in one hand and circles back to her right fifty feet to the spot where she'd climbed out of the pit. Rather than slide down on her butt, she stays on her feet. Hop, slide to a stop. Steadies herself with her free hand. Hop, slide to a stop. It's like a game to her. She's laughing and enjoying the ride.

As Sally slides down, guiding and balancing herself with her free hand, she reminds him of Karen. Neither woman seemed to understand how desirable she was. Sam loves that innocent trait in a woman.

"My morels!" Sally points to her two big bags, which she'd completely forgotten about. "I act like *I'm* the one who was hit on the head."

Sparky stands patiently, reins dangling to the ground. Sally adds Sam's morels to one bag, then ties the two bags' twine strings together near their tops.

"Get yourself in the saddle," she directs. She pushes Sparky over to the rock, and Sam climbs on. She hangs the two pillowcases of morel mushrooms, like giant saddle bags, right behind the saddle.

"And these," Sally picks up both antlers and holds them out front of her. "What a beautiful pair!"

Sam gulps and nods in agreement, wondering if she's thinking what he's thinking…and hopes not.

"Keep my antler, too, okay, for me stumblin' into your morel patch? So now we're even?" Sally hands Sam the reins.

"Nope," he replies. "Every time I get reins in my hands, I end up on the ground. Can you lead us, and I'll just hang on?"

"Sure. Here we go…"

Dusk is approaching. Maureen is at the kitchen sink and spots Sally and Sparky coming down the lane, slowly approaching the yard. Maureen isn't sure what all she's seeing. It's a strange apparition—Sally with a mittful of huge deer antlers in one hand and reins in the other; puffy bags the size of pillowcases hang down each side of Sparky; what looks like a refugee in the saddle, leaning forward on the horn with both hands. Maureen hurries out the front door.

"Look at all this great stuff I found in the woods!" Sally playfully shouts to her sister across the yard.

"What the…? Sam?" Maureen's jaw drops.

"You don't wanna know," he says, closing his eyes and shaking his head.

"I think he needs stitches," Sally informs her sister, while pointing to Sam's head.

"What in the hell did you do to Sam?" Maureen asks. "I just wanted you to meet him someday, not knock 'im over the head and cart him home like a cave woman!"

"It's a long story…" says Sam.

"But a pretty good one," adds a grinning Sally.

CHAPTER 2

MIDWIFERY

When Sam had bought the place down the road from Maureen's six years ago, and Maureen had stopped in unannounced to drop off some neighborly sweet corn and introduce herself, she immediately sensed there was something different but likeable about her new neighbor. He was friendly. She could tell he wasn't hitting on her when he offered her a glass of wine.

However different, they hit it right off. Sam the two-time loser at love, and Maureen, life partner to Joan. He had guessed Maureen was somewhere in age between himself and his daughter, probably in her late thirties. She was attractive in a makeup-less, not-very-tall with just-a-little-extra-around-the-middle way, blonde, lively, and talkative. She'd brought up the subject of Joan that first visit with no apologies.

Maureen and Sam still have late-night, homemade wine-fueled talks a time or two a month, while often exchanging ideas about spiritual healing, the mystical like déjà vu and coincidences that seem like they really aren't, and dreams. Dreams like the one Sam had every month or two that he was going to help a mother deliver her baby.

Until the wine had kicked into second gear back in those early days, Sam had always been a hesitant participant in those enigmatic discussions. He'd brush off Maureen's prodding that he wasn't telling her the whole story. But he confided in Maureen one night (just into their third bottle of wine) that a psychic had told him all people have healing powers, whether they were aware of them or not. The psychic claimed she could sense his were stronger than most.

The psychic had told Sam to think about his childhood hunting dog, which had accidentally been shot by his father. She said, "You held your dog in your arms on the way to the veterinarian."

Sam had nodded in disbelief.

"Your dog got stronger on the way to the vet. You prayed and prayed for your dog, and ran your hands back and forth just above her injured side, and miraculously she hunted again that afternoon."

"Sam," the psychic assured him, "your dog getting shot was an accident, but her miraculous recovery wasn't."

Still not completely convinced his mug should be the first one anyone's baby would see, Sam took the O.B. kit Maureen offered and tucked it into the cubby hole in his bus.

December, 2000

Jody's baby was making its surprise arrival two weeks early, on the afternoon route the last day of school before Christmas break, out in the middle of nowhere. Unless you counted rutted gravel roads, jack pine forests to the horizons, and a trailer house down every other section road as "somewhere".

Why she didn't holler for help before Sam's school bus was six miles of gravel road from the nearest asphalt highway, only Jody Shaw knew. Or maybe at first she blamed her discomfort on the school cafeteria food, complicated by a bumpy bus ride. It was a moot point then anyway.

"GODDAMNIT!!" shrieked the normally shy Stone Creek high school sophomore, rattling the bus windows.

It was the moment Jody screamed from the back of the bus that Sam knew for sure that the dream he shared with Maureen and that moment were one and the same—déjà vu washed over him in a hot wave.

Sam's eyes leapt up to the big overhead mirror. Instinctively, his left foot found the clutch and his right foot the brake. Jody was leaning over sideways in the back seat, poised like she was going to vomit into the wastebasket by the rear emergency door. And she did indeed let her school lunch fly, with a roar worthy of a walrus who's eaten a bad batch of herring.

The other seven passengers, all grade schoolers, immediately bolted up onto their boney little knees and began chancing quick looks over the seat backs. They were bobbing like pop-up targets at a shooting gallery. When a grade schooler heard a high schooler use *that* kind of language at *that* unholy decibel level on the school bus, it usually meant somebody less than four feet tall was about to lose more than their milk money.

"Oh crap!" Sam mumbled under his breath.

He yanked up the parking brake before the bus had even come to a complete halt, shed his seatbelt in one spastic motion, the metal buckle clanging off the side window, and bolted to his feet. When the bus finally skidded to a halt, Sam lost his balance and unceremoniously fell forward onto the transmission shifting knob that stuck out from the floor at crotch height.

"OOF! Good thing I'm not havin' any more kids," he mumbled. Despite the eye-watering ache between his legs, Sam skipped sideways down the aisle made for humans half his width. He hopped like he should be tossing rose petals in an operatic production with fellas wearing tights.

The little kids had seen their bus driver "unhappy" before, like when J. Rod had lit up a cigarette in the back and tossed the match into the wastebasket, starting someone's discarded homework on fire. Even then, J. Rod, a precocious junior who was actually one of Sam's favorites, knew what he had to do when Sam headed down the aisle with the fire extinguisher leveled directly at his face. J. Rod and the wastebasket left the bus together out the emergency door, headed for the woods. Of course Sam wasn't going to "extinguish" J. Rod. He'd just wanted to make a point.

"Jody, Jody!" Sam shook her frail shoulders, and her eyes opened to slits. He brushed her long, blonde hair away from her face. Her hair was damp. There were beads of sweat on her forehead and under her eyes. Jody's fair complexion had turned even paler than usual, to a ghostly white.

"It's time..." she mumbled almost incoherently.

There was a telltale puddle of clear fluid tinged with blood dripping out from under Jody and onto the floor.

"We aren't gonna make it to my house. You gotta help me," she pleaded in a hoarse whisper.

Sam turned to rush the front of the bus. Elisa, the oldest of the grade schoolers, had followed Sam to the back. He accidentally knocked her sideways into a seat. "Oh shit...sorry."

Several times in the past, Elisa, only a fifth grader, had saved Sam from big messes. When a little kid was getting green around the gills, Elisa would hurry to the front of the bus and inform Sam calmly, "Joey's gonna puke. I'll take care of it. Please hand me the paper towels." And she'd hold the basket for the sick kid and even tie the top of the plastic garbage bag into a knot afterwards.

The freckle-faced, red-headed little girl was unperturbed as usual for this emergency. Calmly, she suggested to the frantically retreating bus driver, "You call for help, Sam, and I'll tend to Jody."

Sam radioed in the emergency and their location, then noticed he was parked right in the middle of the road. Well, too bad. The bus would have to stay right there; there wasn't time to move it. He yanked on the latches of the cubby hole beside the mirror, and an O.B. kit fell out. He fumbled it then caught it against his chest.

The other six kids had scurried to the back of the bus and were packed three each in the second-to-last seats, jostling each other and craning their necks for a better view. Sam hurried to the back, attempting to act composed. "Stand aside kids...please." (Sam always said "please" to his kids. That is, if they weren't lighting anything on fire, or farting.)

"I helped my dad pull a calf once," Elisa offered confidently. Sam couldn't stifle a grin.

This was going to be Sam Ryan's first real "rodeo". He wondered why he'd ever wished for it. But that wish had been made twenty years ago, when he'd been younger and dumber.

Another contraction set in, and Jody was wide awake, seeming more angry than in pain. She hissed through her gritted teeth like her head was about to spin around, "THAT... FUCKING...GAAAARRRYYY!!"

Her pain and sense of panic quickly overcame her anger. "OWWW! It hurts so bad! We don't have insurance! I didn't go to classes…I don't know what to do!"

She hiked up her denim, ankle-length dress and pulled her panties aside. The baby was starting to crown.

Sam accepted this fate and regained control of himself with a deep breath. "I know what to do," he promised.

Sam actually did know how to assist a mother giving birth—that was, if the birth went off without a hitch. He remembered back to his firefighter training, and Maureen had given him a quick lesson.

Sam ripped open the O.B. kit. "Jody, I need to cut your underwear off. You okay with that?" He pointed between her legs and looked off to the side.

"Just hurry…I don't give a goddamn shit who sees what!" Jody cried. "Another one's coming. Hurry!"

"Okay, Elisa. You hand me stuff. Are there scissors in there?" Sam asked.

"Yup," Elisa answered, business-like. "Two kinds of scissors. One unwrapped and one in a bag."

"Save the bagged scissors for later," Sam instructed. "Let's get our gloves on."

He handed Elisa a pair, but could only get his partway on. He tugged at them to no avail, wasting precious time. The gloves were size Small, meant for Maureen. Elisa couldn't help but glow as she put her gloves on. They were only a fraction too big for her.

"Come on, Sam! Come on!" Jody ordered through her teeth.

"Scissors," Sam reminded his assistant, managing to sound calm and in control.

He instructed Jody, "Try not to push. Hold off if you can, until I get these off. Don't push until you feel another contraction. Everything'll be fine. The worst part'll be over in another contraction or two. You're doin' great."

Sam, not particularly religious during everyday events, silently prayed that he was right.

Elisa pressed the scissors into his hand, then thinking ahead she ordered like a drill sergeant, "Jimmy! Get the blanket under Sam's seat! Hurry! And don't get any gummy bear slobber on it!"

Jimmy wiped his face with his coat sleeve, leaving a sticky mark from cuff to elbow.

"Save my seat!" he ordered his little buddy as he ran down the aisle.

"Can you find the big padded paper covers called Chux Pads?" Sam asked his assistant while he cut Jody's pants. "They're folded up. Unfold one. It'll be about this big." Sam held his arms and hands about three feet apart. "I'll need one right away to put under Jody's bottom. And we'll wrap the baby in the other one. Make sure you know where the rubber suction bulb is. Find it right now, please. That's more important. As soon as you see the baby's face, hand the bulb to me."

Jody stiffened and gasped, "Would ya cut the crap? The baby's comin' whether you're ready or not! Oh geeeeez! Screw the mess! I'm gonna die if I don't push right now! I know I'm going to friggin' die!"

Sam hastily stuffed the pad under Jody's bottom. "Give it all ya got!" he urged confidently.

Jody puffed hard, gritted her teeth, and screamed while she pushed, "He told me he'd pull out!"

Sam watched the opening tear about an inch near the bottom. Blood trickled out onto the thick pad and disappeared into its layers. The peanut gallery gasped in unison. Sam wasn't sure whether it was the sight in front them or Jody's language that had caused their reaction.

"Perfect." Sam encouraged Jody as she puffed and pushed. Whether that was a white lie or not, he wasn't sure. "That's it."

Sam positioned his hands to cradle the baby's head. It occurred to him that his hand positions were the same as when he helped coach grade school football, a quarterback about to get the ball snapped to him. "Push a little harder. Come on! Some more. You're doin' it! Yes, yes... the baby's head is comin' out!"

Elisa had the syringe out of the package and ready. She stole glances between Sam and the baby, her fifth-grade brow furrowed in worry.

The baby suddenly presented its shoulders. Jody sobbed in relief. With his gloved hands, one on the baby's head and the other on the shoulders, Sam gently turned the baby's head to the side. "Syringe, please."

Elisa's eyes were big as an October full moon, and she was biting her lip. He'd never seen his little bus mother even a tiny bit un-composed before. She whispered into his ear, "Sam, the baby isn't pink." He whispered back, "Babies are always like this, kinda gray, before their first good breath. You'll see. It'll be fine."

The baby's mouth was open and moving, silently. He suctioned the mouth and nostrils. The baby reacted, squirming and making little grunting sounds like a new puppy.

"Everything's just fine, Jody. The baby is beautiful, perfect. You ready to finish this up? Whenever you're ready…"

Jody clenched her teeth and nodded.

"Okay," Sam coached. "Another good push…the best one you've got…"

Jody complied with all her might, her tears and sweat mixing and flowing down her cheeks. "I'm glad he's friggin' gone! That son of a bitch!"

Sam had seen the couple at school together. Gary was always pestering Jody, whispering to her, his hands on her whenever he thought a teacher or aide wasn't looking, or some dumb bus driver wasn't watching in the overhead mirror. Several times, Gary had tried to ride the bus home with Jody.

"You need a bus pass," Sam would tell him. Finally Gary got one, a permanent pass. Coincidentally, that was about nine months ago. But Gary had disappeared from the picture during the tail end of last year, when it became public knowledge that Jody was pregnant.

All the kids were standing on seats and watching over Sam and Elisa's shoulders.

Elisa urged the kids into a cheer, "Come on! We gotta help Jody! Holler with me! JO-DY, JO-DY, JO-DY!" Elisa clapped her gloved hands in sync over her head.

Jody grabbed the top of the seat back and the emergency door handle for leverage. She arched her knees and pushed so hard she thought her eyes would pop out of their sockets. Within a couple of seconds, the baby girl was delivered smoothly the rest of the way into Sam's waiting hands, the umbilical cord trailing from her mother.

Elisa held the second large pad under the baby. Sam settled the infant onto the wrap and Elisa held the baby, first in her hands while Sam folded the cloth over the baby, and then in her arms tight to her chest.

"Here, Jody," Elisa whispered as she carefully set the baby onto Jody's belly and chest.

Elisa cast a questioning glance at Sam, still worried about why the baby wasn't pink, even though she was grunting and moving her arms and legs like any other healthy newborn baby would.

"Watch this," Sam whispered to Elisa. He tickled the bottom of one foot. The baby's eyes immediately squeezed shut like she was being blinded by the sun, and her mouth arched wide open. The baby girl sucked in her first big breath and let 'er rip. She not only pinked up, her face turned crimson. Elisa stood and gave Sam a small kiss on the cheek.

Tears dribbled from the bus driver's eyes. Elisa, back to business immediately, gently dabbed away Sam's eye leakage with a cotton sponge and adeptly tossed it into the wastebasket, like she'd done that a thousand times before for a hundred other doctors.

Elisa fished several more sponges out of the O.B. kit and handed some to Jody. Together they carefully wiped the baby's head and face. The other kids oohed and aahed and cooed to each other. To Sam, it looked like little girls playing house with a doll.

"Your first ride on Sam's bus," Elisa cheerfully informed the baby. The little red-headed, freckle-faced fifth grader was so calm and cool about it. So was Jody. The girls were smiling like best friends at a sleepover.

There was still work to do. Jody lifted her new baby onto the blanket, which Elisa had placed on her belly, and folded it to keep the baby warm, but being careful to leave the umbilical cord exposed. Nestled in her mother's arms, the baby quieted and resumed grunting like a new puppy. Jody's baby girl was already looking for something to suck, her lips formed into a circle and her tongue sliding in and out.

"That's exactly what our baby calf did!" Elisa pointed at the baby's mouth.

Sam was going to ask Elisa for the umbilical clamps, but she already had them in the palm of one hand and the unwrapped umbilical scissors in the other. Jody nuzzled her freshly cleaned and dried baby. If she knew Sam was cutting the cord, she didn't show it.

Sam stood up and pulled his gloves off and so did Elisa. He thought, *Now if that little girl turns them inside out one inside the other and slingshots them into the wastebasket…* She didn't.

"Can we touch her?" Jimmy asked Jody in a polite whisper.

Jody nodded with a smile. Sam got out of the way and the little kids huddled around mother and baby.

Elisa handed out sponges. "Clean your grubby little paws first," she ordered.

The sirens were approaching. "Excuse me, kids," Sam said softly. "I need to move the bus outta the middle of the road."

Sam settled into his seat with a sigh, and looked up into the mirror. It was hard for him to see all the way to the back. So he just listened.

"What you gonna name her?" a second grade girl asked.

"It was gonna be Katie," Jody replied, while brushing her baby's hair softly with her fingers. "But I'm gonna name her Samantha Elisa…Sam E. for short. Get it?"

April, 2003

"That's the third one in a little over two years," Sam told the Boise firefighter, who arrived right as Keith was cutting his newborn son's umbilical cord. The firefighter and his partner took over the immediate post-birth duties: blood pressure, pulse, and saving the placenta for the obstetrician to examine.

Ellen smiled and waved her father over to the side of the stretcher. Sam's grandson had nestled into his mother's chest, the boy's mouth already searching for his first meal. Sam kissed them both on the forehead. Out of nowhere it seemed, his eyes filled with tears. He hadn't had time to cry before then.

"Robert. A nice name. That was my grandfather's name. You never did say what his middle name's gonna be…"

"Nope." Ellen smiled at her husband. "Keith, it was your idea. You wanna tell Grandpa?"

Keith said, "We decided Robert should be his middle name. We're gonna call him Sam."

Sam put his hand over his mouth. He could feel the waterworks starting again.

"Gotta keep your streak going. I hear that's two Samanthas brought into this world with your assistance. And now a Sam. You gonna stop this amateur midwifery at a three-peat?"

"I hope so." Sam crossed his fingers with one hand and wiped under his nose with the other.

"You work in a hospital?" the firefighter asked, as he pulled off his surgical gloves.

"Nope. I'm a school bus driver. Delivered the first baby on my bus. And then one in my little hometown back in Minnesota in the parking lot of the municipal liquor store. Now I carry an O.B. kit with me everywhere."

"You're a lucky man," said the firefighter. "I hope I get my chance someday."

"I hope you do, too," Sam agreed, smiling softly. "But trust me, once is enough…"

CHAPTER 3

WITHOUT SAYING GOODBYE

It wasn't until Sam pulled into Detroit Lakes just before midnight that he knew for sure what day it was. The Minneapolis newspaper in the convenience store where he'd gassed up his pickup truck indicated it was Friday, May 9, 2003. Not that it mattered what day or even what year it was, but the fact that Sam noticed such an ordinary detail meant the attack was finally loosening its grip eighteen miles from home.

He glanced up and saw himself in the store's security monitor. He looked like he'd just fallen off a freight train. Instead of fifty-three years old, Sam Ryan looked every bit of seventy-three. His unshaven face was gaunt, his eyes red, sunken and hollow, and rimmed with black.

The Native American clerk, who looked to be in her forties, was working the cash register keys with one hand while her other one was out of sight below the counter. He supposed either her hidden hand was pressed lightly against the alarm button or her fingers were gripping a pistol. Something about those dark eyes and that firm jaw indicated that she'd use the pistol in a heartbeat if he acted in any way like he was up to no good.

No, Sam was just going home and needed gas in his truck. But he did look every bit a deranged man. And he had been that insane man over the past several days. Since he'd left Boise, she wasn't the first clerk to eye him nervously, suspiciously. Even the ones who'd waited on him in broad daylight.

Sam pulled out from the dusty lot, left the four-lane on the east edge of town, and headed north. He had another half hour drive to get home. The road curved up a steep hill, and there were no other vehicles in sight. It was a dark stretch of road where he could make sure no one was approaching.

He stopped in the middle of his lane, and reached into the open wine case on the floor. In the first slot his hand found, he felt cloth. He squinted and tilted his head, trying to remember what that could be. He reached up and clicked the dome light on. It was the t-shirt he'd had made up for little Josh, his first grandson. Sam thought it was cute. A little stick-figure girl and boy holding hands on a sunny playground, the caption in a child's penmanship, "Make Friends, Not War."

He wracked his brain, trying to remember. He'd left Boise in the middle of the night, without saying goodbye. Drove straight through, he was pretty sure...but didn't remember sleeping since the night the attack began, when he'd left Ellen and Keith's house on foot. He wandered Boise the rest of that night, and the next day...and into the following night until he finally made it back to their house. They must have packed up his bag and the rest of the wine.

Sam folded the little shirt carefully, small enough so it fit back into a bottle slot. From the next slot, he pulled out a bottle. He found a cheap plastic corkscrew in the glove compartment. Bracing the bottle between his knees, he screwed the thing in and pulled the cork out with a "pop." With the cork came a familiar fruity and mildly yeasty aroma.

Sam took a careful sip, held it in his mouth, and let his taste buds explore the flavor. Then with that instinctive habit out of the way, he let the wild grape wine trickle down his throat a little at a time. He hoisted the bottle to his mouth again and took a big gulp, swallowing without tasting it. The alcohol was still minutes away from starting its job, but instantly the wild grape wine warmed his body and soothed his mind. He swallowed once more and dropped the truck shift lever into Drive.

Sam decided to leave the quicker, shorter two-lane route and detoured onto a gravel back road to attempt to put the pieces together. It was a frightening feeling, not knowing where he'd been or how he'd gotten there, like a disconnection from reality that was centered in the pit of his stomach.

He could muster only blurry snapshots of the trip home. The sun coming up when he was somewhere in the flat farm country of southern Idaho…a terrible wreck between a semi and a motor home in the mountains of Montana…darkness falling as he neared Bismarck. The evening of the fight with his brother Russell and his son-in-law Keith, it must have been Wednesday.

No, Sam was sure that his last lucid moments, just before the fight, had been on Tuesday evening. Monday was May fifth, a holiday in Sam's world. When his kids were little, they'd dubbed it Cinco de Morel because the delicious fungi were always growing then. They made it a family outing of holiday proportions and afterward had a giant meal of the delicious mushrooms.

This year's Cinco de Morel feast had been with last year's dried morels and T-bone steaks. It was delayed a day because they were waiting for Russell to get back from business overseas. Sam had never looked Russell up in all his trips to Boise to see the kids. He never even mentioned him. Dinner that night had been Ellen's ill-fated surprise effort to help mend the decades-long rift between Sam and Russell.

"Why did it take me almost forty-eight hours to make the thirteen-hundred-mile trip that should have only taken twenty hours?" Sam asked himself aloud, trying to sort it out. He'd lost a day somewhere, probably in Boise. Maybe he had slept. But where? He didn't have a clue. It was the worst attack Sam had ever had.

A warm glow from the wine soon spread its way through him, like the dope they give you before they knock you out to yank out your appendix. He turned the heater down and opened his window a couple inches. He cruised along the back roads slowly, at twenty, maybe twenty-five miles per hour. Driving back roads and sipping wine or a beer had always been soothing to Sam.

The fog in his head was lifting. It was a welcome relief to finally be able to think again, to process, for Sam to have some control. Except what he was remembering about why he'd left Boise two weeks before he'd planned to was ugly. Even if Ellen had heard about the attacks when Sam was with Karen, he was sure she couldn't have guessed how bad he really got. He thought those attacks had been buried along with his wife. Clearly, they had not.

After Karen, Sam wasn't interested in seeking out anyone as his real family or as his surrogate interest. But something had clicked with Stone Creek, a northern Minnesota town of 527 people and a school. He noticed an ad in the Stone Creek Record for a school bus driver. Fortunately, he still carried that license. Driving a bus when they needed him was a decent enough excuse to get off the ranch he was caretaking that winter of 1996-1997.

The big kids at school had thought Sam was a rebel because he wore his hair down to his shirt collar. In reality, he just hadn't bothered to get it cut for four months. After all, the horses didn't care how he looked. Also, he listened to rock radio stations instead of country or Christian music. When he drove school trips, instead of sitting in the bus sleeping or reading like other drivers did, Sam found himself wandering the museums, amusement parks, state capitol, and the like along with the kids and chaperones.

In some respects, Sam was a kid himself, curious about everything and enjoying their company. On sports trips, he took a place in the bleachers behind the team and cheered them on unabashedly. He was often drafted to be a line judge for volleyball or a base coach for baseball and softball, and became a regular on the "chain gang" at home football games.

He'd stop the bus for a fresh bear track on a sandy back road, a coyote hunting mice, or a family of wild geese and their goslings, so the kids could see them up close. When he took a regular route at the beginning of his first full school year at Stone Creek, he was the only bus driver to visit their homes and introduce himself to the kindergartners and their parents before the first day of school, or when a new family moved in.

Instead of getting Linda and Justin Adams suspended for giving the finger to a logger out the bus's back window, he merely "reminded" them how impolite it was to wave at strangers without using your entire hand. About the only things concerning his bus kids that could rile Sam were farting in winter when the bus windows were up or lighting up a cigarette.

That first spring Sam drove for Stone Creek, another bus driver handed off the 350-mile round trip to Minneapolis, to the live theater with the senior high Shakespeare Club.

Nearing the city, Sam had asked the two teachers, "How about instead of stopping at the usual greasy fast-food joint before we get into Minneapolis, I drop 'em off at the front door of the City Center on Hennepin Avenue. It has a great food court on the third level the kids would enjoy, with every kinda quick food they could imagine, some of it even healthy." With Sam driving, they were ahead of schedule as usual.

Both teachers' mouths dropped open. One stammered, "You'd drive us into downtown Minneapolis? What about the traffic and parking the bus?"

Sam shrugged. "I drove a school bus down there one winter and spring, eight routes a day. Six of the routes were through downtown during the rush hours. I drove like everyone—fast. Except, believe it or not, it's easier to change lanes in a school bus with fogged-up windows on a packed city street than in a car. Just turn on your signal. Give 'em a little fake, and it's like Moses partin' the Red Sea. Nobody wants to hit a darn school bus."

That trip, the kids dubbed him "Sam the Jam" for his *efficiency* in getting them around downtown Minneapolis. The name was later shortened to simply "Jammer", which is what most folks in Stone Creek still called him, even those not connected with him through the school.

To Stone Creek, Sam appeared perfectly content with his life, and many were envious of him. He did extol to the local folk every chance he got that he was living the exact life he wanted—working only half the hours most folks have to, the freedom to come and go as he pleased, living in such a beautiful part of the world, with the woods and the river, making homemade wild grape wine every fall, and picking morels every spring.

He joked to his friends in Stone Creek that to have a wife, even a girlfriend, he'd have to get a real job, a mortgage, and probably have to make minivan payments. Not to mention he'd have to clean his toilet and change his bed sheets more often than every other full moon.

But there was a very private hole in his life behind that happy face, a cavern he explored shortly after Karen was gone. After two disastrous tries the first year on his place in the hills, Sam boarded it shut and left it empty.

Still, that May night, he was very glad to be home in those hills near Stone Creek. But whatever demon had pounced on him when he was with Karen had come back to haunt him out in Boise. It was just as ugly and even more frightening. Sam had no idea how he'd make amends with his daughter and son-in-law…or if that would even be possible. He wasn't sure what all had been said or done that evening, or where all he'd been since.

But during those last few miles home, he decided he needed to go back onto the therapist's couch in order to just hang onto what he had left and, God willing, heal some of what he'd destroyed in Boise.

"Wish me luck!" Sam toasted the nighttime hills with the three-fourths empty bottle.

He drove on past his driveway down the gravel road a quarter mile and stopped his truck on the bridge. He inhaled deeply. "I'm home, dear river." He turned the truck around and drove to his house.

It was shortly after midnight. There were fresh tire tracks in the gravel driveway. Sam assumed they were from either Maureen's or Joan's car from when they'd gathered the eggs and fed his chickens the previous morning. He would drive the trail to their house first thing and thank them. But Maureen would know something went wrong in Boise, and he didn't want to talk about it.

Sam's trail encompassed three and a half miles round trip, including a side loop through his woods and two of the neighbors' woods, including Maureen and Joan's and a county forest tract. He'd cleared the trail with a chainsaw and axe shortly after moving to his house, mostly because the silence had become deafening.

He eventually made it wide enough to drive his little Ford tractor through, which he used to pull a trailer-full of pails of maple sap in March and April. He also used it to haul firewood and sometimes to get a deer home that he'd taken with his bow or gun. And of course, the trail was his highway to the morel mushrooms. Sam liked to drive the trail slowly in his electric golf cart he'd traded stone work for, as a peaceful way to unwind and nurse a few beers or sip on a bottle of wine.

He made a mental note to call the post office and his bus boss to tell them he was home two weeks early. The school was always short of bus drivers, especially that time of year, what with all the spring class trips. He remembered there were two trips to the cities the following week anyway. The other drivers would be more than happy to hand the city trips off to him, and the kids would be delighted to have Sam as their driver, chaperone, and friend.

For Saturday and Sunday, Sam's plan was to decompress—rest, walk in the woods, check on the morels, and canoe the Fox River. The river had tugged at him more than anything else while he was away. She was the love of Sam's life. Her ever-changing beauty, her peacefulness, and her welcoming smile were always there for him with open arms, even when he showed up at midnight, hollow-eyed, smelling of alcohol, and in terrible need of a shower. He knows she will never leave him.

Sam hadn't opened any of the windows when he'd arrived home in the middle of the night. It was early afternoon before he awakened. Sunshine streamed through his south and west windows. The house was stuffy and smelled like the dirt floor basement underneath, humid and moldy. Sitting on the edge of his bed and brushing his hair back with his hands, Sam was reminded that he hadn't showered in days.

When he opened his front door, the aroma was strikingly different. It was pleasant and unmistakably spring-fresh, the damp ground working to compost last year's leaves, smelling like incense. According to the thermometer on the porch post, it was seventy-three degrees, unseasonably warm for northern Minnesota on the tenth of May. There was only a breath of a breeze from the west. A few cottony clouds dotted the blue sky. It was comforting to be home.

Maureen or Joan had stopped to gather the eggs. Seeing Sam's truck, they'd left the basket of eggs on his porch rocking chair.

The ice cold water that doused him in the shower was a cruel reminder he'd forgotten to screw in the fuse for the hot water heater. He did that and let the water heat while he unpacked, then gathered his morel mushroom hunting paraphernalia into his light backpack. It wasn't much stuff—three or four plastic grocery bags, a folding knife, a small plastic pop bottle of wild grape wine, a compact camera, a handful of venison jerky, and three paper towels just in case nature came 'a callin'. Plus, there was already the obligatory corkscrew in the pack, which he left in out of habit, although he certainly didn't need it to get the screw top off the soda bottle.

Sam hadn't had a real meal since the night of the incident in Boise, and he suddenly realized he was famished. He thawed some venison sausage in the microwave and scrambled it with six of the fresh eggs.

Besides Maureen and Joan, nobody else in Minnesota knew Sam was home except his sister Jill, whom his daughter had apparently called when he'd left Boise. Jill had left a message on the answering machine asking how he was doing. He knew he owed her a call. His big sister had always been his rock.

He tried her number in Minneapolis, but she wasn't home. Sam left a simple message, "Tell Ellen and Keith I got home okay and I'm sorry and I'm alright. I'll call you in a couple days."

It had been a foregone conclusion and an easy decision that Sam would miss the black morel mushroom season to attend the birth of his second grandson, then stay in Boise to help out his daughter for a month afterward, like he had with Josh's birth. When Ellen had invited him to Boise for the birth, she'd apologized for the unfortunate timing, but kidded that morel mushrooms hadn't crossed their minds during the conception phase of their baby's journey to Earth.

CHAPTER 4

CARPETS AND CURTAINS

"Forget the Novocain," Sam growls as Maureen inspects the cut on the top of his head. "Just three fingers of brandy, please."

At the kitchen table, Sam sits and leans forward on his forearms. Sally is across the table from him, wincing as if she's the one about to get jabbed with a needle.

"It's *your* head," Maureen says and rolls her eyes. She walks into the pantry and fetches the brandy bottle. On her way back, she plucks two highball glasses from the cupboard next to the sink. One has pheasants on it, the other mallard ducks. She pours Sam's glass half full, enough brandy for three normal highballs. Sally holds her thumb and pointer finger to indicate she wants only a little.

Maureen sets their glasses in front them and the bottle closer to Sam, "Here's more if you need it, cowboy."

Sally cradles the glass between her hands and looks at Sam. "What are we gonna do with all those morels?"

"What do you mean *we*? They're yours. You stole 'em fair and square."

Maureen stands behind Sam and dabs at his wound with antiseptic swabs. He squints and quickly takes a gulp of brandy, lets out an exaggerated sigh, and plunks the glass down on the table top.

"When I was out there and they were everywhere, I got carried away. I was thinkin', sell what I don't want to the co-op, just to get ridda them. And then you literally cartwheeled into the picture. By the way, Maureen, thanks for the pillowcases."

"They'll wash," Maureen answers. "I hope."

Maureen goes to work shaving around the wound with a disposable razor. Sam's not paying attention to what's going on up there.

"I'll make ya a deal," Sam offers Sally. "I'll help you put them up, all of 'em. I've got the screens for dryin' 'em, the vacuum sealer, a big freezer. You take what you want. I can get more."

"You ready, Rambo?" Maureen asks, as she's poised with the needle.

Sam picks up his glass and holds it like he's making a toast. He takes a long swig, swallows hard, and lets out a big "Haaaaah. Dig in."

"You sure?" Sally asks.

"No problem. I love puttin' up morels. It won't take long."

"No!" Sally points to the top of his head. "I mean, you sure you don't want Novocain?"

Maureen pauses just before contact, awaiting Sam's answer.

"Brandy will do," he vows, then takes another big glug, finishing it off. "And the pleasant memories from just before and after I fell down the cliff will kill the rest of the pain."

He smiles wryly at Sally, who rolls her eyes.

Sam nods off in front of the plate of pork chops and freshly sautéed morels the sisters cooked.

It's a combination of only one good night's sleep over the previous five or six days; a pretty good bump on the head; fresh air; plenty of exercise, including rolling down a steep embankment; sights never seen before taking up a lot of space in his brain; and six fingers of brandy, straight.

"Hey, cowboy," Maureen whispers. "You want the couch?"

Sam shakes his head. "No thanks. My own bed." His head slumps again, chin resting on his chest. "It…"

"It what?" Sally asks.

"That's why I came back…already…from Boise…" he slurs. "Who's takin' me home? My own bed…thas what I need…"

The sisters, one under each arm, help Sam to Sally's pickup. He's only a little helpful getting in—he manages to get his butt up on the seat by himself. Sally has to help him with his legs. Maureen buckles him up. Sam's head relaxes against the head rest.

"You want me to follow?" Maureen asks.

"Naw," Sally replies. "We'll be fine."

Sally drives slowly to keep from jostling Sam. The tires crunch on the washboard gravel.

"What am I doin'?" she mumbles under her breath, assuming Sam is asleep. "What are *they* doing, tryin' to set me up? I've got a husband. Things aren't perfect, but…"

She catches him gazing at her by the glow of the dashboard lights, like a lovesick schoolboy. "You're pretty tipsy," she says, with a wry smile crossing her face.

"I'd lie to know the…same thing. Hangin' 'round married women is the safess…s'long as they know the rules and hubby isn't too gooduva shot…"

"Married women?" Sally asks. "How many of those notches have you got on your bedpost? What rules?"

Sam starts fumbling with his seat belt. "Shtop! Shtop right here…!".

"Oh no! You gonna be sick?"

Sally brakes the truck hard and crunches to a jolting stop on the river bridge. She bails out her door and runs around to Sam's.

He's already out of the seat and shuffling to the bridge railing a half of a narrow gravelly lane away. He leans over, swaying in a circle, his hands and arms barely supporting his weight. Sally moves beside him and slides an arm around his waist to steady him.

"Take a slow, deep breath," Sally instructs calmly.

He looks at her curiously. "Huh? No. I' fine. Jus' haf to say…see ya t'murrow"

He straightens up. Sally steadies him, eyeing him. Like a Shakespearian actor (who's overdosed on mead), Sam holds his arms outstretched to his sides.

"M' ladyyy," Sam implores with great aplomb to the rushing water. "My lady…Miss Fox Riveerr, I misshed you…I sshall see ya in the morrow…" He squints in

Sally's direction and sways back and forth. "She's the on'y gir'frind I need…"

He turns to Sally. "Yur com'n with, right?…affer we clean morels…You nee' meet her…"

"The water has to be freezing," she replies, humoring Sam. "What if we fall in?"

"Stan' up an' walk to shhhore," he answers, grinning drunkenly. "Iss on'y two fee' deep…"

"We'll talk about it in the morning," Sally offers. Let's get you home. Next place on the right, right?"

"Right right. I call it Heaven on Earth. It ain' much… but iss mine…"

Sally guides him to the truck door and he's able to slide in by himself and get his legs in. She doesn't bother with his seat belt, and shuts the door carefully.

Sam hadn't left any lights on. Sally parks her truck next to his, pointing it at the front porch. She leaves the engine running and the lights on. "Let me help you in and get some lights on so you don't get another goose egg on that head."

"Thanksh."

She helps Sam's mostly dead weight out of the truck and places her arm around his waist again. They shuffle to the porch and carefully step up onto it. Sam is fading again. He's heavy and reeks of alcohol and antiseptic. She opens the door, feels for the light switch, and flips it on. A bare bulb in the middle of the ceiling comes on. The sudden light revives Sam enough that he lifts his head and looks around blankly.

Sally sees they are in his living room. She takes a few moments to survey the habitat of her new Jackpine Savage friend. Sam seems to be standing up asleep anyway.

The couch, kelly green and threadbare, is along the opposite wall and her plan is to deliver Sam to it. The hard part will be negotiating around the ottoman in front of it. It's made of pine lumber that was scorched with a blow torch before it was varnished, rustic lake cabin furniture. The two cushions either side of the tabletop center portion are mismatched; one's striped in various shades of browns and tans, and the other is plain dark blue.

The dark veneer of a two-tiered end table is scratched badly and peeling on the edges. The lamp is two feet tall and looks like a Roman column wearing a giant hat made of leopard skin. Hunting and fishing magazines are scattered helter-skelter on the lower level. The upper level features several circular interlocking beverage container stains on the veneer.

The wall behind the couch is covered with loud, royal blue, floral wallpaper, probably at least fifty years old. It's peeling in several places near the top and at the seams.

The carpet, crimson with huge, gaudy green and gold palm trees isn't tacked down and doesn't go all the way to the walls. It looks like it came from the movie theater that was remodeled back in the '50s.

The curtains are hand-sewn, patterned with repeating forest scenes with wild animals, mostly forest green, bleached out only over the glass by decades of sun.

It's as if someone had decorated the room purposely not to have anything match.

The one saving grace to the room is the fieldstone fireplace on the wall to the right. Sam had built it the first year he owned the place. Just above the firebox at eye level is the five-inch thick and sixteen-inch deep, hand-peeled, varnished pine mantle that extends half a foot beyond the rocks on each end. Another mantle of half those proportions sits partway to the ceiling. The big mantle holds Sam's three matched sets of large shed antlers, several candles in their holders, and Native American artifacts including stone scrapers and hammers. On the upper mantle sit two antique duck decoys.

Sam, wobbling against Sally, looks around the room with half-open eyes. "Waddya think, Sal…? Am I a decorator or what…?"

"I hate to tell you this, Sam," Sally teases, "Nothin' in here matches—not the curtains, not the paint, not the carpet…"

She helps him around the ottoman and onto the couch, where he plops down clumsily on his butt. He swivels to lie back and puts his feet up. She pulls the crumpled comforter from under his shoes and covers him.

"Sally," he mumbles, "I hate to tell you thiss, toooo… Bu' y'ur carpet dussn't match y'ur curtains either…"

Sally shakes her head and blushes, tilting her head mock-flirtatiously. "Goodnight, cowboy. See ya at 9."

Sam doesn't hear her. He's already snoring.

CHAPTER 5

LIKE THE OTHER MARRIED WOMEN

When Sally pulls into Sam's driveway the next day, he's sitting at a picnic table next to the porch, surrounded by his morel cleaning equipment: a couple of old aluminum dishpans with handles on the sides, a pair of plastic colanders, a large plastic cutting board, and two butcher knives. He's cradling an insulated mug of steaming coffee and smiling at his helper.

It is the makings of a second unusually warm and sunny spring day. And for the second day in a row, Sam had showered. He'd even trimmed his beard and moustache down to a five o'clock shadow. His hair, freshly washed, has dried wavy and flipped up in the back, almost touching the collar of his blue and black plaid flannel shirt with the top three buttons open. He's ready for the day to warm up, wearing a camouflaged t-shirt under it.

"I hope you remembered the morels," Sam kids as Sally exits her truck. "I forgot all about 'em last night."

Her hair is wet and combed back. She's wearing jeans, a baggy navy blue sweatshirt and white tennis shoes, with a touch of light makeup, a nearly transparent coat of pink lipstick and stud earrings with stones in them, light blue, like the sky…like her eyes. And no wedding ring.

"Yup." Sally uses two hands to lift a bulging pillowcase of morels up and out of the truck box.

"Just set it anywhere," Sam instructs. "Have some coffee. Do you need cream or sugar? Hope not. Only got sugar and the mice got into it while I was gone."

"How's the head?" She asks, as he approaches the table with the second pillowcase full of morels. "And black is fine."

They sit one on each side of the picnic table. Sam feels the top of his cap with his free hand. "Hmm? Forgot all about it."

"Not that, silly. The *inside* of your head."

Sam rolls his eyes. "Don't remind me." He takes a long swig of coffee and smiles at the parts of the previous evening he can remember.

"Tell me about all this," Sally says, indicating the array of morel cleaning equipment. "Never put any up before. Just ate 'em fresh."

"Puttin' up morels ain't rocket science, but you gotta pay attention to detail…unless you like eatin' bugs and dirt."

She moves around to Sam's side of the table and sits close enough that their hips touch, barely, although she could have certainly caught the gist of his instructions just as well from across the table. Or even from the porch fifteen feet in front of them.

Sam tries to stifle an instinctive slow, deep breath. Sally hears the air rushing in through his nostrils and gives him a playful elbow to his ribs. "You're not gonna conk out on me again, are ya?"

"I just might," Sam jokes as he reaches for a large aluminum dishpan. "Now, fill a dishpan about halfway with morels. Fill the pan with water. Slosh the morels around. Rinse in the colanders with the hose. Spread 'em on the drying screens. Pull off the bigger ones for halving. Put them back on the screens. Repeat."

They are halving the final batch of bigger morels when Maureen pulls in the driveway. She sees them sitting side by side with their backs to her—closer than they probably need to be—busy at work like an old married couple. She smiles from the privacy of her car. After a few more seconds, she gets out of her car, thinking, *They do look pretty darn good together...I knew it.*

"Hey, you two! I was on my way to the clinic," Maureen shouts.

Both Sam and Sally jump with surprise. They hadn't noticed Maureen drive in and park fifty feet away.

"Thought I better stop in and take a look and my sewin' job."

Sam is on his knees leaning down, holding the canoe tight to the river bank. The bank is half a foot higher than the top edge of the canoe sides.

"Just relax," he gently urges Sally as he adjusts his grip of the gunwales. "I got it."

Their launch point is fifty yards below the dam, upstream from the bridge by Sam's house, a four mile drive and a three hour canoe trip back down. The water is still high from the spring runoff and running fast. Little waves slap at the side of the canoe.

Sally hesitates, sitting on the edge of the bank with her feet outstretched and dangling a couple inches from the canoe floor. She is convinced something bad is about to happen.

"Trust me," Sam promises. "I've gotten in and outta this canoe a thousand times and hardly ever fell in."

"I just want to get in and out of it *once* without fallin' in! How cold is this water?" she asks, stealing a nervous glance at the crystal-clear water running past.

"Cold enough that if we fall in and get soaked we'll have to immediately strip down and huddle together to keep from gettin' hypothermia," Sam teases, but he's not smiling. Instead he's squinting at the floor of the canoe as he flexes his fingers again.

"Well! Why didn't you tell me?" Sally suddenly slides into the canoe with a thud. Sam expected her to slide her butt onto the seat, but she stands with her arms outstretched like a tightrope walker.

"Jeezus, Sally!" Sam scolds as he reaches even further across a thwart. It takes every ounce of his strength to keep the canoe from spinning over and dumping her out. "I was just kidding! Keep your clothes on. Two days in a row of you like *that* and I'll be takin' a long, cold shower every day…which is about five times more often than usual."

Sally settles down onto the canoe seat and peeks over her shoulder at Sam with a devilish grin. "Me, too."

"I'm comin' aboard," he warns. "Just relax."

"I bet I'm not the first woman you've said that to." She wiggles her eyebrows.

Sally can't see that Sam is grinning from ear to ear as he slides his feet into the canoe then scoots his butt over the gunwale onto the seat. Yes, he likes his life uncomplicated. And screwing around with a married woman would certainly be complicated, even if she played by his rules, and even with somebody as desirable as Sally. But these past twenty hours (yes, he's counting) have been the most fun he's had in six years. Three hours to the bridge by his house, Sam thinks…only three hours, dammit.

To Sally, as she gazes in silence down the river, Sam seems safe. He's not going to impose on her or demand anything, and therefore she can be her normal, playful self. She can tell, like Maureen had assured her, that he's the proverbial "nice guy". It might not be fair—to herself, to her husband, or to Sam—to hang out with him like this, even for just an innocent Sunday. But he's just acting like an old buddy, or an older brother without much of a filter, so why not enjoy the company of a new and interesting friend?

Sally had never been unfaithful to Bill; she'd never been unfaithful to anyone before Bill either. Sam had only one demerit in that particular marital department. It had happened toward the tail end of his first marriage. The neighbor lady, in a hot tub. (She'd always flirted with Sam at the mailbox, and in the supermarket.) Sam's wife and kids had been out of town, and so was the neighbor lady's husband. He would argue it wasn't his fault. She'd asked him to change the filter on the hot tub, she was cute, and she'd gotten him drunk on White Russians, which she mixed by the pitcherful.

Is there an attraction here that might be more than platonic? If you asked Sally in strict confidence, she might admit, "I did put on makeup and clean underwear this morning."

If you asked Sam, he might admit, "When's the last time I showered two days in a row?"

Sally feels him settle into the canoe and she relaxes. She reaches down into the water and sends a handful back toward Sam. The water seems almost freezing.

"Hey, as much fun as it was rollin' down into the gravel pit and bein' body-slammed, I've only fallen out of this canoe once, twenty years ago. And I intend to wait at least another twenty years to break the streak, so knock that shit off, please."

Sam hangs onto a tree root sticking out from the bank and lets the current swing the front of the canoe out into the stream six feet. He pushes the bank gently with the tip of his paddle at the right moment to slowly propel the canoe perfectly into a canoe-wide chute of water between the tops of two ash trees that had been felled by beavers.

Sally reaches back for her paddle.

"No need," Sam says quietly. "All you gotta do for the next three hours is relax and enjoy the river. It moves steady like this all the way. All I do back here is steer once in a while to keep us on course. And refill our wine cups."

Sally inhales deeply, and her shoulders visibly loosen. She leans back a little and stretches her neck muscles to both sides. Her long blonde ponytail catches the sunlight and shines a brilliant deep gold.

There are a good many obstacles in the first quarter mile, but nothing serious. Beaver trees every several dozen yards. Sam steers close to them because the wash off the branches creates slightly deeper water. The rocks just barely under the surface give away their hiding places with telltale ripples. He deftly uses his paddle as a rudder and steers around them. What Sam sees on the water and feels through the canoe, the ripples he hears—it's second nature, like being on autopilot, even when he canoes at night.

They approach a rocky riffle.

"Look up ahead, just beyond those rocks," Sam whispers. A school of a dozen fish frantically scatter several yards in front of them, most escaping downstream. Three dash upstream, giving the canoe as wide a berth as they can in the thirty feet of river they have.

"What are they?"

"That's the second run of suckers already," Sam answers, authoritatively. "They're 'red horse' suckers. The white suckers, and most of the walleyes, are gone already. They must've done their run while I was in Boise. I heard we had an early warm spell."

"Gone? Where is there to go?"

Sam likes having a brand new student in the bow with whom he can share his plethora of self-taught river knowledge.

"Yup, they're only in the river long enough to spawn. Then they go back downstream to Fox Lake. Don't be surprised if we have four, five, six close encounters with bald eagles this afternoon. They'll be perched on limbs over the river, watching intently for lunch to swim past. Ever have a totally surprised eagle suddenly take flight ten feet over your head? We might today if we're quiet."

"This your first time down the river this year?" Sally asks.

"Lemme see." Sam ponders for a few seconds. "This is actually my sixth or seventh trip. My maiden voyage was the first week of February. Remember that warm spell?"

"I'd expect the river to be frozen in February—all of February, and all March and April. Northern Minnesota's awfully close to the Arctic Circle, ya know."

"It is frozen bank-to-bank most of the winter. But if we get three or four days when the temperature's above freezing, the middle of the river opens up."

"But canoeing in winter?" Sally asks. "Really, aren't you afraid of fallin' in and freezin' to death?"

"Oh, no more afraid of the river in winter than I suppose you are of fallin' off your horse and breakin' your neck. Canoeing, any time of year…it's just what I do."

Sally leans around and looks at him like he should be committed.

Sam decides that further explanation of his unusual winter river interludes will be helpful. "An ancient Sufi poet named Rumi wrote: 'Siddhartha learned from the ferryman while he was the ferryman's protégé and searching for the meaning of life that *All of life's answers can be found in the river.*' The ferryman didn't specify winter or summer, but I don't think India had much of a winter in fifth century BC."

Sally notes, "You have a cosmic, philosophical side that isn't obvious at first. Where did that come from?"

"Oh, I s'pose it's one part curiosity, and maybe two parts boredom. Winters get awfully long around these parts, even with an occasional canoe trip tossed in. Hey, if I'm gonna live the part of the weird recluse, I should be able to talk with some authority and accuracy."

"Canoeing in winter? You don't think everyone this side of the Arctic Circle thinks that's crazy?" Sally asks. She gazes skyward and points like she's reading something. "I can see your epitaph now: 'Here Lies Sam Ryan, Froze to Death, aka *Canoes in Winter*.'"

"Next winter," Sam offers, "I'll show you. Really, not too many folks know about this river in winter, the magic. It's a different world. And it's somethin' to do after football season when the only channel you get on the TV's running an incessant string of annoying infomercials about glorified food blenders."

For half an hour, the river meanders lazily through a swampy valley that extends a quarter mile each direction. Floating bog, punctuated with swamp grass, cattails, alder brush, willow, and a myriad of water-loving plants and flowers. In the late summer, the open water, flowing or stagnant, will have turned into a wild rice bed, stalks six feet tall, that grow so thick in the denser patches Sam won't have room to reach a paddle forward and dip it back to him. He'll have to grab the stalks to pull his canoe through.

The pretty forested run begins right below the rice bed. Two hours of gliding over rocky, gravely, sandy river bed, with solid river banks and trees growing right to the water's edge and up the slopes as far as you can see into the woods. The evergreens—jack pine, white and black spruce, red pine, white pine, and balsam—dot the landscape. The hardwoods, most just beginning to leaf, dominate though. Only the swamp ash still appear lifeless. They are the last to leaf out in the spring and the first to go bare early in the fall.

Just like below the dam that quarter mile above the rice bed, the beavers have been very busy in the forested part. Wood ducks and mallards take frantic flight seemingly from behind every fallen tree and around every bend. Every rippling run where small rocks cover the river bottom, redhorse suckers scatter like confetti shot from a cannon. A hatch of tiny mayflies is underway. Migrating warblers flit out from the woods, snatch insects, and quickly return to their perches. A tom turkey gobbles every few minutes back in the woods—at crows cawing, blue jays screaming, an airplane flying overhead—hoping to attract a hen's company. A muskrat swims surprisingly swiftly underwater, with a mouthful of fresh greens trailing behind.

Sam steers the canoe onto a gravel bar near the north bank. It crunches to a stop in a couple inches of water. "I'm thirsty. How 'bout you?"

Sally notices he's wearing an old pair of sneakers and no socks. He swings his legs over the edge of the canoe and sloshes up to the front. Pulling the craft up onto where the ground is solid and dry, he offers a hand to help her out.

The sun pours down soothing warmth. "I've taken a few naps right here," Sam confides. He holds his arms out to his sides like a pelican drying its wings from atop a wooden post at the end of an ocean pier. He whispers in his mind, *Thank you, dear river…*

"That was just the first act." Sam leans over the canoe and opens the cooler, pulling out a bottle of wine and two paper cups. He finds the corkscrew under the plastic bags with cheese, crackers, and sausage, all cut and ready.

He pours for Sally first and then for himself. "Here's to morels, deer antlers, the river, and good company."

Their paper cups touch lightly. Sally smiles, but not as brightly as Sam had hoped she would. He can sense a twinge of guilt in her. Maybe she'd forgotten for a moment that she's married, and is now having regrets spending the day with him.

But she toasts as well, her smile a bit counterfeit, "To my philosophical river guide and his great, wild grape wine."

She sips and nods her approval. "By the way, how is the top of your head?"

"I forgot all about it again. Almost good as new, I s'pose. Your sister did a great job as usual. Price was right, too. And I really like the open bar part."

"Did she use that hocus-pocus on you?" Her tone is more direct than an offhand, a curious query.

"I don't know."

"Last night Maureen told me about your talks. I don't get it and I'm not sure about that stuff. In fact, I'm pretty skeptical about this spiritual healin' business."

"I don't go on a soapbox about it like Maureen does. It's just there…if the time and place is right, and I remember to use it."

His eyes seem to be looking far away at a memory coming back to him. "I did go to a weekend retreat about five years ago to learn more and maybe become better at it. I might've been graspin' at straws, lookin' for some 'grand purpose'. I had a feeling it'd be a waste of time and money."

"They give classes on that stuff? I thought you got it from a bolt of lightning, or an angel named Gabriel." Sally smiles.

"That particular modality I studied back then— reiki, it's called. The teacher tried her best to pigeon-hole it. Said she and her teachers owned it, and once 'certified'…" Sam forms air quotes. "…we were authorized to go out and train others. We were given a list of materials to buy and then resell to our students. Seemed like a pyramid scheme to me. At best, it was multi-level marketing. There was very little talk about actual spiritual healing, and only a couple hours of us layin' our hands above each other. She warned us to charge plenty or it wouldn't work!"

Sam shakes his head and can't stifle a grin as he takes a sip of wine.

Sally looks at him curiously. "What is it?"

"I said to the teacher 'Master, please excuse me, but I don't remember Christ tellin' his apostles, 'That'll be three hundred shekels to learn how to perform miracles, and you better make sure those lepers bring you a big fat chicken.'"

"You didn't!"

"Yeah, that was the end of my formal trainin', right there on the spot," Sam admits, shaking his head and still smiling. "The patchouli was chokin' me anyway. And MY GOD, if you're gonna wear a sleeveless sack cloth top, shave your armpits and put on some deodorant."

He fetches the wine bottle from the cooler and pulls the cork out. "Here, some for the road."

Sally settles onto her canoe seat facing Sam, her cup held between her knees, and braces herself with a hand on each gunwale. Sam drags the canoe back into a few inches of water, deep enough that it will float, and he gets in butt first, dangling his legs while the water drips out of his shoes.

Sally's curious to hear more. "Can you tell me about it? Give some examples of when you think it actually worked?"

Sam pulls his feet in and straightens himself on the seat. With two gentle, quiet strokes of his paddle, he directs the canoe into the middle of the river. There's nothing in their path in the hundred yard stretch ahead to the next bend. He places the paddle across the gunwales in front of him and cradles his cup with both hands, his elbows on his knees, contemplating. He hopes Sally isn't busting him for claims that he's raised the dead or shrunken tumors.

"Well, I use it mostly on my bus kids, like if I see in the mirror that little Lexi or Jacob is gettin' kinda pale around the gills."

Sally imitates him, "Hey kid, lemme lay my hands on you! Hallelujah!"

"Not quite," Sam answers, grinning. "I do have a backup plan on one route: Elisa. She'll hold the wastebasket for 'em, but I try to keep it from gettin' that far."

Sam shakes his head, as if he doesn't believe it himself. "You're gonna think I'm as crazy as your sister. This is where it becomes hard to explain. Mentally (or psychically) first I ask the kid's guide or angels, who are always with them, if the kid wants my help. If I get a *Yes* in my mind, I just imagine the sick kid surrounded by healing blue light. Only takes a few seconds, don't even have to take my eyes off the road. It works on the kids almost every time for minor things like potential puking and headaches. Two stops later, the little rascals'll be back pullin' somebody's hair or stuffin' their face full of bubble gum."

"Does it work on animals?"

Sam nods, "It has. I think…"

"Tell me?"

Absently, Sam sets his cup on the canoe floor and gives the water a small stroke to keep the craft pointed straight downstream.

"My second wife and I had a little farm. We kept a few horses. She brought them into our relationship. Had a couple of mares we had bred every year. Got a good-natured sorrel colt we named Scotch, who we thought would be just as smooth-movin' as his mother. He had an overbite, so we eventually had 'im cut. Wouldn't get much for him at the sale, so we decided to keep him for my wife's daughter, who was away at college. We don't know what he went colicky from that fall mornin' (probably acorns) but he was bound up tight. I'm sure you know the drill. The vet did all he could, pain killers plus oil in both ends."

Sally nods, her brow furrowed with concern.

"Nothin' moved. Scotch was miserable. Kept tryin' to roll, but I wouldn't let him. I'd slap him with the lead rope and yank on his halter. My wife put the rendering service on notice. I spent the whole day alternating between walkin' the colt up and down the driveway and pinnin' him in a corner of the stall so I could put my hands on his belly and send healing light through them and into his gut.

"My wife brought me out a beer and somethin' to eat every couple hours. She walked him when I needed nourishment or rest. I heard her whisperin' to Scotch one walk, *He's crazy...but God, I hope it works.*"

Sally's engrossed in the story and has forgotten her wine. Expressionless, she looks Sam square in the face.

"I also spent the whole night workin' on Scotch. My wife checked on me a couple times. Then right after sunrise, the colt and I were in the stall, both of us exhausted, and I had him pinned to the wall. He lunged and got loose from me. Before I could get my hands on the lead rope, he lifted his tail and took a huge, steaming green dump—a perfect shit!

"His ears perked up and he pawed at the floor in front of the barn door. I opened it and barely got outta the way. He charged into the pasture, kickin' and buckin' (and fartin'), his lead rope trailin', and dumped again. I could hear my wife let out a whoop in the house. Her oldest daughter, who never liked me, never did thank me. Scotch turned out to be a helluva good horse for her."

Sally asks, "You think that's what really did it? Or was it just persistence?"

"I don't know for sure. Doesn't matter anyway. All I know is sometimes there ain't no explanation for why sick people and animals get better."

Sam adds, "The trouble with that whole deal was, I slept for almost twenty-four hours after Scotch was okay. And when I woke up, I had pneumonia."

"You mean, performing the healing made you sick?"

"Not sure. Not sure whether it was the healin' part or being up and workin' so hard for twenty-four hours straight. Or maybe I was just s'posed to get sick that day. I wanted so badly for him to live that I might have given him my energy. My life force, so to speak. You know, depleted myself. A healer should never get that personally involved, shouldn't be tryin' to trump the person's or animal's will—or the Universe's will."

"You mean, you should have quit on Scotch?"

"No…it's hard to explain. It's like when my mother was dyin'. There was no hope, we all knew that. Still,

I think my siblings were prayin' for her to miraculously recover. I prayed for her will, and also the Universe's will, to be accomplished in peace. I was not gonna ask Mom to stay and suffer one second more on my account, if it was the time she was choosin' to go.

"My brothers and sisters were angry as hell with me when I told 'em that's how I prayed for Mom. And they really think I'm crazy for prayin' to a different god than they do. Except for one, they disowned me for tellin' 'em I believe their God and the devil are creations—equal creations—of the god I recognize and refer to as The Universe (although I call it God sometimes out of habit, I guess). All their God and devil are for, I told 'em, is to provide platforms, options, to work through and eventually get back to The real source, the Universe, where everything's perfect. Knowin' that's just a start, though. We still have to do the work."

"I have no idea what you're talkin' about," Sally admits with a shrug. "But I'm real sorry about your mom. And I'm glad somebody listened to your prayers for her. Me? I don't do much prayin' anymore, or talkin' to the spirits, or the Universe, or whatever you call all that.

"Now I'll be quiet," Sally whispers as she carefully swings her legs out over the water and pivots to face forward. "See if you can get us close to an eagle, please, and maybe some deer."

They drift on down the forested valley silently, except for the sound of an occasional drop of water off Sam's paddle. When Sally sees something—a fish, a songbird, a mink or a muskrat, painted turtles sunning themselves on logs—she points. Sam's surprised and impressed with her keen eye and also her care in not disturbing the river and its inhabitants.

Four bends in the river after their stop for wine, Sally points toward a tamarack snag with bare limbs and no bark left on it. A young bald eagle, brown and mottled with patches of grayish-white, is perched fifteen feet up on a limb, out over the water. The giant bird, facing downstream, is oblivious to their approach. Sam gently dips the paddle into the stream. He angles it like a rudder, directing the canoe to pass right under the young eagle, careful not to let the paddle scrape the riverbed or bump the canoe.

The plan works. Sally leans back as far as she can and looks straight up at the eagle. Sam has to noisily scrape the river bed to stop the canoe. They would've been discovered in another couple of feet anyway. The eagle takes clamorous flight, the wind under its wing feathers whooshing loudly. Its yellow feet dangle for several powerful, slow wing beats and then, like a jetliner retracting its takeoff gear, the young bald eagle tucks its legs tight to its underside and disappears around the next bend.

"Look!" Sally whispers loudly, pointing up into the dead tamarack.

A single downy under-feather, an inch long and wispy, floats almost weightlessly. Every unseen, unheard, unfelt baby's breath of breeze sends the feather on a new path, this way or that, as it descends as slowly as a crumb of fish food into an aquarium. Lower and lower it drifts toward Sally. While holding her breath, in slow motion

Sally reaches her hand out in front of her. Like a butterfly to a bloom, the feather lands in her palm. Slowly, she pulls her hand to her chest. The tendrils of wispy feather wave in the invisible air.

She cups her free hand over the feather and turns to Sam. Her face is part joy but mostly disbelief. Sally gently directs her breath through her slightly parted lips onto the feather. It rises from her hand as if pulled on an invisible string. A stray, imperceptible breeze catches the feather and it rides the air current slowly upward. Sam and Sally watch in silence as the downy feather continues rising skyward magically—ten feet, fifteen feet, higher—beyond where the young bald eagle had perched in wait for a meal. Out of the forest flies a warbler. It hovers a yard away from the feather for a second, darts forward and snatches the feather in its beak, and flits back into the forest.

Sally turns back to Sam, her eyes questioning. He knows what she's thinking.

"No," he assures her. "A warbler knows a bug from a feather. It'll make great lining for its nest."

An hour into the forested section, Sam noses the canoe into a slot between a deadfall and the shore. It is a place he calls the "high sand bank", a hillside facing south forty feet above the river, with soil too light and an incline too steep to grow a cover of grass or low brush, but not so steep it can't be traversed at an angle. The deer use the high sand bank to get to the river, their trail etched across it at a gentle angle, a path flattened wide enough they can walk the trail up and down.

"You want to go up there and sit for a while, stretch your legs? Maybe take care of business back in the trees?" Sam asks, pointing up the hill.

"Yeah, that'd be nice."

"I'll bring the cooler, give you a head start."

Sam's surprised when, after five minutes, Sally hasn't reappeared at the top of the bank. He ascends the bank himself, but there's no sign of her at the top either. He mulls the possibilities and decides it could be very ungentlemanly of him to go find her. He pours himself more wine.

"Sam!" Sally shouts. "Come here and bring that plastic bag! Morels! All over back here!"

He pours more wine into Sally's cup and follows the deer trail up over the back side of the hill. She has her shirt gathered up in front of her, stowing morels in it like a grandmother might carry eggs in her apron back from the henhouse. The sight of her bare, tan stomach compels Sam to rub his forehead so he can divert his eyes.

"Just pickin' the really big ones," Sally hollers up the hill. "You didn't eat yours last night. Thought you might want a good meal of fresh ones tonight. Can you show me how you make 'em stuffed?"

Sam's caught off guard by Sally inviting herself to supper. He walks down the gentle hill to her and holds the plastic bag open while she dumps the morels into it. Sally grins like a child on Christmas morning as she brushes morel crumbs and bits of soil off the front of her sweatshirt.

"Umm...umm...sure," he agrees. "I'll have to stop in Stone Creek and pick up a couple of things."

It's not that he doesn't appreciate Sally's company. But it wasn't an hour earlier that he sensed guilt in her. And of course Sam has his rules…

"I'm sorry, that was forward of me, invitin' myself to dinner." Sally averts her gaze from Sam to the ground. "I'm havin' such a good time. You have to be wonderin'…"

"Um…I'm not takin' any of this any particular way," Sam fibs as he kneels down to pinch off a black morel with a huge five-inch long cap. He stays close to the ground looking around. "We're just two adults, enjoyin' each other's company, right? No agenda. I have plenty of married women friends I do stuff like this with, pickin' morels and raspberries, canoein', makin' wine. I haven't been hit in the ass with buckshot by an angry husband yet. To those women and their husbands, I must be a gelding. Works for me."

Sally replies, "Obviously, you're not a gelding. You been married twice, right?"

"Half a dozen more," Sam estimates, "and we'll have plenty to fill two cookie sheets."

Then he answers her question in a monotone. "Twenty-one years, one month, three days, and sixteen hours, to the mother of my kids. Did the rebound thing as soon as the ink was dry on the divorce papers. Then I was with Karen, the lady with horses, somethin' around six years. Never did do the math that time. How 'bout you?"

Sally points to another cluster of morels. "Just this one time. Had lots of offers. I'm not braggin', but I turned down three rings before I took the one from Bill. Figured I wasn't gettin' any younger. That was almost three years ago."

"You mentioned yesterday..." Sam says, breaking Rule Number One himself. "Not going so good, huh?" He picks the two biggest morels from a group of at least ten.

"I figured if I waited 'til I was thirty-five to get married, I'd know what I was doin'...and at forty, Bill would know what he was doin'. I knew Bill's family well. Actually, Pop is the father I never really had. Taught me how to ride when I was eleven. Came to all my events and activities at school. After I left Streeter, I still came home for holidays to be with Pop and his wife Emma, just like a daughter would do."

Sam points to another sizable morel and bends down to it. "That should do it."

"You mind if I ask what happened to your father?" he asks. "Maureen and I've never talked about your parents, other than the fact that they're both gone."

"He was a drunk. Died when I was ten. Wrapped his truck around a big white pine..." Her voice trails off.

"And your mother?"

"She took too many pills. That happened when I was away at college. She was always depressed."

"Sorry to hear that." With his hand outstretched, Sam offers Sally the lead up the path back to the high sand bank.

There's a pregnant silence as they walk back.

"How 'bout a bite to eat?" Without waiting for an answer he sits with his legs over the edge of the bank.

"No thanks, I'm okay." She gazes out over the valley and sighs. She sips her wine and sits down next to Sam.

Shaking her head and shifting her focus to her shoes, Sally sucks in a loud breath. "I knew Bill had a reputation. It was common knowledge he could get any woman into the sack. Every time I'd come home to see Pop and Emma, he'd work on me to go out with him. I never did, though, back then.

"Then five years after I left, Emma died. I came home from Oregon for her funeral. After that, Bill sent me flowers and lotsa other gifts and called me a lot, even though he knew I was engaged to another man. Pop had a stroke a year after Emma died. Bill took the farm over, and moved back from Grand Forks to take care of Pop. Except Bill hated takin' care of Pop's cattle. He thought they were a huge waste of time, space, and money.

"It was time for me to leave Oregon anyway. I was and still am convinced that Bill's runnin' days were…are… really over. He was persistent and, I admit, pretty darn charming. A year later we married, I moved in, and Bill went back to his lumberyard job. Bill's brother, Robert, watched the cattle when Bill was gone. And I took care of Pop. That's when Pop deeded 240 acres of the 320 over to me, Bill, and Robert jointly. What happened to the farm after that is a whole other story."

"So, what's goin' on with you and Bill?" Sam asks gently.

"Let's just say Bill isn't as *charming* as he used to be." Sally closes her eyes for a moment. "But I know we can make it work if we just give it some time and space. I can't handle bein' home on weekends right now, and not just because Bill and I are havin' trouble."

"Sorry to hear that." Sam's eyes are squinted a little and his brow furrowed like he has a question. But he doesn't speak further. Out of the corner of his eye, he sees Sally turn to him.

She tightens her lips together and shakes her head in disgust.

"Goddamnit. Two months after Pop deeded us the land, Bill and Robert sold all the cattle (which I guess were technically one-third mine) without askin' me, or carin' what that would do to Pop. They ended up with quite a chunka change and used the money to turn our jointly-owned two-forty and some of the other eighty into a damn four-wheel drive obstacle course, complete with campgrounds, stinkin' port-a-johns all over, and a pole barn clubhouse. Somehow, with the aid of their crooked attorney, they got all the permits and even a liquor license. It's a mess and it's noisier 'n hell.

"Used to be such beautiful, rolling woods, a wonderful pasture, with little sloughs dotted here and there... It was like a park. Now those little watering holes are four-wheeler mud runs and there is hardly a blade of grass in there anywhere. Can't even keep those drunken, drugged-up Billy-Bob wannabe idiots who come out on weekends outta the horse pasture. My other mare, Dakota...they ran her through a fence and she got cut all to hell."

Sally closes her eyes and shakes her head slowly. "I'm not so sure I'd recommend anybody gettin' hitched for the first time at that age...or even married at all. And you did it twice? Do you mind if I ask, what happened with you?"

Her question catches Sam off guard and instinctively he sits straight up and stiff. He wasn't planning on sharing his history, at least not that part of it. He feels obligated to say something and buys himself a couple seconds by lifting the paper cup to his mouth. After swallowing the wine, he sighs and wipes off his lips with the back of his hand.

"Whew...What happened? A question I've asked myself a lot. Other than the fact that it hurt my kids to see their parents break up, I have no regrets at all about leavin' my first wife. I think we married to be like our parents. Even married our parents, in a way. It was safe. We didn't fight, we just went through the motions of bein' not terminally unhappy. Then I got the middle-age crazies, I felt guilty about not really lovin' her, and knew somethin' had to change. Turns out she had the crazies, too.

"My second wife…to be honest, I don't think I was good marriage material after all, although we both found somethin' pretty special that neither of us'd had with our first spouses."

"What do you mean by 'pretty special'?" Sally asks.

"With Karen, I found out what it's like to be married to my best friend. It's pretty intoxicatin' when someone wants to be with you, wants to touch you, just because you are you, when you've never experienced anything like that before. I'm not just talkin' about makin' love, but that does take on a new meaning. It's an entirely different experience when you really care about each other on that level.

"Once, Karen and I drove all the way to Phoenix and back, detourin' to Boise. We never turned the radio on the whole trip, just visited. The little things were so nice, like cookin' together or workin' in the yard."

The pleasant memories allow Sam's shoulders to loosen and a little smile to cross his face.

"One morning, I was listenin' to the radio and readin' the paper at the kitchen table. Karen was makin' the coffee. A song came on, one of my favorites, 'Then You Can Tell Me Goodbye.'"

Sam stares off above the treetops, his eyes beginning to glisten.

"What is it?" Sally asks softly, and touches his shoulder with her fingertips.

"A line in the song," he says, almost in a whisper. "A line in the song...Karen heard me singin' to myself under my breath, *Sweeten my coffee with a morning kiss*. I looked up at her and smiled. She had my favorite cup in her hands ready to pour it full. But first she kissed the rim of my coffee cup. She did that every chance she had from that day on, even when she got up early for work long before I'd be rollin' outta the sack. When I'd get up, my clean coffee cup would be settin' next to the coffeemaker, her fresh lipstick on the rim."

Sally breathes out a barely perceptible, "Whew."

Sam senses it's time to lighten things up. "I did eventually figure out a way to pay Karen back," he says while laughing. "I'd shave 'er legs for her!"

"What? Shave her LEGS?!!"

"Actually, only when the kids weren't home and we had time..."

Her eyes wide with surprise, Sally asks, "Have time? How darn long does it take to shave somebody's legs?"

He grins and winks, "Oh, up to an hour, if ya know what I mean?"

"Really?"

Sam turns away to hide his eyes. He hopes that someplace inside that pretty head, Sally's trying to imagine her and Bill doing any of the things he and Karen had shared. He knows enough about Bill already to know that Sally's shaving her own legs and not sweetening Bill's coffee.

She breaks the ice, asking sympathetically, "So, what happened to you and Karen? You don't have to say if you don't want..."

"I'm still workin' on it...six years later," Sam replies, his eyes trained on the distant tree line. "I'll let you know if I figure it out. What are you guys gonna do, Sally? Counseling?"

"Probably not," she says. "Bill would never go. Heck, we've been tryin' to have a baby since the wedding, but he won't go in for a checkup to see if there's somethin' not right with him. I checked out fine."

Sam chuckles under his breath.

"What's so damn funny?"

"Well, it occurred to me there are a coupla ways you could have *snuck* a sample out of Bill, when he was sleepin'..." Sam continues to chuckle, but after a few seconds of silence from Sally, he regains his composure. "Sorry. I know how serious you are about wantin' a baby."

Sally inquires, "You mean a man can sleep through either of *those*?"

He covers his eyes and shakes his head.

Sam already knows he doesn't like Bill. Not one bit. He imagines Bill to be, if not big and handsome, at least big and a bully, like a football linebacker on steroids. He wishes he hadn't broken his own rule and helped the conversation along. He's not in the mood to hear any more about Sally and Bill, thanks in the most part to his own crack.

Sally offers, "I'll be stayin' home next weekend to see if we can work on our stuff...and just get through a weekend. Also, that should be my fertile time. I gotta wonder if this is as good as it gets for anyone. I got my horses, my dog, my sister, a decent job, good friends...and Pop. What's a little bickerin' on weekends?"

Sam has never discussed "fertile time" with any of the women he hangs out with. He looks around the woods, hoping there might be a replacement topic of discussion in the trees. Finding no such rescue, he asks what's on the tip of his tongue anyway. "You sure he really wants a baby?"

"Course I'm sure," Sally answers confidently.

"Well, then…good luck next weekend!" Sam offers, faking encouragement. But his face can't hide his exasperation over Sally's faith in overcoming her doomed situation. This is the exact reason he runs like hell when a woman complains about her husband, but then assumes she'll somehow make it work with the bastard.

Sam avoids eye contact with Sally because he senses she's glaring at him.

"Wait a minute. You asked about Bill, and now you're givin' me the silent treatment? You mentioned last night in your state of extreme inebriation something about rules for married women. 'As long as they know the rules' is what you said."

"Sorry. A little less than an hour back to your truck." He offers wine. "Might as well finish this."

"No, I need to know about these all-important rules!"

"I'd rather just forget this whole thing," Sam pleads. "I know I'm guilty of askin' too much. The truth is, I…I'm… not comfortable hearin' so much about your relationship, or about any married woman's less than perfect situation with her husband."

"You think I'm hittin' on you, don't you?" Sally's eyes are angry slits. One hand is on a hip while she aims her empty wine cup at Sam's face. "Do you think I'm lookin' for sympathy to trick you into the sack?"

"Nope. Nope."

Sam quickly repacks the cooler and heads across the high sand bank, angling down the hill. Sally follows him down the deer trail only half a step behind like a banty rooster. Sam stops suddenly and turns to his pursuer.

"Okay. Here it is straight," Sam says in exasperation. "I run like hell when a woman starts tellin' me about her asshole of a husband. In fact, if we weren't almost an hour from your truck, all you'd see of me ever again is my ass going over that hill. But you can fix that part by…by not talkin' about Bill again. And I apologize I brought him up. Honestly."

"And if I agree to leave Bill out of our conversation," Sally challenges, "then what?"

"Then," Sam winces, "we're just buddies doin' stuff a couple times a year. But if you ask me to do anything 'husbandly' that isn't part of my personal repertoire, like go with you places, meet you somewhere, do chores, or fix your stuff, my rules state that you will be required to sleep with me, no strings attached." He covers his genitals with the cooler.

A laugh begins building deep inside Sally. She hides her eyes with her left hand and holds her belly with her right hand.

"So how's that workin' for ya?" Sally asks, shaking her head and grinning. "You gettin' laid quite a bit?"

Sam's confused. He eyes her suspiciously, still protecting his crotch. "Umm…enough."

"Define 'enough.'"

"Well…I guess it's been over five years," Sam admits.

"Well, don't look at me," Sally says. "Not that you're not *doable*." She eyes him up and down like a man would a stripper.

Sam turns quickly and heads down the angled deer trail toward the canoe.

"By the way," Sally asks, talking to his back. "Just curious, and don't read anything into this, but did you ride much when you were with Karen?"

"Some," he answers with a shrug. He wades into the river and holds the canoe steady for Sally to get in. "We did trails with some other couples, mostly as gab sessions and to have a few beers along the way. Then they'd all wait for me to get back on after I got bucked off."

Sally grins. "I'm ridin' at the rodeo grounds next Saturday night, barrel racing. I'm helpin' to put the races on during halftime. I'll be ridin' Dakota, the best mare I've ever had. Stop out, if you want. I might even put you to work in the arena settin' barrels when they get knocked. But only if you want to. That way, you won't be obligated to sleep with me." Sally flashes that spectacular smile but etched in it is a little wickedness this time.

"What about Bill?" Sam asks. "Isn't he gonna go help and watch you ride?"

"I'm sure he'll be too busy ruining our two hundred and forty acres with the Billy-Bobs."

"I'll check my schedule," Sam lies.

"You know," Sally asks, furrowing her brow. "How about a rain check on the stuffed morels tonight? I'd like to make some fresh fried morels for Pop instead. Besides, I don't feel like a 'date' tonight anyway."

"Me neither," Sam lies.

CHAPTER 6

SAM'S DAMN RULES

A new set of rules. Or at least some asterisks if he shows up at Sally's barrel races.

A feeling in Sam's gut reminds him of that first summer in his house in the hills when he'd had an affair with a similarly ill-married woman. The sex was okay, but Sam felt used, even though he wasn't in love with her. She was having it both ways. Never had to make a real choice and complained often about her husband, even while she and Sam were in bed together. Sam took up the slack that hubby left.

It was sex, not making love. The act of it reminded him how it felt with his first wife toward the end, with no connection, except the obvious physical one. Sure, that part felt good. But rolling off, and over, without even a goodnight kiss, made it feel meaningless, like he was cheating on himself. With the married woman, it was slam, bam, then she'd set a date and time for their next encounter while she was dressing.

Not that Sam suspects Sally's that kind of woman, sizing him up for a roll in the hay or three. He'd rather go without than just fuck. That's what it always was with a married woman.

And not that Sam knows Bill Hunter at this point, but he knows enough. And Bill isn't Sam's problem anyway. But, it sure sounds like Sally had gone to the pet store looking for a cute and cuddly kitten. But because they were out of them, and Sally had vowed she wasn't going home empty-handed, instead she took home a skunk she found trotting down the white line of the road.

So, why then, Sam wonders, is she surprised that Bill stinks?

Sam's week consists of two full-day school bus trips to the cities (Monday and Wednesday), two days of substitute driving (Tuesday and Friday), and one "Sam Day" (Thursday). On that day, he's left totally to his own devices.

Maybe a solo trip down the river, if the weather cooperates. Pick whatever fruit or mushrooms are in season. Toss a few arrows at the styrofoam deer target. Fiddle with the wine—de-labeling used bottles, bottling, enjoying a glass with lunch. Dream about the winery, cement-in more fieldstone on the walls. Drive the trails, wander off into the woods. A quiet sit in the CBS (Sam's permanent deer stand, the Charlie Brown Stand he'd made totally out of used scrap lumber…and looks like it). Cook up a nice supper that goes well with bourbon and water. Fetch more rocks from the gravel pit the other side of Stone Creek. Maybe a drink in town.

He also does a lot of thinking on Sam Days. Now he'll have one more subject to ponder, whether he wants to or not: Sally Hunter. She's there in a glass of wine. She's naked on top of him (except for a hat). She's smiling with the tiny, downy eagle feather in her hand. She's putting up with the four-wheeler bullshit for the weekend, to have sex with Bill.

Saturday's not meant to be a Sam Day, or a Sally Day, and he makes sure of that. Cleans the chicken coop of the winter's six inches of shit mixed with straw—stifling ammonia, with a pitchfork, prying the eye-watering pack loose from the wood floor and breaking it into chunks with the tines, then wheeling it to the compost heap. Changing oil and filters on the tractor, then greasing it. Same thing on the pickup truck. Raking the leaves from against the house onto a plastic tarp, dragging them into the woods. Switching out storm windows by hauling them to the barn, bringing screens back from there, the extension ladder, the two upstairs windows, too. A load of laundry and a mountain of dirty dishes. Cleaning the shower, toilet, bathroom, and kitchen sinks. The linoleum floors in the kitchen and bathroom, sweep and mop, and the painted wood floors in the bedrooms and hallway. Vacuuming the living room carpet. But there's Sally, dammit, helping him to the couch…

She certainly won't haunt him at the bar in Park Rapids. But two beers later, he sees a poster for the bull ride and barrel races taped to the bathroom wall. And there she is again.

A lanky teenage boy, atop a painted sorrel horse that is oblivious, waves his cowboy hat to keep the spectators' vehicles moving into the rodeo grounds parking area, a grassy field. Sam's is one of the last vehicles to be let in.

The kid nudges his horse into a trot, and reaches Sam where the driveway splits—spectators to the left, contestants and rodeo help straight ahead. The contestants' entrance is roped off.

He asks, "How many old blue Ford pickups are there in this county? You're about the fifteenth one. Are *you* Sam?"

Sam nods, a little confused.

Leaning over toward Sam's window, the kid hands him a rodeo pass. "Sally left this for you. She's parked somewhere over there with the rest of the contestants."

The kid waves his hat at another kid, younger by a few years. "Jimmy!" the teenager hollers, "Let 'im through, please."

Sam assumes the younger kid, also in boots and the proper hat for the day, is working his way up, paying his dues with a less glamorous job. Jimmy lets the rope to the ground and points down a driveway through the trees. "If you're lookin' for Sally, she's toward the back."

What made her think Sam would show up? Was she hoping he would, or hoping he wouldn't? Hell, until forty-five minutes ago, Sam was just gonna have a few too many beers in town and a bad pizza, and that would be his evening. So why did he bring along a bottle of wine and two paper cups?

On the other hand, as badly as he'd tried to keep her out of his head all week, she's just over there.

Horse trailers and campers are parked roughly in maybe six or seven lines with a dozen or so rigs in each. Cowboy hats and boots are milling about. Horses are everywhere—tied to trailers, being led or ridden. Sam drives slowly, peering down each line of rigs.

He sees Sally's gray Dodge and black stock trailer in the last row. She's busy saddling a bay horse, and doesn't notice him drive up and park at the end of the line, two rigs away. She'd brought along Sparky, too, who's already saddled.

Sally's in blue jeans, a wine-colored sweatshirt, and dirty old boots with horse crap stuck in the seam between the leather top and sole. She's wearing an old baseball hat with greenish smudges from horse slobber, her ponytail hanging out the back. Her clothes are a stark contrast to most of the folks on horses, who are wearing starched western clothes, new boots, and stiff, clean hats.

"Hey there, cowgirl!" Sam hollers as he rounds the front of her truck.

She turns with a start. The horses snap to attention, their ears pointing straight up.

She hollers back, smiling as usual, "Come on over here. Want you to meet Dakota. She's my star! Aren't you girl?" Sally gives Dakota a long hug around the neck.

When she looks back, he notices her left eye is banged up, even though she's done a pretty good job covering it with makeup.

"You gonna race Sparky, too?" Sam asks.

Sally shakes her head, no. She catches Sam sneaking a quick look at her eye.

"Then why is she saddled?"

"As long as your head is healed up good enough—it is, right? I figure it's time to get you in a saddle again. I see you're wearin' boots."

Sally touches her eye carefully and winces. "Dang it. When I caught Dakota this morning, and was puttin' the halter on her out in the pasture, she tossed her head. Gave me a pretty darn good shiner!"

She isn't a very good actress.

Sam's not any kind of authority on horse behavior, but for all the world Dakota doesn't look to him like she'd do anything of the sort. He points to his boots. "A lot easier to clean horse shit from the bottoms of these than tennis shoes."

He notices Sally's bruise is turning yellow already. He's sure it's not from today. It must be from yesterday or the day before.

She offers, "You and Sparky can walk along and watch while I warm up Dakota. I let Sparky's stirrups down a little for you."

He points to her discolored eye. "Hmm, when did you say you did that?"

Sally simply shrugs and gives the stirrup a final tug to make sure it won't slip.

"I admit I let the stirrups down at home. I saw they were a little short for you that day we…uh…met in the gravel pit."

She smiles at Sam. "I wouldn't have blamed you if you didn't come, and started paying your insurance by mail instead of coming into the office."

"Don't worry about it," Sam assures her. "I'm a big boy. Just havin' some fun with a new friend. No strings attached, right?"

She nods and smiles tentatively. "Right. And if you think I'm pushing…you know, I get outta line…I'm a big girl. Just tell me. I get carried away sometimes when I'm havin' fun."

Sally plants her left foot in the stirrup and swings up onto Dakota's back, a free and easy movement that flows like a flag in a parade. She leans over and gives her ride a couple pats on the neck. "Hope you're up to this, girl…"

Sam has to hop twice to get his left foot firmly planted in the stirrup. Thankfully, Sparky is patient with him. The mare wouldn't have been the first horse swinging sideways to keep Sam off it. He feels clumsy, compared to the dance-like grace of Sally's mount. Sam's was more like tripping over a tree root.

All week, Sam had compared her to every woman he's known, trying to figure it out. Yes, on looks alone, Sally's as pretty a woman as he's ever seen (naked or otherwise). Even in old blue jeans and a well-used sweatshirt, she'd turn any old man's head.

And atop Dakota, she becomes something that makes Sam almost light-headed. A sudden déjà vu washes over him. She is so perfectly comfortable in the saddle (even more than Karen was, and she'd been a natural).

Sally is confident in the saddle—a trust both ways, between horse and rider. It's as if she and Dakota are connected telepathically. Sam doesn't notice her do anything to cue Dakota from a walk to a trot and finally to a lope. Her body flows with the horse's as she leans forward. It reminds him of water flowing down the Fox River. A beautiful motion that defies words.

Sally brings Dakota up to a stop in front of Sam and Sparky. "What's a matter?"

"I don't exactly know," smiling wryly, Sam admits. "But watchin' you ride, I'm reminded of something else Rumi wrote about."

Sally shakes her head. "Don't you ever read anything from this century? Or this continent?"

"Not much."

They ride at a slow walk back to Sally's trailer. The loudspeakers blare as the first bull rider is introduced.

"S'pose I should get dressed," Sally says. "The first go-round will last about an hour. Then, we barrel race."

She swings a leg over and slides off Dakota. Sam dismounts, too. She slips a halter over Dakota's nose, from the horse's left. She slides Sparky's halter on the same way. Both times, Sam notices, if Sally had gotten butted with a horse head, it was her right eye that would have been in the way.

Sally leans into the back seat of her truck. She brings out two clean western shirts on hangers. "I've got new black jeans and red boots, but which blouse should I wear?"

The first one that catches Sam's eye is the black one with red trim. The other is a white blouse, trimmed in black.

He can't remember the last time a woman asked him what she should wear. It had to have been Karen. He knows Sally will look wonderful in either of them. It's like asking a kid already on a sugar high which candy bar and bottle of pop he wants.

"Black shirt and black hat. Your blonde hair will look great with them. All dark, like the night sky, your hair a shooting star that appears and disappears so fast the other riders won't realize what just went by."

Sally doesn't know whether he's being serious or just blowing smoke. He doesn't know either. "Where did *that* come from? You still have Rumi on the line?"

He grins. "Must be the beer…mixed with the aroma of horse shit."

Sally rolls her eyes, then grabs her clothes, a saddle stand, and a clean spare saddle blanket. She ducks into the stock trailer, tosses the blanket onto the floor to stand on, and places her fresh clothes on the saddle stand. There are open slats all the way around at the height of Sally's shoulders. Unabashedly, she kicks her old boots off and then stands, pulling in her tummy to unbutton and unzip her jeans. She bends over and disappears from Sam's view as she pulls her jeans down. Politely, Sam turns away, thinking he won't be using much hot water next time he showers.

While Sam gets instructions from the husband of one of the other riders, the barrel racers gather at the entrance to the arena. Sam will be tending the third barrel, at the far end of the arena. A rope sticks out from the ground there, he's told. He's to set the barrel touching where the rope sticks out of the dirt and make sure it's level. He is advised to wait against the inside of the fence down several yards so he doesn't get sprayed by pebbles shot from under the horses' churning hooves.

Sam sips a beer, waiting for the last bull rider to finish, so they can roll out and set up the barrels.

Sally spots him. "I could sure use a sip of that. I'm always jittery before a run." Sam hands the beer up to her.

He realizes in that instant that they barely know each other. Still, he hasn't seen any weird looks or sideways glances from folks who might wonder why Sally's hanging around with someone who isn't her husband, and sharing his beer. Maybe they've never seen Bill? Maybe they assume Sam is her husband? Or uncle? Maybe they're used to her bringing along a new male, non-husband sidekick to every event? And Sam is just another in a long line of guys she's flirted into helping her out again.

Sally has drawn the seventeenth spot out of twenty-five riders.

The first rider is announced. Immediately, fast loud music blares over the loudspeakers, urging the rider to really cut loose. The spectators roar and can't help but stand and clap and cheer. They'd have to be dead not to feel the excitement of a cowgirl riding a horse as fast and hard as it can gallop, then screw itself around the barrels with dirt flying from under its hooves like car tires spinning out.

From his post at the opposite end of the arena, Sam has a perfect view of the women and horses barreling out of the half-lit alleyway at full speed and into the bright arena. They cross the electronic timer at a full gallop, and the clock jumps to life—the seconds ticking off, the tenths of a second flashing, the hundredths traveling at a blur, and the thousandths just a streak of red.

Each horse and rider angles toward the first barrel and circles it, starting just a little wide by a couple yards, but exiting the barrel tight. The rider's inside stirrup almost brushes the ground as the horse bends low and digs, and the rider leans. They bolt across the arena to the second barrel, a short run, to also circle it. Then it's full-bore to the barrel Sam tends. Because of the speed, that circle begins another yard wider, but ends tight like the others, before the cowgirls hoot and whip their horses back across the arena, trip the timer at a full gallop, and head right for the metal gate blocking the alley.

No rider lets up until after she crosses the timer. They have a mere seventy-five feet to bring their horses to a stop before they'd hit the steel gate. The cowgirls pull hard on the reins, and the horses slide on their hind legs, turning and rearing just in the nick of time.

Sam had never seen barrel racing in person, only on television. He's surprised he can predict halfway through the fourteen seconds of racing which duos will be the fastest; that is, if nothing goes wrong. Some horses shy at one barrel or another. Sometimes a horse and rider knock a barrel over, which results in a disqualification. It's over so quickly. No wonder there are so many camcorders at the fence. At this speed, with all this frantic action and the winner determined by only a few thousandths of a second, a playback is often the only way to make the call.

The announcer blares, "From a little town just a stone's throw south of here called Streeter, Sally Hunter on Dakota! Let's give this local cowgirl a great big rodeo YEEE-HAWWWWW!"

Sam sucks in his breath and holds it. Suddenly the loudspeaker comes alive with Stevie Ray Vaughn's "The House is Rockin'". The gate swings open and, like an apparition in black, out of the alleyway explode Sally and Dakota. She stretches forward over her horse's neck, Dakota's ears laid back, mouth open. They run fast and level, smoothly as if on rails. So smoothly that Sally's black hat could be a tray full of champagne glasses, and not a single one would spill.

Suddenly, they angle to the first barrel. Sam can see Sally's blonde ponytail flying behind her. They seem to be cutting that barrel tighter than most others have. He worries they'll either slip or knock the barrel. But it's a tight, clean barrel and it seems fast. Sally leans over and grabs the saddle horn with her left hand, as Dakota digs and blasts toward the second. Without the saddle horn, Sam is sure Dakota would run right out from under Sally. That barrel is clean and tight, too.

Sam takes a quick glance at the clock. Sally grabs the saddle horn again with one hand and she and Dakota tear down the arena in his direction, toward the third barrel. That run is three times the distance between barrel one and barrel two. Again, it's like horse and rider are on a rail, except Sally's legs are smacking Dakota's sides in a fast rhythm.

He worries they're approaching the third barrel too tightly. And sure enough, as they enter the turn, Sally's boot nicks the barrel. It tilts and wobbles, but thankfully it doesn't fall. When Dakota digs in, to launch them home, her back hooves shoot a spray of gravel that peppers the rail fence like buckshot.

Sam hasn't taken a breath since Sally was announced. They fly straight away from him, Sally's legs slapping Dakota's sides, one hand on the reins and the other swatting Dakota's rump. The crowd is on their feet cheering wildly as Sally reins Dakota sharply to the right just before the gate. They slide to a stop in a cloud of dirt, and Dakota rears like the Lone Ranger's Silver.

"We have a new time to beat and it's a good one!" shouts the announcer. "14.385! Boy, can that cowgirl ride!"

The crowd goes crazy. The gate opens and Sam sees other riders giving Sally high-fives. Their time is less than a hundredth of a second quicker than the previous fastest time of 14.394.

But nobody beats Sally and Dakota this Saturday night.

Sam trots across the arena with the plastic barrel held over his head. He dumps it by the other two, scales a gate, and walks as quickly as he can without actually running to Sally's truck and trailer. Dakota's saddle is already off. The mare has reverted from fierce Roman, chariot-like steed to her usual role as just another lazy, dark-brown horse, half asleep, tied to a trailer.

Sally's on her phone, talking excitedly. "Yes! Yes, I won the whole darn thing! $650!"

Sam gives her some space, and waits by the front of her truck. He sighs and busies himself scraping the edge of his boot sole on the gravel. He was hoping he'd be the first to congratulate her.

Sally's spirit suddenly droops. She lowers her gaze, pushes her hat back, and purses her lips. She listens for about half a minute. Then she responds apologetically, "Yeah...yeah...okay," and flips the phone shut.

Sam walks up and hold his arms out, offering a congratulatory hug. "That was beautiful, incredible. To think I almost missed it..." He smiles and shakes his head, hoping his compliments will urge Sally out of her funk.

She responds with a short, light embrace, but then quickly turns away. He can hear her sniffle. "What is it?"

"Pop was real excited about the news. But then Bill took the phone from him. I told him we won, that Dakota's back to her winning form... Never mind. You don't need to hear this," she says apologetically.

"What did he say?" Sam urges.

Sally imitated his rough voice. "What the hell? Didn't anybody else show up?"

She runs the back of her hand under her nose, with a shuddering sigh. "I gotta pack up. No rodeo dance for me tonight. Bill's cousin, the regular bartender, showed up too drunk to serve the other drunks. I need to get right home and be there for Pop, so Bill can go tend bar."

Sam offers quietly, "I brought a bottle of wine. Didn't have any idea you'd win. Just tossed it in."

"Can Pop drink wine?"

Sally nods.

"Here, take this home." He wedges the bottle between the two saddles. "See you next weekend in the hills? You gonna stay with Maureen again? The next crop of morels, the yellow ones, should be starting. They're big enough to spot from horseback. No strings attached..."

Sam doesn't know where that came from, offering his services as a surrogate husband, just like that. Breaking his rules for Sally is becoming a habit. And he offers to ride with her, to boot?

"I'll see how Pop's doin'," Sally answers, her smile returning. "Maybe I'll bring him out, if you don't mind. He's the one who taught me about yellow morels...and a lotta other things."

"I'll make sure the electric golf cart's charged up for him."

"Why in the world do you have an electric golf cart? You a golfer, too?"

"Nope. I hate the game, unless there are morels growin' off in the rough," Sam answers, grinning. "The cart's a great way to cruise the trail. Quiet, too."

"Yeah, Pop'll love that. He gets around the farm on a riding mower. Well, I better get goin'..."

Sally slides back into the truck, and hesitates for a moment. "I'm almost gettin' back out for a real hug. But I'm a married woman, no matter how tough it is sometimes. Thanks for bein' here." She starts her truck and drops it into gear.

Sam steps back to let the trailer pass by. But before it has completely cleared past him, the brake lights blink on and the truck comes to a stop. The door opens slowly. Sally swings her legs out and stands, looking back at him. A smile begins to cross her pretty face.

"Ya know," she says, "it was surreal, like I was dreamin'. Felt like we were flyin' through the air. When Dakota and I cleared that first barrel, everything was in perfect sync. She changed leads right on cue. Even after this month layoff, she trusted me, she trusted the footing, she trusted herself. On the run to the finish, she hit another gear I've never felt from her! We were in another world.

"Waddya make of that, Sam Ryan, Rumi's buddy?" Sally's smiling, but seems a bit embarrassed for asking.

"Fana," Sam whispers. "That was Fana tonight, for me. That's what Rumi calls it. Recognizing God-The-Source in something earthly, something so beautiful it makes your eyes leak and your spine flutter. And you and Dakota were Baqa. You were God come to Earth to race the barrels, just because it's so goddamn much fun. He's smilin' tonight. That ride you took him on was pretty amazing. He's probably still tellin' anybody with wings and a halo who'll stand still all about it."

"Yup. You're crazy," Sally teases. "And I need a hug from a crazy man…"

Sam's not sure how close, how firm, how long. He lets her take the lead. Sally holds onto him tighter than he's expecting. He tempers his breath, trying not to let her hear him inhale the faint scent of her shampoo. Instinctively, he squeezes her a little harder, and instantly wishes he hadn't taken that liberty. But she squeezes him back.

When it's over, after about fifteen seconds, she kisses Sam on the cheek. Her lips are soft.

She whispers, "Thanks for comin'. See you next weekend…" Sally turns away, then returns for another quick squeeze. "And thanks for bein' my friend…no strings..."

She avoids his gaze as she slides behind the wheel. He can see her wipe under her nose with her sleeve, then turn to look back at him one last time with a faint smile.

As she drives away, Sam looks down and shakes his head. *What the hell is goin' on?* he asks himself, *besides the fact that I'm standing here in fresh horse shit.*

CHAPTER 7

POP SMILES

Maureen surprises Sally at work Monday a couple minutes before noon.

"Hey!" she shouts merrily as she steps into the insurance office entryway. "Heard you won the barrel race! Way to go! Now let me buy my butt kickin' little sister lunch."

"Sure," Sally answers as she turns quickly to hide her banged up eye. "Let me freshen up first."

They get a booth at the bar and grill on Main. "Sam musta told you, huh?"

"Yup. He brought over some eggs for the rez food shelf this mornin'. Got this glow on his face when he told me about your ride. What's goin' on there?" Maureen waggles her eyebrows.

"Well, nothin'," Sally assures Maureen with a frown. "He's a nice man and all that, and we got a lot in common, but I'm married. Sam and I talked about it; we're just friends. We call it *no strings attached*. And even if I was available, Lord knows I sure don't need another project. I'm sure you know he's been divorced twice. And he's fifteen years older than me anyway. (I cheated, looked in his file.)"

Maureen answers, "No, I didn't know Sam was divorced twice. Did he tell you that?"

"Geez. You've known him a lot longer than me. He never told you about Karen?"

"Oh, I know the Karen story. But I don't think you do," Maureen says. "So, what'd you tell Bill…about Sam?"

"What's to tell? I gotta lot of guy friends. Bill doesn't care, and for good reason."

"How many of these guys clean your morels with you…take you canoein'…go outta their way to watch you ride…to help you out with barrel setting…all within a week?" Maureen challenges.

"We're both just broadening our horizons," Sally answers. "No big deal. Like I said, Sam and I talked about our boundaries. He's got boundaries, too, ya know. Actually, he calls 'em rules."

"After lunch," Maureen says. "Check out the bookstore around the corner. He's a writer, you know. Look for a little publication of local writers, 1999 or 2000. That's all I'm gonna say. You figure it out."

Sally is genuinely curious to hear more about Sam and Karen, but changes the subject. "I'm bringin' Pop out for a day trip this Sunday. We're gonna pick yellow morels with Sam, use his electric golf cart. Pop'll love it."

"Where you gonna be otherwise on the weekend? You gonna hang around the farm and let Bill beat you up again?"

Sally stiffens and looks away. "What're you talkin' about?"

"It's gonna take more than a coupla thick layers of makeup to cover up a shiner like that one," Maureen says through pursed lips.

"No," Sally corrects, "That darn Sparky butted me when I was slippin' her halter on. Didn't Sam tell you?"

"Nope, he never mentioned it." Maureen sits up and folds her hands on the table, her face dead serious. "Just say the word, and Joan'll be all over Bill's crap. How much longer you think I'm gonna sit by and let him pound on my little sister? And don't claim you're stayin' 'cause of Pop. Take Pop with you the hell outta there. It's gotta be breakin' his heart…what those two did to the farm, and what Bill's doin' to you…"

"Well, this lunch is over before it even began." Sally slides out of the booth quickly, pulling on her button-front sweater. "Thanks for the lunch offer. But no thanks for the marriage counselin'."

Sally sits in an easy chair, her legs underneath her butt, watching a rodeo on television. She wears sweats and heavy socks, and has a glass of Sam's wine from the barrel races. Pop and Sheba, Sally's chocolate Labrador, are on the couch, Pop sitting up with Sheba curled into a giant brown ball next to him, close by so Pop can pat and scratch her all she wants.

Sally retreats to her bedroom, and returns with her reading glasses and the book Maureen recommended. "Hey Pop, would you like a little wine?"

He nods, then indicates with his fingers he wants only an inch. "Whatcha readin'?"

She holds up the book. "Maureen's neighbor, that guy Sam who made this wine. He's the one we're goin' morel huntin' with this Sunday. He's got a poem in here. Haven't read it yet, but saw his name in the index."

"Yeah, I met him," Pop offers. "At Maureen's a couple times. Nice man."

His cracked lips manage a small smile. He dares a look out the corner of his eye. Sally doesn't notice Pop watching her. She's already sinking back into the easy chair, curious and contemplative. She begins reading.

I Saw God!

Reflections of a mid-March morning walk after snow overnight, by Sam Ryan

Yes! I saw You there on my walk!
In the fresh snow.
You lay on the branches and boughs,
thick and soft.
The tiniest puff of breeze set You free.
You shimmered like diamonds!

I heard You in the hawk's shrill cry.
The river gurgling.
The swans calling.

I saw You in the tracks on the gravel road I walked—
as deer, raccoons, mice, grouse, coyotes—
signs of life in a place so quiet.

I heard You in the wind over the swans' wings
as they flew low above me.

*I could see You in their dark eyes and
the crinkled webs of their black feet.*

*And I felt You in my lungs
as air so pure. You had no aroma or taste.
Yet I felt You seep into every cell of my body—
into my soul,
awakening me, quickening me,
reminding me to be thankful for this life
and this place.*

*But,
pardon me God,
two things
I would have changed for this morning's walk.*

*To be
with Her,
on two good horses
like she and I used to,*

*The sweet aroma of our horses,
feeling them move heavily under us,
the rich fragrance of leather,
the saddles flexing and creaking,
hooves crunching, squeaking on new snow,
moist horse breath in clouds,
the horses snorting into the woods at danger
real and imagined.*

*Riding alongside Her.
I trust You have new snow, tracks,*

*swans, hawks, fresh air, rivers,
coyotes, and horses in Heaven.
And wonders I can't imagine.*

*Why else would You call her home
so young?*

*And leave me here to walk with You
alone.*

Sally sighs.
Pop asks, "What is it?"
Sally pulls her sweatshirt sleeve down so she can grab the cuff with her fingers. She lifts her reading glasses off and rubs the fabric under each eye.
"Sam…I assumed he was divorced from his second wife, Karen." She dabs under her eyes again while gazing down at the open book. "He didn't walk away from their marriage. She died."
Sally snaps her head up. "Shit! Sorry, Pop! Your wine…"
Pop smiles and shakes his head.

Dear Ellen, May 20, 2003

I'm sorry it's taken me so long to write. I have no excuse for not contacting you sooner to apologize, and to see how you, Keith, and the boys are doing.

I thought those episodes were long behind me. I hadn't had one since right after

Karen died. I'd hoped they were simply a product of her and her family, and that they went away for good when she did. You probably remember I was a mess after she died, even saw a psychiatrist. He said it sounded a lot like post-traumatic stress disorder, because once that trigger was tripped, I became helpless to short circuit the juggernaut that had begun. Had just two therapy sessions, sold the farm, and never went back on the couch. I should have.

But we talked about a lot in those two sessions. He wanted to put the PTSD on my folks, saying they had thoroughly convinced me I wasn't worth a shit. You knew Mom, and you know my dad. They certainly weren't monsters. He said the reason PTSD didn't come out until I was with Karen was because I believed history was repeating itself, her family making it plain they thought I wasn't worth a shit. And then I'd go nuts—go away—reinforcing what they thought.

I guess that's what I thought Keith and Russell were saying to me that night, when we argued about the war in Iraq. What I heard was that my views, my truth, weren't worth a shit, and neither was I. It's not Keith's fault I reacted like that. I hope he doesn't take the blame. And I hope he can forgive me.

I just want you to know I love you and want to get this right. Please forgive me. I have my first appointment with a therapist tomorrow.

Please call and let me know how you are all doing.

Love,

Dad

CHAPTER 8

A THREE-PACK OF CONDOMS

Wednesday, May 21, 2003

Laura, Sam's new therapist, is a throwback to the old hippie days. Sam doesn't ask, but assumes she lives in some sort of commune up in the north end of the county where the ground is rocky and cheap. Her makeup-less face looks to be around forty years old. Her straight, waist-length hair is ninety-five percent gray; that part of her seems at least seventy. Her earrings and necklace look homemade, or maybe from a flea market. She wears a long, beige cotton dress and earth shoes. A faint aura of patchouli surrounds her, but thankfully much less than would qualify her as a human air freshener.

Laura asks her first question, "Tell me about what brought you here today."

He shares what he can remember.

The last picture in Sam's mind is of his older brother, Russell, with a nasty grin—smug and satisfied that he'd been right all along. "You're a spineless piece of shit, and always have been."

Ellen and Keith must have thought they were doing Sam a favor, or maybe they just wanted to help mend that family rift, by inviting Russell for supper that night.

Ellen was a chip off the old block when it came to politics—like her dad, liberal from head to toe and then some. Like Sam's entire family, except for Russell. Sam didn't think the t-shirt was a big deal. Everyone knew Sam had never been a fan of war, for any reason. Had he been drafted into the Vietnam War, he'd have gone to prison first. And if they tried to force his son Matt into war, he'd do whatever he could to keep Matt safe. Sam wasn't an activist concerning Iraq, but like so many others, he privately prayed for people to understand that Iraq was another Vietnam in the making.

First thing after arriving at their house, when Sam had fished the t-shirt out of his bag, he was surprised Ellen wasn't glad for the gift to Josh. Like other clothes he'd given Josh, Sam had expected her to immediately put the shirt on the boy, then Ellen and Keith would make such a big deal out of it that Josh would wear it for many days straight. Instead, she folded it neatly and set it aside with only a polite "Thank you." Sam noticed her take a quick, uncomfortable glance at Keith.

When it was just father and daughter, Sam asked her about the t-shirt. Ellen confided that Keith was not just in favor of going to war, he was pissed as hell at anyone who didn't think America should invade Iraq. Sam hadn't been aware of his son-in-law's political bent, or he wouldn't have brought such a shirt to Boise in the first place.

Ellen suggested Sam didn't join in the conversation if it came up. But the war and the controversy were impossible to ignore, because Keith watched the news channels every minute he could. Apparently Ellen talked to Keith, too, because neither of the men commented on the subject in the other's presence. Sam was glad, because he was quite fond of his son-in-law, who was a good father and husband.

But that night the television showed a Boise city street lined with war supporters. They waved American flags and held up signs reading "Honk If You Love America" and "We Support Our President 100%". The camera zoomed in on a pickup truck that was honking, the driver pumping his fist skyward. It was Keith right there on television, large as life.

Russell smiled at Keith and nodded. Keith was surprised and embarrassed; he hadn't realized he was being filmed. Ellen, breast-feeding Sammy under a blanket, quickly left the room. Sam followed, carrying Josh, who was sleeping on his shoulder.

Russell yelled after him, "Hey Sam, waddya think, huh? Finally someone in the family on MY side! Atta boy, Keith!" Russell was serious, a little drunk, and he wasn't going to let it go at that.

"At least your son-in-law's got some balls," Russell growled.

Sam knew Russell was referring to Vietnam days when Sam had protested against the war. Russell had been in Southeast Asia as an army officer. Being manipulative by nature and college-educated, Russell got himself a cushy job. Never heard a gunshot over there, but came home puffed up like some sort of war hero. And with way more money than he should have. The family never knew for sure what Russell was dealing in over there. But since Vietnam, Russell had held high corporate positions with three different defense companies.

Sam squeezed his eyes shut and shuddered. He turned slowly, his mouth gone dry, and opened his eyes to slits to glare at Russell.

Russell declared, "Anyone who's not FOR this war is anti-American. Those traitors should just get the hell outta our country. Go live in Iraq if it's so goddamn great over there."

Sam replied calmly, "It's our right to disagree, Russell. But it's not your right, or anyone's right, to judge who's a loyal American or not, to even suggest someone should be banished from this country. It's obvious that war never fixed anything for good, except for linin' some fat cats' pockets."

Sam wasn't sure where that had come from. He could feel the blood draining from his brain and his heartbeat pounding inside his ears.

It was too late.

Ellen hurried back into the living room and ordered, "Change the subject. Now!"

Russell ignored his niece, and laughed at Sam, "At least I ain't drivin' a twenty-year-old pickup, haulin' kids in a bus, and callin' it a great day when I sweep and find a quarter."

Keith was dumbfounded over Russell's attack and walked up and put his hands on Sam's shoulders. "Hey, Sam…Sam…?"

Sam misinterpreted Keith's intention, as if Russell had tag-teamed with him and now it was Keith's turn to punch him in the gut. He clumsily brushed off Keith's hands and shuffled backward to the wall, holding his arms out in front as if to fend off an attacker.

Russell grinned evilly. "Sam…you mean if they came over here and were rapin' your daughter, you wouldn't kill to protect her?"

Ellen paced nervously, still breast-feeding the baby. She bit her lip, and tears began streaming down her face. "Just drop it! You'll never agree. Just let it go!"

Sam responded, pointing a finger, "Russell, I'll be the first person to die for peace, to step in front of a bullet or a tank, but I won't *kill* for peace. It doesn't work that way. And neither of you has any right to question my patriotism."

Josh woke in Sam's arms, crying. Keith sighed and hung his head. The toddler reached for his father.

Sam passed the sobbing child to Keith then backed away from the other two men, his arms out in front of him. His face was wrenched with fear, as if a mad dog was about to leap at him.

Russell sneered and nodded in satisfaction at having goaded Sam into an angry reaction. "For a guy who's so against violence, you sure get mad easy…"

Ellen screamed at the three men, "That's it! No more!"

The baby's mouth slipped from her breast, and he began wailing.

Sam felt trapped in their house, and alienated by his daughter. His daughter's screaming and the crying of his two grandsons was a hellish cacophony Sam had to escape from. He put both hands over his ears. All three looked at him like he was insane.

And he was.

Sam grabbed his jacket. Sobbing, he stumbled down the front steps, then ran down the dark street. Two blocks away, he bent over and gave up his supper. He wouldn't return for over two days.

After he'd left, Keith escorted Russell out by his shirt collar. "Listen asshole, you ever mess with my father-in-law again, I'll kick your fat-cat ass!"

When Sam didn't return that night, Ellen called his oldest sister, Jill. She suggested they should put Sam's things in his truck. Let him be, let him drive away if he needed to. It was Ellen who'd put the t-shirt into his wine case. She just wanted it all to go away, anything that would remind her of that terrible evening.

Laura asks Sam to think back. "What about your last episode before Boise. What precipitated that one?"

Sam shrugs, then continues as if he's told the story a hundred times.

"Karen and I were separated, but not officially, not legally. Her dad rented her an apartment in town. He demanded she move outta our place, off the farm. Her family discouraged her—well, hell, they *threatened* her—from goin' to couple's counseling with me. To them it was a done deal that she and I were through. But we kept seein' each other. Spent a lotta nights together once she got the OFP…uh, Order For Protection, lifted."

"Order For Protection?" Laura asks.

Sam bends over and stares at the floor, hands clasped together.

"Karen and I were arguin' one night. I told her she, we, can't have it both ways—us lovin' each other to pieces, but then when they show up, not only am I invisible to them, I am to her, too. That's the only thing we ever really fought about. Those people made it plain every chance they got—even right in my face—that I wasn't good enough for her. I still don't know what strange hold they had over her.

"That night, her niece's wedding was coming up. I told her I was goin' with, whether her family liked it or not, whether she liked it or not. She started hittin' me. Knocked my glasses across the room, tore my sweatshirt. I grabbed both her arms so she'd quit hittin' me. But she was strong, so I left finger marks. A woman she worked with saw the marks, the bruises. Cops showed up the next afternoon and on the spot escorted me off the farm—I never saw it comin'.

"Karen's family showed up at the emergency hearing two days later. That's when they set her up with the apartment, and I was allowed to go back to the farm. She was so impressionable. Took the advocate's advice to nail me, even though she'd been the only one doin' the hittin'. Her conscience, I s'pose—at the next hearing two weeks later, it was her idea to allow contact. Of course I wanted to see her, be with her…but she kept the apartment."

Sam sits back and stares out the window.

"Coupla weeks later when we talked on the phone one night (we talked every evenin' before bedtime), she said she had a headache, a real bad one. I called her an hour later, got no answer. Finally, I drove to her apartment and…she was…just there on the kitchen floor. Dead. A brain aneurysm."

Sam tears up and hunches over, his head hanging with the weight of emotion. He covers his eyes.

After several minutes of silence, he inhales deeply and continues.

"Whew. The next coupla weeks are a blur. Her family stepped right in and took over. Their fancy attorney got the judge to sign an injunction against me having anythin' to do with the funeral. The judge (same one who'd signed the OFP, then lobbied Karen hard not to soften it) only allowed me and my family a fifteen-minute private viewing, the night before the funeral."

Sam sobs into both hands for just a moment, the memories too powerful to ignore, but breathes deeply several times so he can continue on.

"Until Boise, that was the last time I had an attack—right after that. My sister Jill came back to stay with me at the farm. But I bolted. Can't remember where all I went. I was on foot, though. Came home three days later. Karen's family had been there, and had taken all her stuff. Not the horses. They were still in the pasture.

"Karen had two girls. The older one hated me like the rest of her family did. But the younger one, Ally, a senior in high school at the time, was just like one of mine. She'd lived mostly with us those five years. Saw a lotta shit between her mom and me, though. I worked through her to sell the horses, and gave Ally and her sister the money—even my share."

Laura asks, "What did you do next?"

"Had an auction. Sold the farm. Karen and I had taken out life insurance policies that paid off the farm if either of us died. It was her idea, like a premonition maybe. I gave what would've been Karen's half to her daughters.

"I just drifted around that summer and fall, livin' in my old tent trailer, doin' odd jobs. Landed here up north. All my possessions fit in the back of my truck. Spent that first winter takin' care of a ranch in the hills. Bought my place in the spring.

"I don't know if this is helpful. I went to see a psychiatrist shortly after Karen died. Two sessions was all, and it was time to hit the road. He interviewed me for an hour and a half, asking me questions it seemed about every subject known to man. Afterwards, he scratched his head. He said I didn't miss a single answer—only the second person to have a perfect score in his 40 years of practice—and my I.Q. was in the neighborhood of 138 to 140—a borderline genius, the doc told me. So tell me this: If I'm so goddamn smart, why am I crazy?"

Laura smiles and assures him, "You're not crazy. But I think it's best to get together weekly for a while. How about next Wednesday. Same time?"

"Sure. I'm drivin' the senior class to Minneapolis for three days. Leavin' Sunday. We'll be back Tuesday."

Laura taps her finger on the page. "Actually, I'm sorry. I'm gone next week. How about the following Wednesday?"

Sam answers absently, "That'll be fine. Oh shit! Sally and Pop are comin' over Sunday to pick morels. That's the day I leave on the trip. Hope they can make it Saturday instead."

Laura sits straight up, her brow furrowed, questioning.

"Oh, just a woman I met, and her father-in-law. I caught her in my woods—naked—picking my morels.

And I helped her at the rodeo barrel race. She won! You should see her on a horse. Her sister's my neighbor."

Laura looks at her watch and then at her schedule book. "I can get by with half an hour for lunch. Want to talk about Sally? Or anyone else, past or present?"

"Not much to talk about with Sally. She's married. We're not even really what I would call friends...yet."

Laura turns to a fresh page in her notebook and dates it at the top. "Do you think you might ever want to be in a committed relationship again?"

"Oh, yeah. I loved bein' married. I'd do it again in a heartbeat...if the right person came along."

"So, it's been six years since Karen died. Have you dated since then?"

"The first summer in my house," Sam answers while rubbing his beard. "I was still pretty depressed, I guess. And lonely. I was buildin' a stone fireplace in a cabin over on Fox Lake. The neighbor lady who was up for the summer kept droppin' by. Turns out we had a lot in common. And then her husband had to go back to Iowa for a month. On one level it was fun, even exhilarating, when she'd come over in the middle of the night. Yeah, I was fond of her. But to be honest, to me it was just sex."

"What happened to her?" Laura asks.

"She said she was fallin' in love with me. It got complicated. She basically tried to make me into everything her husband wasn't. Even threatened to tell her husband if I didn't agree to meet her in Mankato once a month after summer was over. Said I was forbidden to date while she was home screwin' hubby. I called her bluff, told her to keep it in perspective. And was extremely relieved when she went back to Iowa and I didn't get a loada buckshot in the ass."

"Anybody else you've been serious with?"

"I was on a roll that year, I guess. That fall, I met a lady at the dance hall. She was a cut above the other single women who hung out there. Owned her own business, a string of gas stations. She made all kinds of travel plans for us—Arizona, Mexico. Then a coupla days before Christmas, she snapped. I don't know what to call it, but she confused me with her dead ex-husband who'd broken a few of her bones. The third time she showed up at my door beggin' for forgiveness, I showed her the restrainin' order I was gonna file if she came by or called again."

"Since then?"

"I tell folks it's been so long since I been on a real date, I can't remember who gets tied up! Honest, I still have a three-pack of condoms left from that encounter. Wonder if those things have an expiration date?"

Sam chuckles to himself. "Don't matter anyway. I got *standards* now. I refuse to date a woman who would agree to date the likes of me."

"I think we're missing something," Laura suggests. "You are obviously intelligent and engaging, a genuine people person. I wonder if the PTSD is more of a symptom, and not the real issue at hand. I think I have a handle on your approach to intimate relationships. Tell me about some of your other relationships, work and such."

"Hell, which job you wanna hear about first? Shit, in the fifteen years before Stone Creek, I had at least ten jobs I either lost or walked away from, and never on good terms. Everything from moppin' up in a home for the developmentally disabled to doin' patent research for a lawsuit between two large medical device companies to drivin' a school bus.

"Employers always wanted me on board; I could sell myself to anyone. And more often than not, they'd move me up the ladder real fast, because I was good and I cared. And I'd pour my soul into the job.

"But then soon there'd be some sorta criticism. In my eagerness, I'd step on someone's toes. There'd be a backlash brewin', and I could just sense things were goin' south."

Sam furrows his brow and nods. "Yup, I pretty much got fucked…every time. Oh, excuse my French."

"No offense taken. Okay, so here's what I'm thinking," Laura says, hands clasped and looking straight into Sam's eyes. "I'm wondering if you aren't somehow attracting these unfortunate situations, or possibly even causing them to a degree. It sounds like you tend to test authority figures' trust. You do that by trusting them unconditionally, to see if they are worthy. Does that sound like a possibility?"

"I'm always lookin' for the best in people," he answers with a shrug. "I give 'em my best, and they you-know-what me in the butt anyway."

"Interesting. That's twice you've used the comparison about losing trust in others to getting…taken advantage of sexually. Every person's experience is unique, but certain similarities or common scenarios can point to specific root causes."

"What you gettin' at?" Sam sits back with his arms crossed.

"I'm going to ask something very personal now," Laura warns. "As a child, were you ever sexually abused? Did you have experiences, maybe with an older person whom you trusted, that made you feel uncomfortable, or worse—guilty or tarnished in some way?"

"I mean, yeah I guess. What little kid doesn't experiment with his buddies?"

"Did you?"

"Sure, when you're six or seven, a boner's a pretty mysterious thing. I sure didn't want to ask my dad about it. And if you mentioned it to your mother or a big sister, they'd either slap you or laugh their asses off. So I guess around like fifth or sixth grade, me and my buddies talked about it. Sometimes, we even touched each other. Not a big deal, just curiosity. Then after that, we were much more preoccupied about the mysteries of girls' bodies. Well, and takin' care of our own business, if ya know what I mean."

"Yes, that's all pretty normal stuff. Just one more question. Did you ever do any of that experimenting or touching with someone who was, let's say, significantly older than you?"

"Wow, you're really takin' me to the cleaners for our first session!"

Laura laughs. "Well, I like to know within the first few sessions whether a client is looking for answers and change or they just need a good listener."

He fidgets a bit, and eyes the door. "So, what should I do between now and my next session?"

"We'll begin with having you just observe," she answers, handing him a small notepad. "Be aware of your thoughts, your emotions, even how your body feels when you have those thoughts and experience those emotions. Write them down, just a word or two. For example, when you think about your new friend or when you're with her. When your PTSD episodes come to mind. Memories of Karen. Anything that seems stuck. But don't judge any of it. For now, just take note. Become a casual observer of yourself. And we'll see you and your thoughts and notes in two weeks."

CHAPTER 9

THE FIRE RING

Pop made most of his money as the owner of a car and trailer dealership in Streeter. He'd sold it and retired at age sixty-two, eight years ago. He still has an interest in the business and receives payments every month. After retirement, he stayed a silent partner in the lumberyard in Grand Forks where Bill works. Until his stroke, Pop had spent his spare time running beef cattle on his farm outside town. And of course he kept horses, a nice brace of Percherons, for pulling his wagon in summer parades and for giving the kids rides afterwards.

When Bill had moved back to take care of Pop, he complained about how much grass the horses ate and the huge, round hay bales he had to move with a tractor for them.

Pop had been a wiry-framed guy before the stroke, with gray, wavy hair. He was lean, but looked great in his jeans, western shirt, and hat. You could tell he was most comfortable sitting in a saddle.

The stroke had left Pop with his left side almost totally useless at first. When Sally moved back to Streeter, Pop was confined to a wheelchair, and he could hardly form words. They had to puree his food. But gradually he came around. His sweet Sally became his reason for getting well.

Now Pop shuffles around the house with a walker. He is self-sufficient during the day, except the doctors won't let him drive. The family doesn't leave him home alone nights because he has to take medication to sleep. When he does awaken in the night, he is unsteady and likely to fall and break something, even with the walker. Sheba faithfully alerts the others with barks and whines when Pop stirs at night.

Folks around town assume the day Bill and Sally got married was the happiest day of Pop's life. He finally has the daughter he always wanted, living right there with him. But it's a double-edged sword; he's happy to have Sally back home and officially part of the family, but worried about her with his volatile son, Bill. Pop knew Bill was rarely alone in his Grand Forks apartment.

Bill never hits Sally in front of his father, it's always after Pop is asleep or away. But the marks were evident and Sally's quiet shame broke Pop's heart.

One time, Pop confronted Bill. He warned his son, "If you ever lay another hand on Sally, I'll press charges against you myself."

Bill growled, "Folks in town always thought you were weird with Sally. You get ridda me, and they'll know for sure."

Of course Bill had been lying about Pop and Sally. But providing anyone impetus to breathe such horrible words is the last thing Pop would ever do. He prayed Sally would come to her senses, before something even worse happened.

This past winter, after Sally had taken another fist in the face, Pop tried to talk her into getting the hell out, but she swore she wasn't going anywhere; that she and Bill had said their vows in front of God and everyone; that she knew full well from her own aunts and uncles and cousins the horrible damage divorce causes a family; and she wasn't ever going to be the cause of any of that. Pop reminded her that marriage vows were never meant to be a life sentence—especially if the other person had broken them as badly as Bill had. Sally became angry, challenging Pop by shaking her finger and squeezing the words out between pursed lips, "Bill quit that runnin' around before we got married."

"If that is true," Pop responded sternly, "how could he say like he did last summer when you came home from racing with a big, fat check and flyin' on Cloud Nine. I heard him tellin' you, 'Horses are stupid. And the folks who ride 'em are stupider yet…' And then not even showing up to the state barrel racing finals right there in Grand Forks. Where is the love and honor in any of that?"

Sally's eyes began to moisten and Pop's heart was breaking that he was breaking hers.

"Okay. I'm so sorry for interferin'. You're a big girl who can manage on her own. I shouldn't meddle."

"And I should never talk like that to the most wonderful human bein' I've ever known." Sally kisses Pop on top of his head.

And he never does interfere again. He just prays.

Pop grins like a six-year old with a new bike as he steps on the pedal too hard and the golf cart lurches forward.

Sally covers her smile. Pop instinctively jerks his foot off the pedal and the cart comes to a sudden stop.

"What's this?" Pop asks, pointing to a plastic bottle in the cart's beverage holder.

"Just in case you get thirsty…a little Wild Grape Wine-2002."

"And that?" Pop asks, thumbing over his shoulder to a cooler and cardboard box lashed to the back.

"We'll have a picnic whether we get some yellows or not. Got some chicken cut up and marinated and some veggies." Sam points ahead at the trail beyond the fence opening. "Right through that gate and up into the high hardwoods. Careful you don't drive over 'em!"

Pop steps on it and the electric motor whirs to life. He's soon over the rise and out of sight.

Just past the gate, Sally touches Sam on the shoulder, her head tilted and a genuine smile on her face. "God, I haven't seen Pop this happy in a long time." She lets her hand linger on his shoulder for a moment. He places his hand on top of hers.

Sally sighs contentedly as she pulls her hand away. "We'd better get movin'."

They follow the trail, heading up the first rise. The hardwoods have leafed out, but not completely. The new green grass is pushing through last year's brown. It's an old woods that was last logged at least seventy-five years ago. The overstory is a canopy of treetops fifty or sixty feet high—white oak, red oak, basswood, sugar maple, hard maple, poplar, and birch. The pines are less numerous—jack pine, red pine, white pine, white spruce—just enough to add color it seems.

When the hardwood leaves are full, not much direct sunlight gets through to the ground. Very little brush grows—a patch of hazel brush here and there, some clumps of prickly ash, and scattered ironwood. It's park-like. The grass could be mowed almost anywhere and would look just like someone's well-manicured yard.

When they top the hill, they find the golf cart stopped in a patch of prickly ash, the old-timer on the ground on his hands and knees.

"Pop! You okay?" Sally runs toward him. "What happened?"

Pop turns to her with a huge grin, holding up a massive yellow morel. "Lunch!" he shouts. "Now hand me 'at bottla wine and my ice cream pail." He points into the prickly ash thicket where another dozen large yellow morels await.

She scolds, "You'll be cut to ribbons crawlin' into that mess!"

"Hee hee. What a way to go!" Pop crawls ahead tentatively.

"Wait!" Sam says. "I got somethin' that'll work, back in the barn. Have some wine. I'll be right back." He tosses Sally the plastic bottle. She fumbles it.

He backs the golf cart out of the thicket and heads it home at full speed, only a city block away. "You're gonna love it," he shouts over his shoulder as he disappears over the hill.

Pop and Sally sit side by side, sharing the wine one small sip at a time.

Sam returns quickly with his river can grabber with the two jaws that close when you squeeze the handle. Sam had added two ice pick shafts on one jaw for when stabbing is easier than grabbing.

"You oughta patent this!" Pop reaches into the thicket, closing the jaws around the base of a seven-inch morel. The stem breaks cleanly. He stabs it and drops it into the pail.

For over an hour, Pop zips around the woods, checking every nook and cranny he can get the golf cart into. Each time he finds one, he hollers, "Jackpot!"

If there are some he can't reach, he hollers just as loud, "Need a little help over heeere!"

Sally and Sam search as a team. The walking is easy in the big woods. The yellow morels don't grow as thick as the black ones do at this latitude. Most of them grow alone or in pairs; that first big batch Pop found is a rarity. But they're generally two or three times the size of your average black morel. Cut in half, and fried, they look more like pork chops than mushrooms.

Sam isn't sure if he's imagining it, but Sally seems to be touching him more than usual. A light hand on his back when she points something out. A lingering touch when they reach for the same morel. Not that he's counting, but it had happened exactly five times.

Sally finds a wild violet and pushes the stem through one of the holes in his baseball hat without removing the hat from his head. He gets a pleasant sensation that's not quite a tickle, but gives him goose bumps. Nobody's done anything like that, touched him like that, in five years.

Sam picks a wild geranium. She points to the second button from the top on her blouse. He hesitates. "Hmm, I'd say that's got some strings attached."

Sally just smiles and threads the stem through the buttonhole herself. Pop, up the hill and resting behind the wheel, catches them red-handed and nods his private approval.

Sam's having his best day in six years. He thinks back to his counseling session with Laura. What kind of notes should he make about today? Everything feels good. What is there to dissect about feeling light-hearted and happy? He decides to leave the heavy-duty observing for later. Besides, he left the notepad on the wood stove in the kitchen where he may never find it again.

Sam hollers to Pop, pointing up ahead where three huge white pines grow. "Our picnic spot's up there."

Sam and his son, Matt, had made the fire ring the year he'd bought the place. They'd picked that spot for two reasons. The first reason: the terrain was perfect. It was a flat area seemingly sculpted out of the gentle hill, the size of a city lot, protected from the northwest wind, and with a view to the south, across the distant river valley. The second reason: the giant white pines. They were at least a hundred years old and formed a perfect triangle, twenty-five feet to a side, the fire ring centered between them.

There was also a big jack pine stump about three feet high, on top of which sits a five-gallon plastic water jug and a jar of matches.

"What's in the bucket?" Sally asks, pointing to the base of the stump.

"Newspaper and kindling…and my book of Rumi," Sam answers, smiling. He walks to the plastic bucket and pries the lid off with his fingers.

Pop ponders the configuration of seats, eight large flat rocks surrounding the fire ring, two steps back from it. "Are the seats lined up with the compass points?"

"Yup." Sam crushes a sheet of newspaper into a wad. He points to the southern rock. "If you sit on that one, the north star lines up with the notch in that one." He points to the north rock, which has a sharp indentation in the close edge.

"Why?" asks Sally. "Why go to all this trouble just to have a campfire?"

"It just happened," Sam shrugs as he crushes another sheet. "Once Matt and I got into it, it all fell together in a weekend. We hauled rocks from a pile in the field. Then we made a fire and cooked venison sausage, drank beer 'til after dark. Matt says in a thousand years someone'll find this collection of rocks and attach some sorta significance to the layout, when all we wanted was a quiet, pretty place to cook sausage and drink beer. Linin' up the rock seats with the compass points was to trick 'em… make 'em think we ancient humans were intelligent." Sam approaches the fire ring with the bucket and begins stacking twigs onto the wads of newspaper.

Pop smiles wickedly, "Now if you'd put the rocks about twenty degrees to the right, maybe they'd figure out it was actually the Republicans who wiped us out."

"Now, Pop!" Sally teases. "What if Sam's a Republican? We're his guests!"

Sam smiles as the butane lighter clicks to flame. "Not a chance. Not a chance in hell."

She adds, "Hey! Bill's a Republican."

"Figures," Pop mumbles.

"What if *I'm* a Republican?" Sally asks, arms crossed defiantly.

Sam replies as he adds slightly larger kindling to the growing flames, "Well then, if you don't have a Dale Earnhardt tattoo in the small of your back (and I know you don't) or a membership to the NRA, you better get 'em. They check for that stuff now at the GOP caucuses."

Each taking an arm, they help Pop out of the golf cart and into a lawn chair. Sam fetches four chunks of split jack pine from a small pile stacked at an angle against one of the white pines. Sally wanders off to search for more wildflowers. Pop takes a deep breath and closes his eyes for a moment.

"Tell me about your winery," Pop asks Sam, who's carefully settinging the chunks of firewood on top of the growing flames. "Maureen mentioned it. Is that what the stone building will be for?"

"Yup. I'm hoping to be in commercial production after the 2006 harvest. We'll see how the vines I bought are doin', the ones I planted two springs ago." Sam turns to the golf cart and fetches a bottle of his homemade wild grape wine along with a corkscrew and three juice glasses.

"You can grow grapes up here?"

"Well, the wild ones grow okay, but they're tricky to transplant and get fruit from consistently. I'm still learnin' and still pickin' grapes here and there around the countryside. The vines I bought were developed by the university. French vines crossed with northern wilds, they say. But mostly I'm hoping the wild vines I cut and planted will do well enough under cultivation so the wild grape can be my primary wine."

Sally returns with a fistful of wild geraniums and ferns. She empties the wine left in Pop's bottle into one of the glasses Sam has set on the stump. She fills the bottle with water from the spigot on the jug and pokes the flowers and ferns in. Carefully she sets the bouquet on the south rock. Sam has the wine open and is pouring into the three glasses.

"What got you interested in a winery?" she asks.

Sam delivers a glass to Pop. "It's a family tradition. Not that anyone brought it over from the Old Country. My dad was the first. Makin' wine was his hobby even way back when I was little. He was very scientific about it. Tried makin' all different kinds—rhubarb, dandelion, any kind of fruit and vegetable you can imagine. Even made wheat wine, which was actually pretty good.

"But after dozens of varieties he settled on just one: cranberry. He'd make two hundred gallons a year in his basement. Went to the bogs in northern Wisconsin every fall and brought back garbage cans full of cranberries from the commercial growers. Dad blew off the wild grape wine for the most part. Too much work to get the fruit. Except one year we stumbled across a mother lode. I helped him and he turned out a heckuva batch. So when I moved to where my second wife and I lived and there were wild grapes growin' all over, he gave me his old recipe."

"Recipe?" Sally accepts a glass .

"Unlike regular wine grapes, where you simply crush 'em to release their juice, if you did that with wild grapes, you'd end up with somethin' that would take the paint off your car…not to mention what it would do to your insides."

Pop holds up his glass and gazes into the clear, deep purple liquid. "This stuff's real good. I think you're onto somethin'…givin' me a good buzz."

"Thanks. I really think it'll sell well. Lord knows how much I've given away the past five years or so. Hope people haven't been crowin' about it just 'cause it was free and full of that feel-good stuff. I'm gonna call the wild variety Two-Glass Wine. After one glass, you feel it warmin' you up. Two glasses and you gotta lie down. Three glasses and you don't care who you lie down with!"

Sally says, "Another glass, please!"

Pop remembers, "We visited a winery once, south of the cities. Small family operation in the rolling hills. Real pretty country, kinda like these hills. Walkin' trails. Folks cross-country skied in the winter. Always thought that'd be a perfect place for a team of horses, maybe give wagon and sleigh rides. How much trail you got here?"

"'Bout three and a half miles round trip from my place to Maureen and Joan's, including the loop."

Pop, always the businessman, figures in his head as he strokes his chin. "Wouldn't have to be that long of a ride to get folks into the wine-buyin' mood. In nice weather, twenty minutes to a wine-tasting, maybe deliver 'em right here. In winter, come up with a decent hot-spiced wine recipe. Bundle 'em up, and charge 'em plenty. They're gonna love this wine and love it here!"

He takes another slow sip as he scans the countryside. "Mmm-hmm, they're gonna love it. I can even see folks gettin' married on this hilltop. Brought in by a team pullin' a wagon…"

Sally smiles widely, knowing something Sam doesn't.

"Tell ya what. I'll make you a deal," Pop offers Sam. "I'll turn over my Perch team to ya. Bill wants 'em outta the pasture anyway. Do you have some pasture land? Doesn't take much of a fence. They're the gentlest animals on Earth. I'll buy the hay in the winter, and the oats year-round. I got the wagon, and I even know of a sleigh for sale…"

Sam replies, "But…but…I've never driven a team, or even hitched one. To be honest, horses don't really like me and the feelin' is…well, mutual."

Sally jumps in. "This could actually work. Think about it! Your barn has a wide enough alley to park the wagon. Drive it in one end and out the other. Easy to build a couple stalls for bad weather. I can help with that."

"But…er…"

"No buts about it!" Pop orders. "When you got time to come down for a lesson on hitchin' 'em?"

"Umm…anytime, I guess. But, you know, I'd have to pay you."

Pop holds up a hand. "Here's the deal. All I want is to be able to come up and drive 'em once in a while. You supply the wine. I only need to know they're bein' looked after and used for what they were born to do. And when I die, they're all yours…under one condition: You deliver me to my final restin' place in that wagon, pulled by my horses."

"Oh, Pop!" Sally shakes a finger at him. "You ain't going nowhere…"

Sam purposely doesn't tell the high school seniors his birthday will be during the class trip on Tuesday. Lord knows there'd be no end to the jokes and shenanigans if they knew. He's advised Matt not to mention it when they go to dinner with the group Monday night.

Sam is the last person into the hotel lobby. The seniors are uncharacteristically quiet for a group waiting to register and get to the pool. The crowd parts as Sam approaches. He eyes the kids suspiciously.

Sure enough, right on the desk in full view sits a vase of flowers, the envelope reading, "Happy Birthday, Cowboy Sam!" Two small plastic horses and riders top long plastic sticks—one a cowboy, the other a cowgirl. Sam covers his eyes and drops his head.

"Hey, Jammer? You jammin' somethin' besides the gears in the school bus these days?" asks Steven, the class clown.

The kids break into uproarious laughter. Even the two class advisors laugh out loud.

Sam turns eighteen shades of red. "I…uh…I got no idea where these came from. Must be a mistake…"

Steven reaches for the card. "Well, lemme find out for ya…"

Sam is frozen in his tracks, speechless. Mrs. Clausen, the bubbly junior high English teacher a couple years from retirement, comes to his rescue—sort of. The kids love her because she is innocent of, and oblivious to, everything besides teaching English.

"Now class, if Sam's been sneaking around with some cowgirl behind our backs, that's none of our business." Mrs. Clausen screws her face into a question. "Do I know her?"

The kids roar again.

Mrs. Clausen hands him the card. Sam quickly stuffs it into his shirt pocket.

"Um...I better go park the bus..."

He drops his bag and hurries toward the revolving door. His mind whirring, he forgets to exit the door the first time around, prompting more laughter.

Mr. Jensen, the young history teacher, remarks "Whew. Must be serious!"

The kids all move to the windows to watch Sam climb into the driver's seat and open the card. He smiles and shakes his finger at them, shuts the door, and pulls away.

Sally's cell number is on the card, along with a note indicating she wants to take him out that night for an early birthday dinner.

He calls her from his hotel room. "You sure are fulla surprises! Thanks for the flowers, but dinner tonight...It's a long way just to take me to dinner. Where the hell are ya anyway?"

"On my way to Buffalo, matter of fact," Sally replies. "Hey, it was a last minute deal. It's a good payday in Buffalo if me and Dakota do anything right. My girlfriend talked me into it. We're stayin' in her fancy trailer. We don't ride 'til tomorrow morning and I don't have anything to do tonight, except find someplace for dinner and someone to share it with."

"I s'pose Maureen let you know where I'd be. But my birthday... Nobody knows my birthday."

"Except your insurance agency! So, are you busy tonight or aren't ya?"

"Nope. Tonight's just pizza and pool party. Clausen and Jensen can handle it. Later, I was gonna hit a little club off the edge of downtown, a band I like."

"I know the hotel. And a fun little sidewalk café in Uptown. You gonna ask me to join you after I buy you dinner?"

Sam's head is spinning like the revolving door in the hotel. "No strings attached, right?"

"Right. Just consider tonight my way of thankin' a new friend. My sister's good neighbor, Pop's future horse-drawn cortege driver, and my canoein', morelin', wine-sharin', and good listenin' buddy. How's 7:30 sound? Pick you up out front."

"Um," Sam replies. "Better make it the side door on Fifth Avenue, as far away from the pool as possible."

"It's a date."

Sam opens the truck passenger door to find Sally stunning in new blue jeans and a light blue western shirt. He loves that she doesn't have to make a statement with fancy clothes. Her shiny blonde hair hangs below her shoulders, and is tucked behind her ears. Her smile, as has become habit, takes Sam's breath away. She's wearing lipstick—understated, a soft pink. The earring on his side dangles, shiny silver with three blue stones, matching her blouse…and her eyes.

"You're somethin' else," he says. "Never had a friend like you do anything this nice for me. Hate to say it, but it's the kinda thing Karen and I used to do for each other, little surprises. You know the way to Uptown?"

"Yep. I went to college down here, so I know my way around." Sally adds, "I hate to say *this*—I've never done anything like this before. I wouldn't have done it without our…rule."

Sam's belly is part flutter and part tightness, like just before a first kiss. He wants to capture the moment, so he can describe the feeling to Laura at the next appointment…and remember it for other reasons. Maybe among his other issues, he's got a bad case of arrested development.

"You're awfully quiet over there," Sally says. "Whatcha thinkin'?"

"Whew. Déjà vu all over again. You remind me of Karen in so many ways…except she had brown hair."

"Karen… Which reminds me, I've gotta apologize."

"For what?"

"You know, that day on the river. You told me about the great connection you two had. I assumed you were divorced. And I thought, *What kinda guy would bail outta that, then miss her so bad and talk about her so much.* But then, I read your poem…"

Sam sighs. "Who knows if we would've made it. Anyway, I should be the one apologizing. I admit it…I *do* let people think I divorced her, 'stead of the truth. Seems like a handy, natural barrier to put up, like don't even think about goin' there with Sam the two-time loser."

"Go where?"

"Any kinda serious thing. Laura says maybe I don't feel worthy. Says for a man like me to stay single this long and not even date, there's gotta be a reason. So, this friendship that's washed over us so fast…I think it works for me."

"Laura?"

"My therapist. Every Wednesday. Too much information, huh?" Sam asks. "You sure you still want to go to dinner…with a crazy man?"

"Yep." Sally flashes a smile. "I'll just have the waiter put a cork on the business end of your fork."

The Italian café is on Hennepin Avenue. They sit outside at a wrought-iron table. It's a perfect late-spring evening to spend the last hour of daylight dining at a sidewalk café—blue sky above, just a hint of a warm and inviting breeze. No need to bring a sweater or weight down the napkins with the salt and pepper shakers, and as comfortable as the dining room at home.

Hennepin Avenue and Lake Street direct an irregular stream of folks such as theater-goers or people seeking food and drink, listening to local bands, taking a walk, or window shopping. This part of town has especially good people-watching, with plenty of young folks and a melting pot of cultures and lifestyles.

"So, did you take Pop back to the farm?" Sam asks.

"Yeah, I did, but…"

"What is it?"

"Same shit, different day. Bill was all over me, wanted me to stay the weekend and holiday, so I could watch Pop and he could hang out at the campground. I'm sure the neighbors could hear us arguin' about it."

"What's it like for Pop when you guys fight over who stays with him?"

"Well, we didn't tell Bill it was actually Pop's idea for me to come down to see you. Actually, dinner's on Pop (although I wasn't s'posed to tell you). He really likes you, you know.

"If Bill has to run off to the damn four-wheeler deal, his brother Robert only lives a couple miles away.

Considering Robert doesn't dare risk getting booted outta the will, he'll come over once in a while and sleep on the couch to keep track of Pop at night."

Sam offers, "I realize I don't know you all that well yet. And just tell me to shut up if you want, but…why you tryin' to have a baby with a man you don't dare stay home with or he'll…"

Sally straightens in her chair, avoiding his gaze by looking across the street. "Or he'll what?"

"…smack you around."

"Who says he does that?" Sally demands, her chin held high in defiance.

"Oh, come on. If Dakota had given you that shiner, it would've been your other eye."

"So what? You some kinda private investigator now?" Sally crosses her arms tightly.

"Nope. But no strings attached or not, I'm starting to care about you…" Sam admits softly.

She stares directly into his eyes. Her eyes narrow a little. Her mouth is set firmly and her chin quivers slightly. Sam looks down into his beer, trying to think of a way to apologize.

"Listen, I'm married to Bill. It might not seem like it this weekend, but I'm gonna stay that way—forever. Please don't misunderstand…"

Sam pleads, "Do you really think he's gonna change? I mean, you plannin' on spending the next thirty, forty years like this?"

"I think if we have a baby together, that'll change everything. Being a father'll soften him up. It has to. Kids are a miracle."

Sam responds softly, "A baby never fixed a broken marriage. On the other hand, I seen a lotta bad marriages mess up a kid for good."

"It'll change him. I know it will."

"A wise old Bohemian once said…"

"Oh, here we go again with ancient philosophy." Sally throws her hands up and rolls her eyes.

Sam repeats, "A wise old Bohemian once said, *There are only two things we can change concerning another person. The first is our perception of that person. The second is our proximity to that person. Everything else is up to the other person to change himself.*"

"Where'd you hear that one? Was Rumi Bohemian?"

"Nope. It just came out, outta…nowhere…"

He takes a breath, lets his shoulders loosen, and relaxes his hands. "Hey, I'm gettin' hungry. How 'bout you?"

Sally visibly relaxes as well. "Yup, I'm starvin'. I recommend the tortellini stuffed with sausage."

Their order is delivered and conversation between bites is light, almost like they're old friends who've had dinner dozens of times. They make plans to take Pop down the river on the next nice weekend. Sally recites the horse events she'll be competing at over the early summer. She invites Sam to attend, and enlists him to help bring Pop to one or two.

Sam mentions he's got plenty of time on his hands this coming summer, that he doesn't have a stone job lined up yet, but that's okay with him.

"I'll fiddle with layin' some rock on the winery, get the fence ready for the horses, and build the stalls and a tack room in the barn."

Sally asks, "So, if you don't mind my askin'…how do you get by? I mean, work, money seems rather unsteady for you. Even your bus drivin' is a question mark 'cause you said you're just a substitute driver now."

"Well, the farm's paid for. Had just enough money from my half of the life insurance. When I get low on cash, somethin' always seems to come along, extra bus trips or a stone job."

"What about saving a little nest egg, some security in case somethin' goes haywire? You should be puttin' something away every month. You are, aren't you?"

Sam shrugs. "Never seem to have much extra. Just spend what I have, when I have it. What little extra there is goes into grapevines and the winery building. S'pose the winery's my retirement account. Past couple years, I been saving ahead a coupla months for the essentials. You know—electric and propane, insurance, phone. Stuff it in a sock."

Sally ignores the sock statement, and doesn't believe it. But it's true—that is where Sam puts his extra money.

"But what about when you're ready to go into wine production?" Sally asks. "That equipment can't be cheap."

"I'll buy more socks. Heh heh."

Sally frowns.

"Something'll come along. It always does. I remember one time 'bout four years ago, I was down to just 35¢."

"You were?"

Sam leans back so the waitress can take their plates. He thanks the young lady, then picks up the story where he left off.

"I had enough gas in the truck to get to Stone Creek maybe twice in case I had to drive a summer bus trip. But I had running water, wine, venison, morels, chickens in the coop, a garden, enough toilet paper. Phone and electric weren't due 'til the next month. I read somewhere that when things go haywire, don't fight it. Instead breathe it in, experience it, feel it all the way to your soul. It's like a chance to heal your negative perception of whatever's gone wrong. And then it just goes away."

"Did it?"

"After a little meditation at the fire ring, I took the 35¢ and flushed it down the toilet."

"Oh geez, you are nuts…or were you drunk on wild grape wine?"

"I thanked God for that particular human experience, bein' broke as hell. The toilet tank hadn't even refilled and there was a knock on the door. It was a contractor I did stone work for once in a while. Another stone mason had crapped out on him. Just like that, a four-sided see-through fireplace, twenty-eight feet to the ceiling. He wrote me a check right then, a down payment for $3,000. Said he'd even have his helper unload rocks for me, bring 'em up the scaffold—and mix my mortar and clean the mixer—a luxury I'd never had. The total I made on the job was $12,000."

"So you can commit to something, huh?" Sally asks.

"Heh heh. Well, maybe for a couple months…if the price is right."

The waitress returns and sets the check in front of Sam. Sally reaches across the table to grab it.

"That was one of my best years in recent memory," Sam continues. "Bought my little tractor and trailer with the down payment. Drove it to the job every day—stopping at the gravel pit, to or from the job, to gather rocks—whichever trip compelled me to stop. Bought my first ever cement mixer. And still had more than enough cash (along with my bus check) to get me through that winter...'bout three socks full. I even took a month in winter to see friends in Colorado, and detoured to Boise to visit my daughter and son-in-law. Skied and ice fished in the mountains."

Sally asks, "But now, what if you want a decent truck? Or a trip to Europe? Or a new house?"

Sam shrugs. "Had all that. Worked my ass off for it. Made my first wife happy as anything that I worked two jobs for it. But when the money quit flowin' so nicely, it made her mad as hell. I worked that hard for her, not for myself. It was the only way there'd be peace in our household. And the only way I would get a piece. I knew I didn't need all those things to be happy and feel useful."

"So, with Karen, you lived modestly, right? Was she okay with that?"

"She was, but her family wasn't. We had bigger plans, but had to scale back. I was soon on her family's shit list. I got real sick. The doctors couldn't figure it out. Sore all over, couldn't sleep, heart goin' goofy, brain fog, depression. Six months later they finally decided I had Lyme disease. That was back before they knew much about it. In the meantime Karen sold the El Dorado and took a second job."

"I've hearda that Lyme stuff," Sally says. "Nasty."

"At the time, I wondered if that's what it felt like to be dyin'. But six months after that, I was pretty well mended. But by then we were behind on everything except the mortgage. Owed thousands in doctor bills, taxes, utilities…sold some horses, farmed out the others. Worst day of my life when I had to give my son back to his mother—Karen's worst day, too, when she had to turn her daughter over to her ex-husband—because we couldn't afford to feed 'em. Eventually had to file bankruptcy. Karen worked her ass off. Saw us through it all and never complained."

Sally sniffles and digs through her purse looking for the cash Pop had given her. She finds a stray tissue and quickly dabs at her nose.

"Life's a trip, huh?," Sam says. "I learned the only thing in life anyone can guarantee is love—whether you're with someone or not. I love my first wife, but certainly don't want to be with her. I have a lot to be thankful for. I still love her, in a fashion, even though she's generally a pain in the ass at family functions. Finally figured out why she has that pained look on her face every time our paths cross. She needs more fiber in her diet."

That comment breaks the ice. Sally smiles at Sam and dabs at her nose again. She chuckles softly.

Sally asks, "So, back to your tough times with Karen. You're sayin' if Bill got sick and we were goin' broke, if I really love him, I would graciously sell my horses, if it came to that? Is that what you're lookin' for? Holdin' out for another woman who would sell her horses for you?"

"Maybe I am," Sam replies. "Is that the kinda woman Bill has?"

"I dunno...I just don't know..."

"Looks awfully crowded," Sally worries aloud as they walk past the club door. Folks are lined up down the sidewalk almost half a block away. "Think we'll be able to get in?"

"We'll go around back. I forgot to tell you. Guy I grew up with, Rick, is friends with the band. We're meetin' him here."

"What kinda band is it?" Sally asks while Sam knocks. "Mosta those folks waitin' look about our age."

"Rock and roll. Lots of great electric guitar, a stand-up bass, and a drummer from outer space. Rockabilly. Maybe just a little bitta redneck."

Sam adds, "I'm not much of a dancer, but Rick is a maniac. He'll only stop at the table to take on some fluids and change women. You ready to dance with him? Of course, I get you back when they slow it down..."

"Gosh! I haven't danced since...since my wedding reception. Always have to rush home after the rodeos, never stayed for the dance after."

The door finally opens. A shaft of smoky, yellow light envelops them.

A big guy with a crew cut and a gray Security t-shirt asks, "You Sam Ryan...and Sally? Right this way..."

Sam steps aside and gestures for Sally to enter first.

The bouncer leads them in from behind the stage. The band tinkers with the equipment, getting ready for the show. Before Sam's eyes can adjust, Rick calls to them from a table in the front.

"Hey, Sam!" Rick jumps up and rushes over to give Sam a bear hug. "So glad you could make it!" He turns to Sally and smiles. "Yup, Sam wasn't exaggerating about you."

Sally asks, "Oh yeah? What'd he tell you? You know about the gravel pit?!!"

"He said that you have the most beautiful smile he's ever seen." Rick winks at Sam.

Sally blushes. "Well, thank you both." She lets her hand find Sam's and gives it a squeeze.

Rick's girlfriend is several years younger than him. He wears his hair combed back. It's curly at the ends just above his collar, like Sam's—salt and pepper on top, thinning in the front, and graying on the sides. Similar to Rick, Denise is dressed in biker attire—mostly black, leather vest, western boots, with shiny dangling earrings and bracelets on both arms. Rick and Denise are a handsome couple.

Denise asks Sally, "You're in town to ride, to barrel race, huh?"

"Yeah, out in Buffalo tomorrow."

"Well," Denise says, "We'll have to take our Memorial Day bike ride to the west of town, huh Rick? You gonna be able to get away, Sam?"

"No, unfortunately not," he replies. "We got the Twins game tomorrow. It's a noon start."

Sally's smile dissolves into a bit of disappointment. Sam's wheels begin to turn.

"Well, wait a sec. We're only six blocks from the Metrodome. I won't need to drive them there. They can take the Skyway if it rains. Lord knows there isn't much trouble they can get into at a baseball game. I don't think I'll be missed. What time, Sally?"

First she bites her lip to ward off the tears trying to escape, then her smile comes alive. "Really! You can drive the bus to Buffalo? The draw's at ten. Could be ridin' any time after that."

"It's a date. I'll have to watch where I walk though." Sam points to his tennis shoes. Rick and Denise share a curious glance.

The house lights dim. Suddenly a spotlight shines on Jim, the lead guitar player and primary vocalist. He looks right out of a '50s prison movie. The clean-shaven, stone-faced chain gang guard, but without the badge and gun. A felt fedora, mirror aviator sunglasses, white t-shirt with a pack of Camels rolled up in the sleeve. A half-smoked cigarette with a long ash dangling from the corner of his mouth. Perfectly polished black pull-on boots, with a pant leg caught in the top of one. The drummer beats click, click, click. And the night is on…

Rick reaches for Sally's hand. "Come on!"

Sally leaps up to join him, smiling widely. Sam's amazed at how easily he leads her into an intricate swing dance, like they've been dancing together forever. Her blonde hair swinging, she never quits smiling.

Denise moves next to Sam. She cups her hand and says into his ear, "Just a friend, huh?"

"I don't know. It's confusing."

"Two things. Believe what she does over what she says. And be patient. This is a huge deal for her."

After the first two dances Rick takes the obligatory swig of beer and changes partners. Sally is more than content to sit with Sam and take in the music. She slides her chair close so their hips touch. It isn't until the fifth song that Jim slows it down.

"Shall we?" Sam asks.

Sally nods, smiles shyly, and slides her chair back.

His arm instinctively knows where to rest at her waist, even though he hasn't danced in over six years. Sally's hand fits perfectly in his. It's like they've danced a hundred times before. She looks up into Sam's eyes. He sees that hers are shining and wonders whether it's from the cigarette smoke, or something else. She lays her head on his shoulder.

"Oh geez," Sam whispers. "Where are the nuns to slide a book between us when we need 'em?"

Sally returns her head to Sam's shoulder with a contented sigh. "Think I'm gettin' the hang of this no strings attached business. Feels better than I thought it would."

They leave the bar at midnight. Sally pulls into the alley behind the hotel. They linger against the tailgate, side by side, their bodies touching at a few points. Sam puts his arm around her waist. She turns and melts against him.

Sally sighs. "Shit…I s'pose I better go."

With their hands linked, she presses a light kiss on his lips. It's more than a quick peck, but less than a signal promising anything more. She slides into the driver's seat and drives away down the alley.

Sam touches his mouth and tastes the faint remnants of Sally's lipstick.

The rib joint is on the north edge of downtown. The senior class walks ahead a half block, with Sam, Matt, Clausen, and Jensen following.

"Hey, Dad," Matt asks. "What's that on your shoe? Looks like horse crap."

Sam hadn't mentioned a word about Sally to his son. He'd even hidden the birthday flowers in the hotel closet.

"Nnn…nnnothing…"

Clausen pipes up. "Sam, you missed a great ball game this afternoon."

Jensen adds, "And a fun pizza and pool party last night."

"Hey, ol' man," Matt asks suspiciously. "I repeat—what's up?"

"Gosh, those flowers are beautiful!" Clausen gushes. "…those little plastic horses with a cowboy and cowgirl. How creative!"

Matt says, "Oh. Yeah, the kids found out about your birthday. But why would they put plastic horses in your birthday flowers?"

"They didn't know it was my birthday," Sam says, "'til we got to the hotel and the flowers were waitin' for me at the front desk."

Jensen says, "Can't picture you on a horse, Jammer."

Matt sighs loudly. "Okay. Why haven't I heard about her?"

"Oh, we're just friends."

Clausen and Jensen are enjoying the father/son conversation, following a step behind like two mice listening from a hole in the wall.

At the corner, they pause for a red light.

Matt turns to his dad, his arms crossed. "So, where did the horse crap come from?"

Sam admits, "Rick, Denise, and I went to her barrel race in Buffalo this afternoon. Hmm? S'pose I should be more careful where I step, huh?"

"And the pizza party?" Matt asks. "Where were you last night?"

"Oh! Oh right, now I remember. She took me out for my birthday…to dinner. Then we went dancin' with Rick and Denise. Oops! Light's green. We better catch up to the others!"

Matt lays a hand on Sam's shoulder and holds him back.

"Geez, Dad. This feels a lot like—when was it, five years ago? The married lady. Nobody knew a thing about her…until she was stalking you."

"Well, son, this time's different. No strings attached… just friends."

He starts across the street and the others hurry to follow.

"Please tell me she's not married," Matt begs.

The four adults stop in the middle of the crosswalk, their heads snapped to attention. The other three form a semicircle around Sam, eager for his response. The light turns red and cars honk. The four of them scurry to take refuge on the concrete median.

"Hey!" Sam yells at a taxi driver. "Don't you know it's rude to wave with just part of your hand!"

"Dad!"

"Yes, she's married. But we're *just friends*. She's my neighbor Maureen's sister. Turns out she's also the receptionist at the insurance office. I did her a little favor, took her and her father-in-law out morel picking."

"What else?" Matt demands.

"Nothin'. Not any big deal."

"Come on. Spill it!"

The light turns green. Quickly, Sam proceeds toward the other side of the street, his audience hurrying behind him like baby ducks after their mother.

"You aren't gonna believe how we met…" Sam stops on the sidewalk. "I mean, I'd seen her in the office. Really, I thought she was single. Then I found her in my morel woods, sunbathing…naked. I rolled down into the gravel pit and she fell on toppa me like that."

"Wait…naked?"

"Next day, she canoed the river with me. And the following weekend, I helped out at her barrel race, which she won. Oh God! You should see her on a horse. Wowee!"

Sam bolts toward the students, half a block away.

"And…?" Matt shouts at his father's back.

"Just Saturday she brought Pop (he's her father-in-law) over to pick yellow morels and have a picnic. And Pop's givin' me his team of Percherons, the harnesses and the wagon."

Sam jogs ahead, still a ways back from the pack.

"And where's her husband been through all this?" Matt starts to pant.

"He's not very nice to her," Sam yells over his shoulder.

"Dad! You really do want to get shot in the…"

"He's not even nice to his own dad," Sam adds, finally slowing to a walk.

They reach the next stoplight. The kids have slowed and are only a quarter block ahead of the adults, waiting.

Matt, breathing hard, puts a hand on his dad's shoulder. "Assuming you aren't sleeping with her...yet...did it ever occur to you this woman's probably just having you take over for the missing parts of her marriage? This puppy dog look...I'm worried you really like her. But she doesn't have any intention of leaving him for you. They never do. I don't want you to end up crazy when this woman finally dumps you. Which she most certainly will when her husband finds out."

"I don't know the guy," Sam admits. "But Sally let it slip he's got a history of playin' the field. He lives and works in Grand Forks during the week. On weekends he's home, but he's always runnin' off to who knows where with who knows who."

"Oh! Well, why didn't you say so earlier?" Matt replies. "As long as she sleeps with you outta revenge...hey, that changes everything!"

Sam grits his teeth. "Listen here. We are NOT sleeping together!" He adds in a whisper, "Darn it..."

Clausen whispers to Jensen, "Well, I'll be darned."

"What?" Sam demands, whipping around to address them directly.

Clausen responds sheepishly, "Well, to be honest... everybody in Stone Creek thinks you're gay! You know—Sharon Johnson brought you those chocolate chip cookies right after you moved in, wearing Daisy Dukes and a halter top. You didn't even let her in the door. So she went 'round and told everybody you're obviously gay."

"Good Lord," Sam replies with disgust. "Of course I didn't let her in! Who the hell knows what mighta crawled off that woman?"

Sam turns to Jensen. "What would *you* have said to her?"

Jensen runs a hand down his beard. "I actually asked her, 'Does two percent milk go with those cookies?'"

Clausen splutters, "Jensen! You little...you little...slut!"

"Hey!" Jensen protests. "Mrs. Johnson even slept with the P.E. teacher, Sandra."

Clausen and Sam stop in their tracks. In unison they ask, "Butch Beebe?"

Clausen shrieks as she swoons, "Oh my goodness. You mean...Sandra's a *lesbian*?"

Jensen shakes his head, laughing to himself. "Why you s'pose the kids call her Butch?"

"Well, gee, I thought it was on account of her short haircut..."

CHAPTER 10

ELVIS AND ROY

The following Saturday.

Pop peeks out the back door and his face lights up to see the golf cart being towed on a trailer behind Sam's pickup truck. The plan is to surprise Sally by making the trip to watch her ride. That is, after Pop introduces Sam to the Perch team.

Bill is walking down from the pole barn when Sam pulls to a stop. Turns out Bill's actually a sawed-off little runt with a tiny head—so small that his beer hat is on the tightest notch. The plastic adjuster pokes straight out behind, like a horse's tail just before he launches a steaming pile of shit. Bill can't be over 135 pounds soakin' wet, and 5'7".

These past weeks, Sam hadn't tried one bit to give him any kind of benefit of the doubt. And now he's instantly satisfied he didn't. Bill's walking like a rooster with a set of giant balls between its legs. He holds his head back with a permanent smirk, like a prizefighter who just dodged a punch. For some reason, Bill's grinning widely, as if Sam's an old and cherished friend who's finally paying back that money he owes, with interest.

Besides all that, his beady eyes are strangely close together, his mouth is just a tiny sideways slit. He hasn't shaved in days. And his belly...like an anorexic girl who's six months pregnant. It's obvious to Sam that Sally hasn't "married up".

Bill pulls off his right glove and eagerly sticks out a clammy hand. "Well, hey there. You gotta be Sam, the lucky devil whose pasture those two grass- and oat-wastin' fleabags are gonna crap in from now on! Boy, am I glad to meet YOU!"

His voice is annoyingly high-pitched and screechy, making Sam wonder if the runt had maybe lost something going over a barb-wire fence and that's why he walks funny. Like fingernails on a chalkboard. Add to that, Bill apparently doesn't have a volume control.

Sam forces a smile. "Yup."

Bill adds, "Now, if I could just get you to take those other two goddamn horses..."

"Not Sally's gamers?" Sam asks.

"Jesus, talk about a waste o' time and money..."

"I hear she's pretty good with horses. Wins more than her share of races."

"I wouldn't know," Bill answers. He squirts a stream of tobacco juice out the left side of his mouth. "All I know is, she ain't around much when I'm here. How's 'at for a wife who wants to have a kid? Never even home to let me pound that fur patch of hers enough to get her to settle. Ha, ha, ha..." He chuckles at his clever entendre.

Sam feels his blood begin to heat up. He lies, "Well, nice meetin' ya. And by the way, I won't be takin' the team home 'til I know how to handle 'em good, probably later this summer."

"Whatever." Bill turns quickly and struts back to the pole barn, walking like he has a terminal case of monkey butt.

Sam looks up to the house. Pop holds the back door open. His cowboy hat is on, and there's a jacket and plastic bag hanging over the walker.

Sam shouts, "Gimme a minute, Pop. Be right there."

He hurries to the front of the trailer and loosens the come-a-long that's attached to the frame of the golf cart. He pulls a pin on the trailer tongue, and steps up and into the golf cart. He releases the foot brake and inches the cart backward. The trailer bed slowly tips. Sam rolls the cart onto the driveway. The entire process has taken less than a minute. He drives to the back steps.

"Pretty slick!" Pop says.

Pop eases himself into the cart and drives so Sam can be the gate opener. Just inside the pasture, Pop whistles up the two big horses. They pull their heads up and lope over, not light on their feet but still graceful. They are both grayish-white. One horse approaches Pop for a kiss on its nose. The other introduces himself to Sam with a sniff of his shirt sleeve. Just beyond the far edge of the pasture, they can hear the racket of four-wheel drive trucks revving and churning.

"That's Elvis," instructs Pop, pointing to the horse by Sam. "This one's Roy. They're full brothers, a year apart."

"My gosh!" Pop says after patting Roy's nose a bit. "I wondered what Sally was doin' out here so long the other evenin'. Look, she combed out their manes and tails. And shaved their bridle paths."

"How can you tell who's who?"

"First of all, they got different personalities. Elvis there's more confident. See how he came right up to ya, a perfect stranger? He holds his head a bit higher when they're runnin', or doing anything besides drivin' or eatin'. And Roy here has a pink snip on his nose. Won't be long, you'll know who's who without even lookin' at 'em. Elvis is always hitched to the right."

They drive up to the barn next to the abandoned cow yard.

Smiling, Pop shakes his head, "Geez."

"What?"

"A week ago, even the damn cats couldn't make it from one end of the alley to the other, all the goddamn junk Bill and Robert left lyin' around. Sally again…gettin' it ready for you to learn the team. If that kidda mine had half a brain…"

Sam thinks to himself, *Half a brain sounds just about right.*

"Last I saw of 'em, the harnesses were in the old milk room." Pop points to the furthest corner of the barn.

Pop urges the golf cart to the doorway, while Sam follows on foot. They both peer in. Sam's not sure what he's looking at, but Pop knows. Not only are the leather straps and rigging dusted and laid out, the leather has been freshly oiled.

After only a quick inventory of the rigging, Sam helps Pop into his truck, then loads the golf cart. Neither wants to miss Sally's rides. She's at a Fun Show today, with all different kinds of games. No money involved, except a small entry fee to cover the winners' ribbons. Sally's excited to see if Dakota can do something besides barrel race—like run the poles, do the keyhole, and master the egg and spoon.

The guys make a quick stop to get coffee at the convenience store in Streeter.

Pop gratefully accepts the brew, blowing on it lightly. "You know, your friendship with Sally means a lot to her," he says as Sam puts the truck in gear.

"And hers to me," Sam says. "But I have to keep it in perspective. I mean, how many married women are out there, in less than perfect situations, who find something away from home. But we're not doin' anything like that, Pop."

"Well…Lord knows what that kid of mine's doin' evenings and nights up there in Grand Forks. Got no idea where he picked up that habit. Or why Sally seems to be oblivious to it."

Pop continues, "I sure hope they don't have a baby. God, that would seal the deal. I can't believe Bill really even wants one."

"Sally mentioned," Sam offers, "that she went in to get checked and was okay. But Bill won't go…"

"He's more than okay," Pop assures. "Got two girls pregnant…that I know of. The first one willingly went for an abortion. Second one wanted the kid, and wanted to get married. But of course, Bill didn't want any part of her or the baby. Got nasty. She hired a lawyer. Then she miscarried. What a shame…"

"Sally would make a helluva mother," Sam says. "I can just tell—the way she is with the horses."

"Maureen told me about your work, and all you do at the school. And deliverin' three babies! Not surprised you and Sally finally met and hit it off. You're a lot alike, people-people. Too bad it didn't happen four years ago…"

"Aww, I'm too old for her anyway." Sam laughs self-consciously. "What's Sally? 37? 38? I'm 53. Trust me, she wouldn't want to settle for an old fart like me."

Pop smiles. "She ever tell you 'bout the guy she left to move home from Oregon, after my stroke? Paul. He is seventeen years older 'n her. She'd been with him five or six years. Sally would probably still be out there in Oregon with him, except he refused to have kids with her. He already had two kids from his first marriage; they were almost as old as Sally. That's why she never went through with it. She wanted her own family. Even if I hadn't had the stroke, she was fixin' to give up on Paul anyway."

Sam asks, "Are you and I the only two men in the world who realize what a treasure she is?"

"Looks like it. Sometimes I wonder if she really wants kids. Or maybe she unconsciously picks men where it either ain't gonna happen—like with Paul—or it shouldn't happen—like with Bill. I dunno. She came from a real tough place…"

They drive into the dirt lot at the fairgrounds, Pop directing the way past empty white buildings of livestock stalls and closed-up exhibit halls with giant green 4-H clovers painted on them. He points toward a high, slab-wood fence with an opening. "Through that gate."

Sam spots Sally's silver truck and black trailer at the other side of the arena. Dakota's tied to the trailer and saddled.

"Is she out ridin' Sparky?"

"No. Sparky must be at Maureen's. Sally isn't goin' back to the farm tonight."

Sam parks out of the way, behind the judges tower.

A friend of Sally's, Kate, recognizes Pop and trots her horse up to the truck. "Hey, Pop! You gonna have time to make a halter for Kylee's pony?"

Pop grins. "'Course! You got the rope?"

"Sure do. Surprised to see you here. Sally said you weren't comin.'"

Kate turns to Sam, who's at the front of the trailer unhitching the come-a-long. "You're Sam, huh? Don't worry! I'm not p.g. But there's a lady over there who looks like she's 'bout due!"

"Heh heh. Nope, I'm outta that business…I hope." Sam wonders how much Sally has been talking about him.

Kate says, "Sally's over behind that big trailer with the water tank on top, givin' some girls a lesson in horse massage."

Pop slides from the truck into the cart's driver's seat. They head for the big horse trailer.

Busy massaging deep under the shoulder blade of a sorrel, Sally doesn't see them approach at first.

"Oh my God!" she shrieks when she notices their golf cart approaching. "You made it!"

She wipes off her hands and hurries over to give them both big hugs.

"Thanks," she whispers in Sam's ear.

He whispers back, "Wouldn't have missed it for the world…"

Kate watches from atop her horse, smiling.

"Hop in!" Pop says to Sally. "Lemme give you a lift. I wanna go see Dakota."

Sam says, "You guys go ahead. I'll fetch the walker, chairs, and cooler and meet you there."

"Naw! We'll go get 'em with my new legs here!" Pop pats the golf cart's dashboard, steps on the accelerator and the cart lurches forward. Sally has to grab her baseball hat to keep it from falling off.

Sam gets sidetracked on the way to the truck and trailer, by one of the Stone Creek seniors from the class trip. LuAnn's brushing her horse.

"Hey Jammer!" she shouts. "Funny meetin' you here!"

Sam grins and walks over to her. "Please, do your best to keep the fact that I'm not gay from Mrs. Johnson."

"Yup. I see who your girlfriend is," LuAnn teases with a devilish glance. "Nope, you're not gay…not even close."

"She ain't my girlfriend! Honest, we're just friends."

LuAnn pauses for a few seconds then offers her eighteen-year old advice. "Ok then. Two things. Somehow you'll need to keep your hands off each other. And second, you'll need to practice your lyin'. You really suck at it, Jammer."

Sam shakes his finger at her, but can't hide his smile. "Good luck, LuAnn."

When Sam gets to the truck and trailer, Dakota's unhitched. The bay horse is nuzzling Pop, whose eyes are moist.

"You're a helluva horse," Pop whispers into Dakota's nose. "You take good care of our girl…"

Pop nudges the golf cart to the fence. Sam, Sally, and finally Dakota line up down the fence beyond the cart. Sally is so confident and focused when it comes to barrel racing, it's strange for her to be unsure of herself with the other games. She and Dakota are running late in the draw for the first event, pole bending.

"Gosh, you went to all this trouble. Hell, I haven't a clue how me and Dakota will do. She may get past the far pole, jump the fence, throw me, and end up in Iowa, for all I know."

Sam watches Dakota, who for all the world seems to be concentrating on the other horses as they weave the poles, almost as if she's memorizing the pattern.

"First thing—look at her. She's got it," Pop assures Sally. "She'll be fine. Second thing, I don't come to these things thinkin' you have to win for it to be a good day. All you gotta do is get up on a horse and smile, and I'm happy."

"Really?"

"Really."

"Ditto," Sam offers as he nods.

"Well, here then." Sally hands him her camcorder. "Cover us on these poles. I need to warm Dakota up. Just remember, I'm only gonna lope her, so don't expect much."

From the golf cart a few yards away, Pop adds his two-cent's worth. "Hey cowgirl, if she wants it, give Dakota her head. You remember how it's done. Let 'er know at the fifth pole she's gonna be circlin' the sixth to come home. Sit back in the seat a bit. Nothin' to it. I can't hardly wait to see you two flyin' home!"

Finally, it's their turn. Once inside the arena, Dakota prances, anxious to run. Sally reins her into a tight circle. "It's fine…it's fine…"

When Dakota's nose is pointed at the first pole, and instinctively she's about to explode into a blur of speeding horseflesh, Sally drops the reins; when it's obvious Dakota's being over-anxious, she puts some pressure back on the bit to slow her down. Settled down enough, it does look like Sally's only loping Dakota—they move so effortlessly.

On the final turn, Sally and Dakota cut it too tight, knocking down the last pole before their eye-watering dash to the finish line—a five second penalty.

Even with that mistake, Sally's visibly shaking with excitement after they slide to a stop. Dakota snorts and blows, spinning twice after they halt, but Sally keeps turning her body so she can see Pop and Sam. Dakota's first attempt at pole bending is beyond anybody's expectations, except maybe Pop's. Even at three-fourths the speed, their time would have been less than two-tenths off the winning time.

The afternoon becomes lazy between Sally and Dakota's other runs. Pop makes not just the halter for Kylee, but another to go along with her first-place ribbon for the junior barrel race. Sally shows the little girl how easy it is to put it on her horse. She beams at Sally like she's Miss America and the first woman president all wrapped into one. Pop tools around the grounds, visiting with the children and grandchildren of old friends.

Halfway through the afternoon, Sally and Dakota easily win the senior barrels. But after that race, she worries about another event her mare has never encountered, the speed and action race. Before they leave the trailer area, Sally grabs Sam's beer and takes a long swig.

"I'm gonna need that, I think. I hope she's not too much horse…and I'm enough rider."

Sam starts the camera as they enter the arena. As he's learned about Sally's best steed ever, when it's time, Dakota can hardly wait to run. The mare prances nervously, like she's about to explode. Sally reins her in two tight circles and pats her on the neck. She nudges Dakota into a ten by ten starting space, marked at the corners with flagpoles, the perimeter drawn in the sand with a stick.

Sally wears a nervous smile as she pulls up on the reins and puts a little pressure on the bit. Dakota finally stands with all four feet still. Sally whispers to her and pats her on the neck, then sits up relaxed and leans forward. Dakota's ears spring erect; she knows Sally's about to drop the reins and she gets to perform what she was born to do.

Dakota rears, her front hooves coming off the ground a couple feet and flailing for terra firma when they touch down. Again, Sam worries, just like at the rodeo, that Dakota's going to run right out from under Sally. The horse is already at top speed when she crosses the timer three strides in front of her. Sally's leaning out over her horse's neck, one hand full of reins, the other gripping the saddle horn.

They're on a heart-stopping dash to the single barrel at the other end of the arena they must circle before heading back through the timer.

In a single stride, Dakota's at full gallop again and Sally's hanging onto the horn with one hand. Half an arena away is the timer. Sam had noticed that most riders began bringing their mount to a stop several yards before the timer. But Dakota and Sally run like they've got forty acres to come to a halt instead of just thirty feet beyond the timer, where they are supposed to come to a dead stop back in the square.

When the front of Dakota hits the timer, Sally's hand on the horn instantly and gracefully joins her other hand on the reins. She pulls and leans back herself. Dakota's front feet fly off the ground, flailing the air, her torso nearly vertical, while her hind hooves dig into the ground and go into a skid, sending the arena dirt flying. The two race monitors, who stand just outside the square turn to run away.

Dakota drops her front hooves back to the ground while her hinds still skid, then puts the brakes on the fronts, too. She and Sally come to a halt in the middle of the flagged square. It looks like Dakota isn't going to keep herself from bolting and jumping the arena fence and running off to who knows where before she uses up her adrenaline.

Sally whispers and pats Dakota on the neck. The monitor, an older gentleman who carries a small flag on a stick, has suddenly forgotten it's his job to count the three seconds steed and rider must stay completely in the square for their ride to count. He tips his hat to Sally, then remembers to hold the flag up and finally drop it, signaling they can leave the confines of the dirt square.

Sally makes Dakota mind her manners and walk out of the square toward the gate. Halfway there, she lets out a "Whoop!" and pulls back on the reins, Dakota's cue to rise up on her hind feet and dance.

Nobody else comes close to their time.

A half dozen riders excitedly escort Sally and Dakota back to the horse trailer. Pop is already out of the golf cart and quickly shuffling to the trailer with his walker. Sam fumbles with the camcorder, trying to shut it off. Pop gets the first hug, Dakota gets the second, and Sam the third. Sally notices Sam hasn't shut off the camcorder and reaches over and pushes the button.

Sam hands her his beer. She takes a big swig, passes it back, and is instantly surrounded by congratulations from the other riders, and questions about how she has such perfect control of such a strong horse.

A little cowboy about seven years old, under a huge, black hat and on a horse that seems five sizes too big, rides up to Sam. He's wearing chaps to match his hat, real spurs on his boots, and a gun belt with a pair of plastic six-shooters. He has a wad in his cheek of what Sam hopes is chewing gum.

The little guy leans onto the saddle horn, one leather-gloved hand upon the other. He looks over at Sally, who at that moment is stealing a glance at Sam, smiling that incredible smile.

The little cowboy declares through one front tooth, "If I hath to get mawwied thumday…I wanna wife wike yourth, who'th justh ath purdy, an' can wide wike that!"

With that, the kid spits a stream of blue juice at the ground, kicks and lazily reins his horse around, spurs it, and lopes away like he's been riding and contemplating his prospective wife since he got done taming the entire west last week.

Sally and Sam help Pop into Maureen's house. He has brought a bag with his pajamas, slippers, and medications, and is looking forward to a nap.

Sally settles him onto the couch. She carefully spreads a blanket over him, and gives a kiss on his forehead.

He smiles and whispers sleepily, "A very, very good day…thanks…" He's snoring within two minutes.

Sam sits at the kitchen table with Maureen, who asks, "You got any ideas about supper?"

"Chili?" suggests Sally.

"Good idea," Sam says. "I'm overstocked with tomato sauce. Wanna take the cart over to my place?"

Maureen adds, "A jar of peppers, please. And some of your home-grown garlic."

"We're gonna need a roadie," Sally says. "I'd like one of those quiet rides you told me about. I'm beat…"

They take their time on the trail, spending over half an hour on a trip that usually takes just fifteen minutes, both feeling the afternoon's beer and fresh air, and sipping wine.

Whirring along lazily, Sally confides, "I'm gettin' used to havin' someone there for me at the horse shows. I like it. Thanks. Really…"

Sam answers, "I love to watch you ride. And to… just…be around you."

She slides her arm around his waist. "Trail's a little bumpy. I better hang on." She squeezes his shoulder and slides a little closer.

He sighs, partly out of contentment, partly in frustration. "But Sally, you don't know the half of me. The half that's on the therapy couch every Wednesday. You don't need to be gettin' mixed up with a nut case like me. Not even as friends."

She squeezes him tighter and tilts her head against his. "Well, the half I do know, I'm real grateful for. But I do feel like I'm leanin' on you too much. Feels like there's somethin' secret going on behind Bill's back. And I guess there is, in a way… It feels way better to be with you than it should. I always look forward to seein' you. But I wouldn't blame ya if you just tell me to take a hike, to go home and either fix my marriage or get the hell out. Or at any rate, to quit my whinin' about it."

"I'm a big boy," Sam assures her as they drive past the gravel pit. "I know what I'm gettin' into." He points to the scar in the soil going down the gravel pit embankment, where that first fateful encounter took place. He grins. "Or, more correctly stated, what I'm not gettin' into.

"But seriously, I understand. Even though it's against my rules—a lotta rules. It's a big deal—fix it or fuck it. What does a person do? We all hope and pray for something to change, because we have a huge stake in our marriages. Took me five years, no ten, to finally leave my first wife. I was still in denial, right up to the day I told her I was done. My friend Mark, who was my best man the second time around, kept tellin' me to get the hell out because things would never change. About a year before we separated, I told Mark I had a plan."

"A plan?" Sally asks.

"Yeah, we were both married to 'Catholic chicks', as Mark called 'em. At least in our circle of friends, nobody who was married to a Catholic chick got much lovin' (mainly just on birthdays and anniversaries); twice a month would give a guy braggin' rights."

"You guys talked about how much sex you had with your wives?"

"Wasn't much to talk about!" Sam laughs.

"So, your plan...?"

"What I hadn't told Mark yet was, I'd already implemented the plan two months before. I told 'im I cut her off! Mark couldn't believe me and said she probably hasn't even noticed! And then scolded me that they can go FOREVER without sex, reminding me the nuns teach 'em in Catholic school, if you go a month without having sex with your husband, you got grounds for annulment."

He stops the golf cart and looks right into her eyes. Her mouth is open and eyebrows raised.

"Give you one guess what my first wife went and got from the church. Hell, we hadn't even gone to church for about ten years. I must have been a bad influence."

Sam shakes his head and laughs while gently stepping on the accelerator.

"Oh geez. Really?"

"True story," Sam confirms, still smiling at the irony of it all.

Sam gives Sally a tour of his house beyond the parts she'd already seen.

"Don't chew on the woodwork," he warns, "there's probably lead in it."

Sally admires his antique wood-burning kitchen stove, which is covered with at least a month's worth of mail and newspapers, empty wine bottles, rolls of tape, scissors, a smattering of pens and pencils, a small flashlight, and who knows what else under the heap.

"I've always wanted one of these...but for cooking," she teases.

"It's pretty darn obvious I'm a minimalist as a housekeeper and decorator," he admits. He points out the framed photos and knick-knacks with at least two years of dust on them.

"You don't have a dog? Or a cat?" Sally asks as he digs in the pantry.

"Nope. Never met a cat I liked more than the mice who occasionally move in and crap in the butter dish. Haven't had a dog since my old Lab Misty had to be put down, just before I moved in here."

"Seems like a perfect place for a dog, back roads, all this land to roam. Someone to come home to who's always glad to see you."

"Didn't think it would be fair to a dog, I reckon', with me away so much on bus trips. Hate the thought of caging it in a kennel when I'm gone."

"They're fine with that! Gosh, ten minutes of attention more than makes up for you bein' gone for a day. That's their job, to wait patiently."

"You don't think maybe I'm commitment-phobic, even so far as having a dog, do ya? Laura wonders if that might be the case..."

"So you think unless your soul slaps you upside the face with somethin' or someone perfect, you might never commit to anything substantial again, like a nine-to-five job, a dog, or a partner?"

Sam turns toward her, raises his eyes to the ceiling in serious thought, and replies, "Nope. Maybe. And most definitely."

"Huh?" Sally asks.

"Definitely 'No' to a real job. Maybe, to a dog—if I can find a yellow Lab born of nice, calm parents, who isn't gonna grow up to be the size of a buffalo. I do look forward to havin' a partner again someday. When I get my shit together, and the right person comes along…who's not married, of course." Sam winks.

"Excuses, excuses…" Sally rolls her eyes.

———

Sam has a pretty good wine buzz going as they putt-putt slowly along the trail back to Maureen's. He stops the golf cart at the edge of the gravel pit, gazing out over the expanse of sparse grass, boulders, and the few spindly jack pines, including the one her horse had yanked out of the ground.

Sally lets him be for a moment, then leans over, putting her arm around his shoulders. "Whatcha thinkin', friend?"

He scratches his head. Gently covering her hand with his own, he speaks softly without looking at her. "It just occurred to me what's happenin'."

"What do you mean?"

"It was the spring equinox. On that day, the sun sets due west at this latitude," Sam recalls. "I was sittin' on the east rock at the fire ring at sunset. So many times I've written down my intentions, wishes, and desires on paper. Some mystics say, if you burn those wishes with a little wild sage and send them to the heavens as smoke, the spirits will make sure they come true.

"I admit, nothin' much has come true that I've wished for since I've been in Stone Creek. But then, I haven't wanted much beyond what I have here—a pretty simple, predictable existence. Sometimes I feel like this is gonna be *IT* until I die—not bad, but not wonderful either. So this year, I simply wrote, 'I give up—surprise me.'"

He sucks in a deep breath and lets it out, "Whew…"

"What?"

"Helping deliver my grandson—unbelievable. Then there was that episode, the reason I came home from Boise early. I'll take that guilt to my grave. And then meeting you…"

"What episode? No, you don't have to tell me about it if you don't want to."

Sam sighs, voice wavering and eyes moistening.

"This baggage I have… After Karen died, I started seein' a counselor. Told my therapist about the two times with Karen when I snapped, both times after a huge fight about her family. And after she died. I'd go into this uncontrollable grief—sobbing, lyin' in a ball in bed, wanderin' the countryside, mind roarin' like a freight train. I was inconsolable. Happened again at my daughter's when Sammy was about ten days old. My oldest brother, Russell, was there. He dredged up some shit. Never been able to stop those attacks once they're triggered."

"Wow. So what did the psychiatrist say?"

"Post-traumatic Stress Disorder."

"What caused it?" Sally asks. "Were you in Vietnam?"

"Nope. Had a few brushes with death otherwise, but never put two and two together. He also wondered if it might be some sort of emotional trauma from when I was a kid. We never got to the cause of these attacks before I sold the farm and left that part of the world."

"What does Laura say about it?"

"Probably the same. She's diggin', but I don't think she'll find the reason. It's just how I am."

Sally kisses him on the cheek. "You didn't need to tell me any of this."

"I'm sorry to lay this crap on you…"

"No, no. That's not what I mean. I think you trust me."

He forces a smile. "Yup. Yup. Well, I'm sure Maureen's waitin' for the sauce and stuff…"

Sam pushes lightly on the accelerator, and they edge forward with only the low whir of the electric motor.

Joan's pulling into the yard in her dark-blue SUV as they drive through the gate.

"Hey, you guys! I hear we're havin' a party. Good! I need a distraction from crooked lawyers' legal briefs and affidavits from their lyin' clients. Don't even get me started on the guardian ad litem's boneheaded recommendations…"

She holds up a brown-bagged bottle. "A real good cognac, for dessert."

Joan heads for the house, lugging her bulging briefcase in her other hand.

By the time they finish supper, it's nearly dark. Joan stays in the kitchen to soak the dishes, while the rest retire to the living room, brandy snifters in hand. No one's feeling any pain, having consumed two bottles of Sam's wine with supper before pouring the cognac.

"Hey," Sally suggests, "anybody want to see the video of me and Dakota today? I've got the rodeo on this tape, too."

"Yeah!"

"You bet!"

"Wouldn't miss it!"

"Wait for me," Joan hollers from the kitchen.

Sally hooks up the camcorder and rewinds the tape. She hits PLAY, and there she is at the rodeo from two weeks before. A friend's husband had been commandeered to record her. Sam hadn't noticed he was being filmed when he'd handed his beer to Sally, as they waited for the last bull rider to finish.

He's a little tipsy, and embarrassed about seeing himself on the screen. He watches carefully, trying to remember whether he'd scratched himself inappropriately, or put a finger in his nose. (It was pretty dusty on the rodeo grounds.)

But the only thing he's doing is gazing up at Sally, like a lovesick puppy. He stands with his hands in his pockets as she takes a careful sip of beer.

The camera zooms in on Sally.

"Whew!" Joan says. "Lookin' pretty darn sharp there, cowgirl!"

A little looped, Sally admits, "Thanks! Sam dressed me!"

Everyone laughs, except Sam. He covers his eyes, head down.

"Well, not exactly…"

"Darn it," Sam mutters under his breath, staring into his brandy snifter.

"No! Sam picked out my outfit. He didn't help me into it!" Sally clarifies.

"…or out of it," Sam laments. "Darn it again."

The others laugh harder.

Maureen suggests, "Come on. Let's see that winnin' $650 ride!"

The camera guy had been recording from the fence behind the second barrel. Sally fast-forwards through a couple of her girlfriends' rides, then plays hers.

Sam starts to experience the same wonderful warm and fuzzy feeling from that day at the rodeo barrel races. He leans forward, mesmerized into a trance.

After the race is over, Sam notices they're all staring at him, smiling. "What?"

"Remind me," Maureen teases, "never to ask you to operate any machinery larger than a can opener after you've watched my sister ride."

He says, "Can't help it. You guys ever seen anything so beautiful?"

"Oh, cut it out!" Sally blushes. "Just another cowgirl on a darn horse…"

"How about today?" Pop asks, then adds, "Sam did the taping this afternoon."

Sam says, "Oh God, I hope it turned out. Drinkin' beers all day, you know. And I wasn't real sure how to operate the thing…"

Sally pushes PLAY. The picture darts all over the place. They hear TV Sam say, "Hey Pop! You think this thing's on?"

TV Pop responds in the background, "Check for a red light."

Suddenly TV Sam's face fills the screen. "Oh fuck. Oh yeah. Here it is Pop! It's on!"

Good-natured laughter once again fills the room.

"Stop the tape, PLEASE!" Sam pleads.

Sally does as requested. "Whatsa matter?"

He covers his face and shakes his head. "I had no idea the thing recorded *sound* along with the video."

"Ya THINK?" Joan laughs.

"Oooooh!" Maureen says. "I gotta feelin' this might be good…" She leans forward, sloshing her cognac in the snifter.

"I'm just gonna go home now," Sam announces as he gets up from the couch.

"Hold on there, Mr. Cameraman!" Sally orders, as she pulls him back down next to her by his shirt.

"Joan," Sam calls out, holding up his brandy snifter. "I think I need more. Bring the whole bottle, please."

Sally restarts the video.

The picture's still jerking all over the place spastically. The arena loudspeaker blares, "Now here's Sallyyy Hunterrr…on Dakotaaa!"

TV Pop frantically tries to coach Sam, while the picture zips all around. "She's comin' in the gate! Over there."

"Shit," TV Sam says. The camera suddenly zooms in on the ground in the arena. "What was that buzzin' noise? Does that mean it's on?" Then TV Sam's nose fills the TV screen, shot from slightly below.

Sally pauses the video. "Nice nostrils!" Her body convulses with laughter.

Maureen shrieks, "Ouch! I could have made it through an entire life just fine without seein' that shot!"

"Me, too," Sam agrees. "Keep goin'. Just get it over with."

Suddenly, there are Sally and Dakota. It's actually a decent shot of them, already zoomed in. The camera quickly jerks to TV Pop, TV Sam informing him, "Yup, got 'er figured out!"

Quickly again, the camera jerks back to Dakota and Sally, just as she cues her horse to run.

Sam doesn't try anything fancy—leaves it on full zoom the entire run, which makes it look like Sally and Dakota are gonna run over him on their way to the first pole, and again on the dash to the finish line. Both frames TV Sam flinches wildly—the first time mumbling a simple "Oops". The second time, he's caught off guard, and is a little harder on himself, calling himself a "dumb shit." When Sally and Dakota slide to a stop, he says to himself, "Oh my God...that was sooo beautiful..."

Sally narrates, "Next is the barrel race. I can hardly wait to see what our illustrious play-by-play man has to say this time."

"Only the Lord knows..." Sam responds.

Sally and Dakota are back in the arena. She bends to her horse's ear, talking softly. Dakota's ears are back, and she prances nervously, spinning twice, as if she's going to explode if Sally doesn't cut her loose soon.

Meanwhile, TV Sam prompts himself, "A little tighter now." He zooms way in as Sally and Dakota are facing away. "Whew! Those've gotta be the two nicest rear ends in Becker County."

The crowd in front of the TV roars—except for Sam and Sally. She gives him a sideways frown.

He has his hand over his face and is peeking out between his fingers. He holds up both hands in defensively in front of his face.

TV Sam's commentary continues during the first part of the run. "Beautiful…just beautiful…perfect. Oh God, yes, YES! Come on now!"

When Sally and Dakota turn the third barrel, TV Sam's voice builds in cadence and intensity. "Good… GOOD! GOOD! NOW BRING HER HOME! OH GOD! OH GOD! OH…MY…GOD!"

Finally TV Sam whispers, "Whew…"

Sally stops the tape and turns to him with a bemused look.

There's a pregnant silence. Everyone is looking at Sam with various amused expressions.

Maureen breaks the ice, "Hey Sam, sounds like you was havin' yourself quite a special moment there!"

The room bursts into hysterics, with considerable thigh-slapping, eye-rolling, and soon tears of laughter. Sam takes a big swig of his cognac, and covers his eyes again. "I need to go to the bathroom."

Pop remarks, "I s'pose you do!" More laughter ensues.

"I'm almost afraid to play the last race!" Sally confides.

"Let's get it over with," Sam pleads.

"Now, this is the event I was really worried about, the speed and action. I had no idea whether Dakota would even enter the square at a walk, let alone on the way back, go from a dead run into a slide-to-a-stop back into the square. Watch her…"

"Oh, Mister Wide World of Sports Commentator," Sally addresses Sam. "Anything we need to tell the censors ahead of time?"

"I haven't a clue," Sam admits, shaking his head and staring at the floor in front of him. "I haven't a clue…"

The tape begins rolling just before Sally enters the arena. She forces Dakota to walk slowly while Sally bends over and pats her on the neck, speaking quietly to settle her down.

TV Sam zooms in and mutters, "My god, what an angel."

Dakota walks right into the square. The mare obediently stops still when Sally lifts the reins only an inch, without any pressure on the bit.

TV Sam whispers, as if in church, "Look at those ears—Dakota knows. She knows. That lucky bastard horse, got Sally's beautiful long legs wrapped around 'er."

Sally turns to Sam, "You got a certain *streak* I never woulda guessed!"

"Umm…um…that wasn't me," Sam lies. "There was this cowboy standing by me. I'm real sorry."

Sally has to turn away to hide her smile.

"Oh God, Sally…oh God…" TV Sam says as Sally and Dakota explode from the square.

He follows them perfectly with the camera. He even zooms in when they turn the barrel, then pulls back for the dash home. "Okay! Brakes!" TV Sam yells.

When the dust clears, both Sams having been holding their breath on the dash home, they sigh in unison, "So beautiful…"

TV Sam shouts, "Pop! Pop! Can you believe what we just saw?"

The camera zooms back and focuses on Pop, who pulls out his hanky out and dabs his eyes.

The room is quiet, then Pop raises his brandy snifter. "My heart soars like a hawk. To my beautiful and talented daughter-in-law, and her incredible Dakota. May you have a thousand more races together…"

"Here, here," the others concur.

Sally swipes her eyes with the back of her hand. She kisses Pop on the cheek and they hug tightly.

At 8:30 am, Sam's surprised to hear the whirring of the golf cart's electric motor and the crunch of gravel outside his door. He'd left the cart over at Maureen and Joan's the night before.

He hurries outside and finds Pop, who seems to be in a helluva hurry. In so much of a hurry, he'd forgot his walker.

"Hey Sam! Gimme a hand into the house before they come lookin' for me!"

"Coffee's on." Sam wraps a steadying arm around Pop's waist to walk him inside, then helps him to a kitchen chair.

"What brings you out so early?" Sam asks, pouring two cups. "Do the girls know you're gone?"

Sam fetches the sugar bowl from the cupboard, and inspects it for mouse turds. Pop strains to look into the bowl, and sees several dark droppings.

"Black is fine," Pop says. "Nope. They're still sleepin'. Left 'em a note though."

Sam dumps the sugar into the sink and rinses it down.

"Two things I need you to help me with, without them knowin'," Pop whispers. "One thing, you're gonna think I'm nuts. And the other one, you're gonna think I'm crazy."

"Why are we whispering?" Sam asks.

"Oh, right. But it's a secret, ok?"

Sam nods as he blows on his coffee. "Oh, I forgot. Got some Bailey's, a little something sweet for your coffee." He fetches a bottle from the refrigerator and shakes it.

Pop holds his cup out, and Sam pours in a short shot.

"I wanna give Sally a real fancy horse trailer for her birthday. It's a gooseneck, with a little tack room in the back, and living quarters up front like a camper. They have a repo at my old dealership. It needs a lotta work. I want to add a water tank, pump, hot water, and a shower, plus a holding tank for the gray water. I'll pay you. That's why I asked you the other day if you had a rock job lined up for the summer. I'll have the dealer haul it up here this week."

"But she'll never believe I've suddenly gone into the horse trailer finishing business," Sam says. "Sally will know something's up."

"Don't worry about Sally guessing it's for her," Pop assures him. "Already worked out a deal with her friend, Kate. She's gonna say it's for her sister-in-law in Rapid City. I'll even have Kate's sister-in-law's name painted on the door before I have 'em bring it here."

"That could work. How much time we got?"

"Until her birthday, June 25th. I'll help, too."

"Whew!" Sam exclaims. "That'll be tight, but I'm lookin' forward to it. I'm almost afraid to ask what your second request is. I hope the trailer's the more difficult one of the two."

"Oh! Right. I'd like to smoke a doobie. I think that's what they're called..." Pop looks Sam square in the face for a reaction.

Sam laughs nervously. "You're pullin' my leg, right?"

"Nope! I saw on the TV they're tryin' to legalize marijuana in some states for medicinal purposes like pain relief. That's why I can't sleep, 'cause of the pain. Have to take those darn pills every night to knock me out. And then when I wake up, I'm so out of it somebody's gotta help me."

"Sorry, Pop. I don't have any. Never been a big dope smoker myself."

"How 'bout your neighbors? Someone's gotta be growin' it in these hills. I know this area. There are way too many hippies, vegetarians, and artists over here for there not to be one or two growin' marijuana."

Sam snickers. "Yeah, you're right about that. Did you talk to Sally about this?"

"Afraid to."

"Well, I think she'll be okay with it. You know, for medicinal purposes."

"How we gonna break it to her, that her father-in-law wants to be a toilet head?"

"That's *pot head*, Pop."

"Whatever you call it, I need to do something 'bout gettin' to sleep without turnin' into a zombie."

"Come to think of it, there looks to be some wild pot growin' that we can see from the river. You feel like a canoe trip today? Could you talk Sally into it? I'll just point it out casual-like…and we'll go from there."

"Perfect," Pop agrees.

The phone rings and Pop jumps like a bomb just went off under his chair.

Sam answers. "Yup, he's here. Wanna talk to him? ~ Fine, just fine. ~ Havin' coffee. ~ Said he was gonna head back in a bit. ~ Yup, I'll send a jar. ~ Okay."

He tells Pop, "That's your cue. S'posed to send back some tomato juice with you. Sounds like there's at least one hangover over there. Not sure if you can talk Sally into the river today…it sounded like she's not feeling so great."

"I hope I don't have to play *that* card."

"Which one?"

"The *I'd-like-to-do-this-before-I-die* card."

"Good luck. If I don't pick up the phone, it's 'cause I'm workin' on the fence for Roy and Elvis. Just come on over, whenever. I'll borrow a neighbor's kayak for Sally. And I'll see if he gives out samples of his cash crop."

After the river trip, they have a late supper at Sam's. Sally had brought some things for her and Pop so they could stay if necessary.

"According to my neighbor, we prob'ly won't need both of these," Sam says, eyeing the two perfectly rolled joints in his palm.

He hands one to Pop, who examines it carefully then takes a sniff. He approaches his first smoke like an archeologist ponders a newly discovered mummy, from every direction, inside and out. Sam and Sally watch, shooting little smiles at each other.

"So, how do we do this?" Pop asks. "I seen it on TV. You suck it in with a big breath, right? Then hold it in?"

"Now Pop," Sally says, "If this works, you don't have to worry about rollin' them—I'll get you a one-hitter."

"A what-hitter?"

"Comes in its own case about the size of a cigarette pack, and holds a little extra dope in a compartment, too. Just cram the end of the pipe into the dope, and light it while you inhale. I think I know where I can get you one."

"Where?"

"My dresser," Sally admits.

They all laugh.

Sam teases Sally, "Well, you do the honors then."

Pop hands the joint to her. She lights it carefully with the butane lighter. Takes just a little hit, then checks to see if it's going good. It isn't. She lights it again and takes a slightly bigger hit, then hands it to Pop. He smells it and contemplates the pungent smoke drifting around him.

Sally exhales, then urges Pop, "Better keep it goin'. It's not gonna hurt you."

Pop takes a tentative drag, then while holding his breath, he checks the end to see if it's still burning. Sam reaches for the joint.

Pop exhales, then quickly takes a sip of wine. "Whew!" he exclaims. "Haven't smoked anything for about 20 years. Burns a little."

They each take another hit, then let the joint go out, about two-thirds of it burned away.

"See Pop," Sally assures him. "It's not like when they put you out for surgery. Pretty gentle, huh? I think this is nice stuff."

Pop rubs his temples with his fingertips. A little smile creases his lips. "Hmm. Had to check. Feels like the top part of my head's goin' numb."

Sam and Sally check their own heads and agree, nodding.

"Anything else, Pop?" Sally asks.

"Just feels warm and fuzzy all over. Kinda like what two fingers of whiskey used to do to me on an empty stomach, but doesn't take as long."

Pop plucks the joint from the ashtray. He examines the third that's left of it from every angle, oblivious to Sam and Sally intently watching his every move. He relights it himself, inhaling the smoke more deeply than before, and holding it longer.

The other two potheads, curious about how Pop's doing, wave off another hit when he offers it to them. After Pop exhales, he seems pleased—very pleased—in a private sorta dreamy way. He watches the orange glow fade while he holds the remaining one-fourth of the joint with his thumb and fingertip. His face relaxes into gentle contemplation, like a drunk dog watching TV. He cocks his head to one side a little, then asks no one in particular, "Now…why is this stuff illegal?"

Sally doesn't stir from Sam's couch until the countryside is already waking up. Songbirds are calling and the two roosters are crowing in the coop. She glances at her watch, and is surprised to hear Pop rustling around in the kitchen.

"Pop! You okay?"

Sam jumps into his sweatpants and hurries out from the bedroom. Pop's pouring water into the coffeemaker. He's dressed and his hair is combed, all ready for the day. He smiles at them over his shoulder. "Just fine. You didn't even hear me get up last night…or this morning, didja? No pain pill hangover!"

Over coffee, Pop tells Sally the white lie about the trailer and says it will be delivered to Sam's today. Since they're making the trip from Streeter, Pop says he's decided to have the dealership guys stop by the farm and haul Elvis and Roy up to Sam's.

"So, Pop, you gonna come home tonight?" Sally asks, her eyes searching the floor.

"Well, I wanna make sure Elvis and Roy are good with their new home. But I tell ya what. How 'bout you come back here tonight? I'll have the dealership make another trip and bring up the wagon and rigging. Then I'll give ya both a lesson hitchin' and drivin' the team. How's 'at?"

CHAPTER 11

ROBERT

Sally returns home to the farm to get ready for work. Robert's fiddling with nothing in particular in the pole barn. If he feels sorry about Sally's situation with Bill, he's never shown it. She often catches Robert staring at her, leering actually. His eyes always seem to be looking somewhere besides her face.

Many nights Sally senses she's being watched through the windows. Sheba would growl, the same low growl she gives every time Robert came over to putter around the farmyard. The hairs on the back of Sally's neck always stand up when Sheba growls like that.

A couple years younger than Bill, Robert had difficulty in school, and never did graduate. Most folks just figured Robert was a tad slow in the intelligence department. Besides working the four-wheeler course and campgrounds, he worked at the co-op for his regular job, loading feed and other goods off trucks, then loading them back into customers' pickups and trailers. That job suited him fine.

Unlike Bill, who was soft around the edges of his scrawny physique, Robert was strong, like he could break your arm with his bare hands. His eyes were small, under a bony, prominent brow, his jaw square, and his hands were rugged and strong as oak stumps.

He'd been married once, to a woman named Marcy with two daughters. They met through an internet dating site. After only a two-month, long-distance courtship, she moved up to Streeter from Des Moines, to get out of the city, be together, and give the girls a father.

Robert didn't mind her roundish figure, missing teeth, and stringy hair; she was a woman who showed a genuine interest in him. That had never happened before.

Marcy was socially inept, emotionally stunted, and unemployable, except in the simplest, most structured environment. She didn't know who the father was for either of the girls, although she was pretty sure they weren't full sisters.

The girls, Mindy and Karla, were eight and ten when Robert and Marcy got married three months later. Folks had doubted Robert would be much of a stepfather. But the girls took an immediate shine to him, as he did to them. He bought them candy and any little toy they asked for. He played with them constantly.

Some folks around Streeter joked that Robert had finally found friends who were on his own level. Others thought it was quite touching to see him so outgoing and loving, instead of lurking around the perimeter of life like a stray dog.

Marcy found work immediately after moving to Streeter. Second shift at the potato processing plant, cleaning the offices and bathrooms, while Robert babysat the girls. A few months into the marriage, Mindy told her mother about a new game called Bucking Bull that they played with Robert just before bedtime. Mindy was upset because Robert never let her be on the bottom.

Mindy explained the game. Robert would be on his hands and knees on their double bed. She would ride on top, just like a bull rider. Karla would ride below, her legs encircling his waist tightly, and her arms wrapped just as snugly around his neck. Then Robert would bounce up and down, trying to throw them off.

Marcy didn't confront him, but she was curious. At work for half her next shift, she feigned illness, and drove home early. She watched through the window.

At first the game seemed harmless enough, lots of laughing and giggling, with Robert roaring and snorting like a mad bull and tossing the girls off. They were all in their nightclothes. Then Mindy slid off Robert, down his backside, accidentally pushing his pajama bottoms down to his thighs. Robert kept bucking and roaring, and Marcy saw he was sexually aroused.

Marcy ran around to the front door as fast as she could, and burst into the bedroom. By the time she got there, he had already ejaculated, spilling some onto Karla's nightgown. He was still bucking as Mindy was trying to climb back onto him.

Marcy immediately contacted the police, but when she realized the girls would have to give statements and most likely also have to testify, she worried that anything they said could be twisted against her, and she might somehow lose the girls. Marcy then refused to cooperate, claiming she'd been mistaken and everything was fine. But she threatened Robert that if he came home before they could clear out the next day and move back to Iowa, she would kill him. He knew she meant it.

There was no arrest, no trial or official publicity, but word got out. When Pop found out, he forced Robert to file for divorce through an attorney friend. Pop took care of the legal fees and sent Marcy and the girls $5000. Sally had heard the story in town shortly after the incident took place, on one of her trips back from California, three years before she came home to Streeter for good.

Robert hurries to catch Sally before she gets into the house. As usual, he looks like he slept in his clothes. One work boot's lace is loose and dragging. The tail of his crumpled blue work shirt with the co-op logo on the front hangs out the back. Greasy hair sticks out from under his hat at odd angles. He hasn't shaved for days, and probably hasn't showered either over that time. His eyes are narrowed to slits and his jaw is set firmly; his chin sticks out in angry defiance.

Sheba barks furiously behind the door into the entryway.

"Where you been?" Robert demands. "Where's Pop?"

"We stayed over in the hills," Sally answers. She continues walking toward the house, picking up her pace. "Why is Sheba's doggie door nailed over with that board? When did you barricade her in here?" Sally demands. There is a pitchfork leaning against the house between the entrance door and the doggie door it.

"Lock her in, hell!" Robert yells. "Yesterday I had to go to the can and I bolted her door inside, and the fuckin' bitch still got in! At least she respects a pitchfork."

Robert narrows his eyes and asks, "Where were you while your fuckin' dog was tryin' to kill me when I'm tryin' to keep an eye on this goddam place? At Maureen's?"

"No, we were at Sam's, the guy who's gettin' Roy and Elvis."

Sally turns and yanks the screen door open. Sheba keeps barking, as if she wants a piece of Robert's hide for breakfast.

"I gotta feelin' about you…" Robert waggles his finger. "And take that goddam dog with if you want her alive next time you come home from cattin' around all weekend. Can't get nothin' done around here with that fuckin' bitch following me 'round all the time and growlin'".

Sally opens the wooden door and talks to Sheba, calming her down. "It's okay, girl…okay…"

"A feelin'? What kinda feelin'?" Sally closes the screen door and locks it.

"Somethin' funny's goin' on. You're never 'round when Bill's home. That ain't right for a wife."

Robert stares blankly at her breasts through the screen door.

Sally doesn't feel she owes him any kind of explanation. She slams the big door and bolts it, watching through the kitchen window as Robert finally leaves in his beat-up old Plymouth four-door. She lets Sheba out. The hairs on Sheba's back stick straight up as she sniffs where Robert had been standing next to the porch.

There are scratches from Sheba on the outside of Sally's bedroom door. She enters the bedroom where she never leaves her closet door open, in order to keep the old house cat out of there. But Boots is curled up on Sally's nightshirt on the floor of the closet, which she's certain she'd left lying out on the bed like she always does. The bed otherwise has not been slept in or touched. The tissue box lays on the floor in front of the nightstand. The bottom of the screen on the bedroom window is out of its slot. She's certain someone has been in their bedroom and it wasn't Bill sleeping there.

She goes into the bathroom to put on makeup for work. The toilet lid is up and there is a wad of tissue floating in the bowl. Even Bill, with a dog and a cat living in the house, knows better than to leave the lid up.

In the afternoon, Sam puts together a thick wild rice and chicken soup while Pop naps. The three of them hurry through supper so they can get at hitching the horses.

Even though Elvis and Roy haven't been driven for over three years, they are as obedient as guide dogs. Sally and Sam are both surprised that, with Pop's careful instructions, what appears to be a jumble of tangled lines goes easily over the horses' heads, hooking here and strapping there. They're underway with two hours of daylight remaining, Pop sitting between his students. Sally puts her arm around Pop and gives him a squeeze. She reaches further and rubs Sam's arm.

On the way to Maureen's via Sam's trails, they take turns driving and putting the team through all sorts of paces—big arcing turns, square turns, standing, and backing. No one is home at Maureen and Joan's. They've lost track of time and the sun will soon dip behind the treetops. They drive the team up the driveway and take the quicker route home, following the gravel road. They let the boys trot a few hundred yards just to get the kinks out. It's dark before they get the horses unhitched and the rigging all stowed.

When they get inside the house, Sam's answering machine blinks to indicate three new messages. The first one is Bill. He sounds drunk.

"Hey Sam! Can't thank you enough for takin' those fleabags off the place already. I need to talk to Sally or Pop. Tell 'em to call me pronto."

The second message is from Maureen.

"I'm real sorry, but I had to give Bill your number, Sam. I must have just missed you guys. He called here mad as hell. Robert must've told him Sally and Pop are out there."

The third message is Bill again, sounding even more intoxicated. "Listen, just tell the ol' lady to get 'er ass back to the farm…and quit dragging my old man around like he's a goddamn puppy…fuck. Oh yeah…I think this is the weekend we're s'posed to make a baby, so she should probably stay home fer a while."

The three of them trade glances in heavy silence. Sally sighs and puts a hand over her face, massaging her forehead. Pop rolls his eyes and seems worried.

"You really gonna stay there this weekend, Sally?" Sam asks.

"No, not this weekend," Sally corrects. "I will be in two weeks again though. Stayin' at Maureen's for a bit."

Sam shakes his head and comes closer, wanting to shake her by the shoulders. "Remember Saturday, you said you'd never just stand by and let life pass me by anymore. You *almost* convinced me I got somethin' of value left to give or receive, and that you know what you're talkin' about. Well, I'm not buyin' that crap from you anymore.

You gotta walk your talk before you start givin' out advice like that. I can't listen to another thing like that." He points to the answering machine.

Sally stares straight ahead, her lips pressed together firmly. Pop has seen her stubborn side before, and can tell she's digging in.

Sam is losing his temper. He continues sternly, "If it's just about havin' a baby, for chrissakes have one with someone who loves you! Or anyone besides that asshole! Or even have one on your own!"

Sally breathes heavily, her eyes narrowing with anger. She heads for the door. "It's time to go, Pop."

Pop doesn't move. "I'm sorry. I'm stayin' here tonight. Gonna get Sam started on the horse trailer in the morning. Will you pick me up on your way home from work tomorrow night?"

She nods and hurries to the door, but not fast enough to beat the tears welling up.

She turns and warns, "Now don't you two start gangin' up on me! I don't know where any of this is going. Yeah, my marriage is…is…*fucked* up. But I don't need this kinda pressure. Matter of fact—Pop, I changed my mind. Find your own damn way home! Or don't—I don't care."

She slams the door shut.

Sally calls from work the next day when Sam and Pop are having leftover chicken soup for lunch.

Sam instantly responds, "I'm real sorry…"

"The flowers are pretty…thanks."

"I had no right…"

Pop does his best to hide a smile.

"Yes, you did," Sally says. "But I need time. Okay?"

"What do you want from me in the meantime?" Sam asks.

"I honestly don't know. But I do know this hasn't been fair to you. In the meantime…I did buy you a puppy today."

"You WHAT?!!

"Just what you ordered, a little yellow Lab. The smallest one in the litter. She was the only one of eleven who woke up from her nap when I asked, *Who wants to pee on Sam's floor so he'll finally get the mop out and wash it?* She bounced over to the fence and started whinin'. She's sleepin' in a box by my desk right now. Déjà vu all over again, huh Sam?"

"You know," Sam says, "how about that's what we call her? Déjà vu—Deja for short."

After work, Sally comes over to deliver the little girl.

"First thing I'd do is roll up all these rugs. Especially the big hideous one in front of the couch. It should be hung outside and beaten daily for about a month anyway. And then taken to the dump."

Deja sniffs enthusiastically all around Sam's living room, like a bloodhound on the trail. The tiny puppy suddenly stops, drops her hind end, points a little tail about forty-five degrees above her target, and pees a little yellow puddle. Luckily, the rug's so dirty, the anointment sits on top like a puddle of mercury. Sam's first instinct is to scold her, but Sally quickly claps a hand over his mouth. "Shhh!"

Little Deja runs up to Sally, tail wagging, and begs to be petted for doing such a nice job on the rug. Sally picks her up and hands her to Sam. Deja eagerly licks his face all over. Her puppy breath brings back memories.

"Well," says Pop. "Don't think anyone here will be gettin' much sleep tonight. I'm goin' home…"

Deja squirms to get down.

"Sally," Sam says, "I've never…I mean…nobody…Just get over here and let me give you a hug."

He holds her lightly, then whispers in her ear, "I hope that's not too much pressure for you?"

Sally looks up and grins. "Just a little more…there you go. And you're so welcome."

Pop tries to act like he isn't paying attention. But they can see him smiling as he ties his plastic grocery bag to the front of his walker.

CHAPTER 12

SIDAS WAPBO

Laura begins, "Okay, we skipped a week because of the holiday. How did it go? You told me the holidays are difficult for you. Did you do anything special?"

"Lemme see…" Sam contemplates. "Nope. Not much since I saw you last."

"What's with the grin? Oh gosh, don't tell me…the married woman?"

"We didn't do nothin'!"

"Care to elaborate on *nothing*?"

"Just took her and her father-in-law morel huntin', like I mentioned I would, then we had a picnic. Not a big deal. She took me out to dinner, and I took her dancing after…"

Laura writes feverishly, her brow furrowed. "Um, slow down a little."

"My friends and I went to her barrel race that Monday. Umm. Lemme see. Umm…"

At that moment, Sam realizes two things. First of all, he and Sally had been spending an awful lot of time together. And second, he isn't sure how much he wants to tell Laura.

It's like she reads his mind. "Don't filter it. Just spill it…"

"Then the next Saturday, me and Pop (that's her father-in-law) surprised Sally at her races in Detroit Lakes. I got to meet hubby at the farm that day. Whatta sawed-off pin-headed dipshit…"

"I see. Does he know you had dinner and went dancing with his wife?"

"Oh hell no! They hardly ever see each other. He's not a nice man at all. Beats 'er up sometimes. He works in Grand Forks. Comes home on weekends to run his campground and four-wheeler course. That's when she gets the hell out, usually to her sister's place, down the road from me about a mile and a half."

"Slow down," Laura requests. Her pen had run out of ink. She fumbles in a cup of mismatched pens for a new one. "Okay…"

"She does stay home about every fourth weekend to be with him, when she thinks it's her fertile time. They want to have a baby…"

"What?" Laura looks up, her pen poised mid-stroke.

Sam says, "You know—a little tiny person. A baby!" He holds his hands about a foot and a half apart.

Laura shakes her head and cringes. Sam waits for her to quit writing. He's learning to pace himself just right.

"Anyway, she won a couple races that day. I did the videotaping. Then we all had dinner at her sister's. And cognac afterwards…"

"Okay," Laura sums it up. "Her father-in-law is okay with you hanging around her. And so is her sister…"

"She's a lesbian, in case that matters. And so is her partner, Joan."

"Okay. Go on…"

Sam fills Laura in about the horse trailer and helping Pop find a dope supplier. And the phone calls from Bill.

"What happened next?" Laura asks.

"Nothing…really," Sam fibs. "We had a fight over her husband, and I sent her flowers, we both said we're sorry, and Sally bought me a puppy. That was Monday."

"Okay." Laura has caught up and is calculating in her head. "Okay. That was less than two days ago. Do I need another note pad to write down what's happened since?"

"Shouldn't. She's only called about four times, to see how Deja's doing. I dreamed about that name the night before she found the puppy for me. She's bringing Pop out tonight because he and I are gonna work on the trailer tomorrow. Pop's gonna give us another lesson hitchin' and drivin' the team tonight. She'll stay overnight again."

"I'm almost afraid to ask. What are the sleeping arrangements?"

"Don't worry about that," Sam assures Laura. "She's married!"

"Give me a minute to digest this." Laura flips back two pages, and begins scanning her notes. Sam sits in the armchair, twiddling his thumbs, as if he's waiting for the bank teller to count out the cash for his paycheck.

"So. Except for the pot-smoking father-in-law, this appears to be a classic case of a married woman seeking something from another guy, the things her husband doesn't provide. I would suggest, at this early stage of your therapy, you keep this 'friendship' in perspective."

"Might be too late," Sam admits. "I had another dream…about me and her…"

Laura glances at the clock. "I tell you what. Let's save that dream for next week, okay? In the meantime, I want you to step outside of this thing with Sally. Examine it like an objective bystander, if you can."

Sam asks, "You're thinking this is a SIDAS WAPBO, aren't you?"

"A what?"

"Those are initials. I made it up. It means Self-Inflicted Dumb Ass Situation With A Predictable Bad Outcome. You might want to write it down. Could come in handy in this business," Sam jokes.

Laura can't hide a little grin as she does as Sam instructs. "That's a good one…"

Pop catches on real fast with the one-hitter. He can open the box, pack in a hit of pot, and take a drag in less than a minute. He keeps it by his bed for easy access. He calculates that the $100 he paid for the dope, which looks like it will last him at least a month, is half the cost of his prescription medication…and a lot more fun to use.

Bill has started to become a real pain in the ass for Sam. He'd called four or five times both Tuesday and Wednesday, leaving messages for Sally. Hell, she has a cell phone if he wants up-to-the-minute updates of his wife's whereabouts.

Finally, Sam answers. "Quit calling my goddamn house!"

When Sally calls to check on Deja Thursday morning, Sam asks her why Bill keeps calling.

"He knows I'm home," she replies tersely. "And, you know you could've been a little nicer to him last night. You know he works awful hard, long hours. And to be fair, I haven't been around much in the evenings 'cause I been workin' the horses. It's not a crime, you know, to call around lookin' for your wife."

Thursday morning, when she drops off Pop, it's like Sally and Sam have never even met and don't care to. They don't exchange their customary hugs, coming or going. Sally seems impatient to get to work.

After she leaves, Sam asks Pop as gently as he can muster, "What the hell's goin' on?"

Pop looks down and pinches the bridge of his nose. "She says he's changed."

"What? Changed into what?"

"Tuesday night he called her, said he'd signed up for an anger management group. And he said it's time to remodel the house, start thinkin' 'bout puttin' on an addition for a nursery. Says he has the money saved up. Even asked her for some decoratin' ideas."

"She believes him?" Sam asks incredulously.

"Sally's been lookin' at carpet and paint, and furniture. It's like another woman took over her personality. What you gonna do, Sam?"

"You know, she told me she'd been workin' her horses all those nights. Don't think I'll even talk to her about it. I was an idiot to get into this 'friendship' with her in the first place…SIDAS WAPBO."

"What?"

"Oh, nothin'…"

It's Saturday morning. Pop admits he's been overdoing it. Still, he wants to see Sally race. He and Sam detour to the farm for Pop to get a change of clothes.

Bill and Robert are working on a tractor in the pole barn. As Pop and Sam drive in, Bill hurries over. He doesn't seem as glad to see Sam as the first time they met. Robert ambles over and stands a few yards behind his brother, for all the world looking like a dog prowling up on strangers. Pop uses his walker to head for the house.

Bill doesn't pussy-foot around. He gets in Sam's face, exhaling the stench of chewing tobacco and stale alcohol.

"Back off," Sam warns.

Bill slowly steps back one step. "Ya know, Robert here might not be book smart, but he knows shit. Says you and my ol' lady got somethin' goin' on."

Sam remains expressionless, leaning against the truck. Robert moves closer so the two brothers stand side by side in front of him like prison guards.

"We been friends. Good friends. Nothin' wrong with that." Sam crosses his arms over his chest.

Bill accuses, "You got no business bein' friends with a married woman…havin' her stay at your place. And Pop…"

"Yeah, what about Pop?" Sam challenges.

"Why's he so damn nice to you?" Robert asks. "You better pay for them horses. That's money right outta our pockets when he dies!"

A thousand things race through Sam's brain, including the way they treat Sally, hate the horses, and only want

Pop for what's left of his farm and money. On his way out of her life or not, he can't stand the thought of Sally getting beat up again.

"Here's the deal," Sam warns Bill through clenched teeth, "You ever lay a hand on Sally again and I'll…"

"Tell ya what, old man," Bill interrupts as he steps closer, his face only inches away. "I'm lookin' forward to taking you down."

Sam's eyes remain steady on Bill's. He slowly uncrosses his arms. Robert paces nervously, fidgeting his hands.

Sam repeats his vow, calmly. "Like I said, you touch her again, and I'll come lookin' for you. That's a promise you don't want me to have to keep."

Bill backs away a few steps, then begins side-stepping back toward the pole barn. "We'll see, old man. We'll see…"

Pop had heard the confrontation from the kitchen window. He motions Sam to come over.

"Don't pay him no mind. Bill's actually chickenshit. He's never picked on no one but women and guys half his size."

"It's not me I'm worried about," Sam replies.

Sam wouldn't have gone near the races today if it weren't for Pop. He hopes Pop doesn't feel like some kid being dumped off from divorced parents who have something better to do.

When they get to the race, Sally seems distant and preoccupied. And she isn't riding worth a shit. Sam records a couple of her rides, without commentary. Pop's unusually quiet and hardly spends any time with Sally between rides. It's like they'd broken up, too. Not once does she ask them how her ride looked.

But Sam hangs around the entire day, so Pop has a companion.

"Next weekend," Pop says, "I'll be stayin' at the farm with Sally and Bill. Father's Day."

Sam nods. "Good idea. Yeah. Okay." But it's like a knife in the gut to hear Bill and Sally's names spoken as if they're a real couple. Maybe Laura was right. He shouldn't have gotten in so deep. He'll ask Pop to take Roy and Elvis back.

Sam takes Pop to Maureen's after the races, where he'll wait for Sally. On the drive, Pop won't listen to a thing about taking the team back. Maureen asks Sam to hang around for a drink. He has one short brandy with them. Sally drives in just as he finishes his drink, and he gets up to leave. He turns down dinner with the gang at Maureen's, like they did before. Sam lies that he made plans with some teachers from Stone Creek to play poker tonight. Sam lies again that he will be up north Sunday, to help get a friend get started on a stone barbecue in his yard.

Sally meets Sam at his truck and trailer. "Gonna be a beautiful night," she comments, like every damn thing in her Mary Poppins world is perfect. "Not too many mosquitoes this year. Too dry for 'em, huh?" She talks to Sam like he's a stranger.

"Yup. Too dry. I'll leave the cart for Pop," he says without looking at her.

"No need. We're going to Fargo first thing tomorrow. Gonna pick up some paint, maybe some wallpaper for the bathroom. We'll be headin' back to the farm after shopping and pickin' up Dakota and Sparky here."

Sam nods and slides into his truck, half expecting the hills to come alive with the sound of music.

"I dunno what got into him," Sally comments, with a light and happy tone in her voice. "It's like Bill's changed overnight."

"Well." Sam forces a smile. "People do change. Sounds like your dreams are comin' true. Good for you guys."

He puts his truck in gear, and checks the side mirror as he pulls away, watching Sally stare off into the heavens like a star-struck teenage rock'n'roll groupie.

Sam hadn't gotten good and drunk at the campfire since the previous autumn. But that time it wasn't planned. He'd crushed his final batch of grapes and started them fermenting on a gorgeous Indian summer evening. Yes, he'd been a little depressed. He and Karen always celebrated by a campfire after the last batch was perking, by getting a little tipsy on wine they'd saved from the year before. It was their silly way of thanking the grape gods, and another excuse to be with each other under the stars, under layers of blankets. To hold each other. To make love.

The irony that his friendship with Sally is the reason Bill suddenly started being nice to her sticks in Sam's mind like pinesap on his hands. He hopes two bottles of wine will rid him of that image—Bill and Sally, acting like honeymooners.

He's loaded Deja's food bowl full, and brought along her water dish and a cord to tie her up if he has to. At dusk, they arrive at the fire ring, Deja's first visit.

He sets his supplies on the jack pine stump, and Deja's bowls on the ground, then builds the fire. Deja sits mesmerized by the flickering flames, just close enough to feel the warmth.

A big gnarly, dead jack pine about eighteen inches in diameter stands on the side hill above the fire ring, at the very edge of the gas lantern's glow, fifty feet away. Sam has been meaning to chop it down. The trunk and limbs will be excellent campfire wood, the branches good kindling. He pours another cup of wine and ties Deja to the stump. He settles his puppy on a sleeping bag-lined chair, facing the fire.

Sam walks a little cockeyed to the big jack pine, the single-blade axe in one hand, his cup in the other. Satisfied that her master isn't going too far away, Deja settles her head on her paws, and watches the fire.

Sam makes several trips back to the fire ring to fill his paper cup, toss wood on the fire, and pet Deja. By 1:00 am, he isn't quite halfway through the jack pine and loses his balance when he turns to look at the fading lantern that is running out of fuel. He needs to open the second bottle if he's going to do it up good.

He declines to fill the lantern. Tonight the hiss of the lantern annoys him. It interferes with the crackling fire and the night sounds—coyotes, owls, distant loons, whippoorwills, frogs, crickets. Half a moon shines down. Along with the glow from the fire, that will be ample light to continue to chop.

Sam stumbles on the way back to the jack pine, spilling half his wine. He swears at the ground that tripped him, then gulps the rest, losing his balance once again when he tips his head back to drink. He feels around on the ground with his hands and finds the axe lying in the woodchips at the base of the tree.

"Okay, motherfucker," Sam warns the tree. He takes a mighty swing like a baseball player, and misses the tree, losing his grip on the axe. The axe sails toward the fire ring…and the lawn chair where Deja's sleeping. THUMP, onto the sleeping bag. The chair flops over. Deja yips. The axe bounces into the fire.

"Oh fuck oh fuck oh fuck." Sam stumbles down the hill toward Deja.

He kneels next to the chair and frantically feels all over the cloth. He finds the warm spot on the sleeping bag where Deja had been—the blade has cut the fabric right through. Frantically, he pats the ground in the shadows. "Deja! Deja!"

Suddenly, she appears between his legs, the odor of fresh puppy shit wafting upward. He turns back to see that it covers the toe of his boot. By the good grace of God, Deja had gotten up to do her business, just before the axe slammed into her nest.

Sam mumbles a thanks. He cleans off the toe of his boot with a twig and then straightens up the lawn chair and sleeping bag. They sleep until the morning birds wake them, just as dawn begins to break. Then they drive home in the predawn, Deja curled up in Sam's lap, asleep.

Sally talks Maureen into an early morning ride on the trail before she heads to Fargo with Pop. They notice a wisp of smoke wafting up from the fire ring and ride up to check. The axe handle is burned off except for a couple inches near the head. An empty wine bottle lies next to the stump. Another bottle is half full, its cork on the ground. A sleeping bag lies in a jumble next to the lawn chair.

Neither sister comments. Sally is the first to wheel her horse around, and lope back to the trail toward Maureen's.

"Yup, I know you saw the truck at the bridge on your way to Fargo and back home," Maureen tells her sister over the phone. "It's dark and I just checked. There's a thunderstorm brewin'. The truck's still there. What the hell do you care anyway?"

"What's that s'posed to mean?" Sally asks. "He's my friend. Of course I care."

"Exactly how many 'friends' like Sam didja have in Oregon?"

"I beg your pardon!"

"It's time we had a talk, little sister."

"And you're the expert on relationships, right?" Sally replies. "My lesbian sister! Ha!"

"Oh, that was a cheap shot. But I'm gonna let it go this time."

Maureen continues, "You been with so many idiots, abusers, and liars. And when you found all three wrapped into one, you married 'im. I'd like to say yours is a marriage of some sorta convenience. People do that all the time. At least they're gettin' something out of it. But, other than Pop, there ain't one damn thing in this marriage for you. Same goes for Bill. Except 'least he's got another woman to screw in his spare time."

"You don't know Bill's bein' unfaithful," Sally snaps.

"If you can't see it, I'm not even goin' there," Maureen responds. "Listen, Sam has been my friend and neighbor for a lotta years. He'd do anything for anyone, long as there's an honesty about it. You sure didn't act like you were married when he brought you those first two bottles of wine. You flirted with him and led him on. That was your cue to say, *My husband and I will enjoy this wine*. And when he asked you to go down the river, after he found out you're in such a terrible marriage you don't dare go home when Bill's there, that was when you shoulda said, *No thanks* and just gone home."

"I've never told Sam anything other than I don't know what I'll do…and we agreed what the deal is."

"MY GOD! Seriously? What about when he recorded your rides at Detroit Lakes? Could it have been any more obvious he was fallin' in love with you?"

"I'm not leavin' Bill. He's changed. If Sam hasn't figured that out yet, that's his problem."

"My guess is that he did. But don't you dare do anything for him for Father's Day from the puppy, or call and ask about her, or find any other excuse. Just walk away and stay away."

Sam's taking a longer than usual canoe trip. Instead of putting in at the dam like he always does, he has the pot-growing neighbor drop them at the headwaters of the river upstream, twenty-some miles by road. Sam has always wanted to canoe the river's entire length. He won't make it to the bridge by home until the next morning if he paddles all night, too. After a day's rest, he plans to do the last twenty miles below his place.

When the storm hits just before midnight, Sam uses his raincoat to make a tent for Deja to huddle under. He paddles near the lee shore to stay out of the gusty winds. Finally, when the rain quits, Sam changes into a dry sweatshirt. He settles Deja inside his shirt to keep them both warm.

They arrive home at dawn. Sam drives the golf cart up to the fire ring and cleans up the mess he'd left Sunday morning. Examining the axe, he realizes it will need a new handle. In the nearby mud, he notices two sets of horse tracks.

He calls Pop.

"I can handle it for a few days," Sam offers. "How about Thursday?"

Pop agrees. The remodeling is nearly complete anyway.

CHAPTER 13

CANOED ALL NIGHT

"Sam, you look a mess."

His eyes are hollow, with the bottoms rimmed in black. He hunches forward in the therapist's chair.

"Got a wild hair up my butt. Decided to canoe the river from where it starts up north, all the way to where it dumps into the Crow Wing. Forty miles by road. Through ten lakes. Not quite forty hours in all. Two portages around real dams. Four or five portages around beaver dams. Lost count of the deadfalls I had to maneuver around or over. You ever canoed at night? Then took a day off and canoed all night the next night?"

"And Sally?" Laura asks.

"SIDAS WAPBO. It's over…"

He adds, "Had a lotta time to think on the river." He takes an envelope from his shirt pocket and pushes it across the desk it toward Laura. "Here's somethin' I wrote during my winter takin' care of the ranch. It's really nothin', but if you want, maybe we can talk about it next time."

After Sam has left the office, she calls the front desk. "Hold my next appointment until I call."

Summer 1957

"Tell Ma you found me...under this tree... dead from a broken neck," the little boy said with detached numbness. "Maybe I'll just fall outta here right now..."

His sister stood below the tree fort, which was fifteen feet up in a huge, sprawling white oak. She pleaded, "Why do you keep doing this? You're really gonna get it this time."

She was his oldest sister. He was eight, she was thirteen.

He gazed ahead, as if intently watching a fox in the meadow on the other side of the swamp. She could see the clean streaks the tears had made when they'd run down his grimy face.

She warned, "I can't lie to her. Just come home and get it over with."

"Was Daddy mad I wasn't home when he left for work?" the little boy asked.

"Yup. Plenty. I told him I'd write down your chores and give you the list."

She thought for a few seconds. "Hey! I got an idea. Why don't you go to the chicken coop and start cleanin' it? I'll tell Ma that's where I found you! That you overheard 'em talking 'bout it...and went right out there on your own and got busy on your way home from Sparky's."

His sister sensed she was being watched. She turned and looked up the hill toward the house. Their mother was standing in her house dress and apron not twenty feet away, arms folded and her face chiseled into a glaring frown.

The girl gasped. Instinctively, the little boy peeked around the tree trunk, thinking she had seen a garter snake. He saw it was Ma. The little boy returned to his expressionless gaze. He closed his eyes and bit his lip.

Ma ordered the girl, "Get back to the house! The twins are throwin' a fit."

The girl hurried up the hill past her ma, without looking back.

"As if I ain't got enough to do, I need to come down here and round up a bad little boy tryin' to get out of his chores. Boy, if you aren't on those porch steps right behind me, your bicycle's goin' to the dump..."

She turned and leaned into the hill as she marched up it, holding her house dress in a knot thigh-high with one hand to keep it from tangling in the raspberry bushes.

The little boy hesitated. Maybe I'd rather be dead, he wondered. Would it feel like I was flying free as a bird that half second before I hit the ground with the top of my head, snapping my neck? And then what? Heaven? I doubt it. Hell, most likely. That's where bad boys like me end up.

Or maybe there's nothing at all? What would that be like? To not even BE?

His ma shrieked, startling the little boy from his reverie. "Don't forget to find yourself a switch!"

That was a delicate task, finding the sapling you'd be spanked across the bare butt with. Too wimpy of a switch, and you'd have to go back into the wood lot and find a bigger one, then get switched harder. Too big of one, and you only caused yourself more pain.

He scrambled down the tree like a squirrel. Where there wasn't a branch to step on, he and the neighbor kid Sparky had nailed 2x4s as foot- and hand-holds.

He didn't know for sure how old Sparky was, except that he was two or three grades ahead of his big sister. Sparky wasn't really a neighbor. He was from Minneapolis. Got into some sort of trouble and was sent to his grandparents for the summer. They both worked and weren't around much, and there wasn't much for Sparky to do way out there in the country. The little boy had just been glad for the new neighbor kid to be the big brother he needed. And so were his ma and daddy.

But soon there were things about the new neighbor kid that troubled the little boy. Sure, he'd put old wagon wheels and a handle on the wooden milk crate for the little boy to put the water bucket in for the chickens. And together they built the tree fort.

But Sparky also caught big fat tadpoles just to squash 'em with his fist on the old barn's concrete steps. He urged the little boy to do it, too, threatening that if he didn't, he'd tell little boy's ma he'd caught him lookin' at dirty pictures.

Sparky had also showed him some pictures of women who were undressed. The little boy could tell by Sparky's long leers that something wasn't right about looking at them. But he didn't know what.

And then Sparky had asked him if he'd ever seen his sisters undressed. The little boy didn't want to see the new neighbor kid anymore after he made him look at those pictures. But his ma and daddy sent him over there just about every day, to get the little boy out of their hair.

The little boy hurried up the hill. His daddy had cut down a red oak at the edge of the yard two summers before. And from around the stump grew a couple dozen suckers. They were as tall as the little boy then, and about as thick as a man's forefinger where they rose from the stump edge. Stripped of their branches and leaves, they snapped like a buggy whip.

Sometimes they were hard to break off, so the little boy left a little camping hatchet stuck in the stump. He learned that the last thing he wanted to do was spend time jerking and yanking and twisting at a stubborn switch while his folks waited, getting madder and madder.

The little boy knew the drill. His ma sat in the armchair, with the ottoman in front of her. For the moment, he held the switch like an altar boy carries a candle holder, and stood in front of her, facing away.

The other older kids except for his big sister, busied themselves at the dining room table. His big sister coaxed the twins out onto the porch with crackers and lemonade. But the third sister, the spoiled one, sat on the couch and pretended to watch television. From the corner of the little boy's eye he could see she was smirking.

His ma yanked his pants down to his knees and gasped, "Oh! What a damn stink! What a stinkin' mess!"

He closed his eyes and shook like willow leaves in the wind. He wasn't yet bent over the ottoman, but expected something to sting him or send him reeling, probably the switch or his ma's hand, and he didn't know where it would land.

He hadn't eaten since lunch, before he was sent to the older neighbor kid's five hours before, but he felt like he was going to vomit. He wretched, but nothing came up, his eyes feeling like they were popping from their sockets.

"Your underpants!" shrieked his ma. "Where are they? I thought we were down to just two who need diapers!"

The last thing the little boy remembered before he woke up in the shower, with his big sister washing him, was the twins crying and his big sister screaming, "Leave him alone, GODDAMNIT!"

After he was clean and dried off, both the little boy and his big sister got beat with the red oak switch, she through her jeans, and him on his bare bottom. They got beat again in the morning when their daddy woke up after working the night shift.

Sam's already in the trailer when Sally pulls up. She doesn't get out of her truck to check on their progress or greet Deja, who stands in the doorway, wagging her tail in excitement.

"Have a good day" is all she says.

Still, as she drives away, Sam feels an emptiness in his chest that longs to be filled. He can fill it with sorrow and self-pity, a bottle of wine, or work. He's not in the mood to step outside what he's feeling and examine it objectively. Mercifully, Pop wants to get right to work.

All the plumbing is in, so they air test it then install the paneling. They fill the water tank on top of the trailer, and make sure the pump and hot water heater work. Trim around the shower needs a second coat of polyurethane. They already know the refrigerator works. A twelve-pack of beer to toast their efforts cooled nicely in it when they installed it a week ago. The dealership will come fetch the trailer Friday and park it there while the painter replaces the name of Kate's sister-in-law with Sally's.

"I'll have 'em deliver it to the farm soon as they're done, Tuesday or Wednesday, so Sally can use it on her birthday weekend. Need to spill the beans a couple days early, so I can have the gooseneck hitch installed on her truck, and she can get used to drivin' it before she goes back to Detroit Lakes for the district barrels."

Sam nods.

"Want me to give you a call so you can be there when she realizes it's hers, since you worked so hard on it? Bill won't be around."

"Naw. I'm just gonna…stay out of it, Pop."

"I understand. Anyway, you did a helluva job. Now, where's that beer? I'd like to get just a little drunk with ya."

Laura gets right down to business. "You've told me about a few episodes of pretty intense anger, and some recent drinking binges."

Sam shudders and shakes his head.

"Those behaviors are not necessarily simply PTSD. We may actually be dealing with a couple of things. The story you gave me to read—did those things really happen to you?"

Elbows on his knees, Sam gazes blankly at the floor. "That's me…that's everybody, including Sparky. And I went along with that on my own. I mean, I didn't do nothin' to stop it."

"Why did you write that?"

"I just needed to finally tell somebody. That first winter after Karen died…on the ranch…I sent it to Jill. She got so angry, she confronted Dad. I wish she hadn't done that. That's when he disowned me for good, wrote me off as crazy, as did the rest of my sibs, except for Jill. I still write to Dad every couple months, but I never heard back from him since then."

Laura asks, "That's not the whole story, is it?"

"No," Sam whispers. "There were other things Sparky did that I didn't put in the story—the first stuff."

He massages his temples and takes a deep shuddering breath. "I had no idea what it was all about. He would sit on the toilet, and make me watch. He had me touch him, too…and help him. Called it 'whipped cream', and we both laughed about that."

"How did you feel about being there when he was doing that, and asking you to help him?"

"I felt there was something naughty about it, that somehow it was wrong, but didn't know exactly what.

"Then one time Sparky came over to our house. He asked my big sister if she liked whipped cream, busted out laughin' when she said *Yes*. Guess I was s'posed to laugh, too. But I couldn't. Somehow I knew I'd done somethin' real bad."

"Why did you feel you couldn't go to your parents?"

"You gotta understand," Sam explains, "We were a big family, seven kids. Mom and Dad both worked so hard. They didn't have time to put up with any baloney from us kids. You screwed up, you got beat. That took care of the problem real quick. I got beat more than the others. I was always screwin' up, being out in the woods and forgettin' to come home on time, gettin' less than perfect grades at school, bustin' things around the house playing ball."

"How did that make you feel about yourself, bearing the brunt of their anger?"

"Honestly? Felt like I wasn't worth a shit. Every wakin' minute, I lived in fear of screwin' up…and gettin' beat. I didn't have anyone to protect me. My oldest sister, Jill, was the closest I had to a protector. But she was no match for Ma and Dad."

"So when Sparky became your friend, a kind of big brother, and did nice things for you, that was pretty special, right?"

"Of course. None of the other kids ever did anything fun with me. I was given a lotta leeway when I was with Sparky. I s'pose my folks were glad to have me outta their hair. Trust me, they weren't monsters. But I felt everything was my fault, even being taken advantage of by Sparky. I knew if I'd told 'em, I would have gotten beat."

"How long did this go on?"

"Just that one summer and he went back to the city."

"How did you break away from him? How did that friendship end?"

Sam gazes out the window, unblinking, a tear forming at the corner of each eye. Finally, he turns to Laura.

"The day…the day he raped me," Sam admits hoarsely. "Well, thank God my folks wouldn't let me outta the farmyard after that. I was grounded the rest of the summer. No bicycle. Extra chores. No swimmin' lessons with the other kids. I pretty much worked all day. When Sparky did come over, there was no place for him to get me. Jill sensed something horrible had happened. I think she mighta scared him away with our little 22 rifle."

Sam buries his face in his hands and begins sobbing. His shoulders shake. Mucous drips from the corners of his mouth. Soon he can't catch his breath. Laura lets him weep for several minutes without interfering.

Eventually, he sits back up, blows his nose, and wipes his eyes. "That's why I love kids so much. That's why I'm there for them. I can pick an abused kid out of a crowd from a hundred yards away. Kids…gosh, they're all so perfect. No kid I know will ever have to keep a secret like mine 'cause he's afraid he'll get beaten. I get so angry when I hear about a kid gettin' hurt."

Laura offers, "Now I can see the pattern, and how it's all interconnected—your PTSD-like episodes, hypersensitivity to criticism, and maybe even the part where you choose jobs that don't last very long…and intimate relationships. Or, on the other hand, why you now avoid serious commitment altogether. What you went through back then, and the burden you've been carrying…we can't change the past, but we can learn to live with it and even thrive."

Sam suddenly sits straight up, and stares out the window. Laura can tell he's remembering something by the faraway look in his eyes.

"What is it?"

"Somethin' I said to Sally when we're having dinner on my birthday—about her husband's behavior. I'm wonderin' if I shouldn't take my own advice. I told her there are only two things we can change with respect to another person. First is our perception of them, and second is our proximity to them. And the rest is up to them…"

Laura's questioning look tells Sam she isn't catching the drift.

"It's like I've been irrevocably married to my past," Sam explains. "I've been leaving it up to the past to heal itself, which it hasn't. And I've tried to remove myself from the past, and admittedly have done a pretty good job of it for the past five or six years, but… Do you think it's possible I can change my perception of the past and find some semblance of peace with it?"

"You just put our work here in a nutshell. And yes, I believe that you, of all people I counsel, can find the peace you're finally seeking."

His eyes moisten and he reaches for the hanky in his back pocket. "Where do we begin?"

"The key to managing this is to continue observing your thoughts and feelings, a conscious step you interject between the trigger and the reaction. We already know the triggers. They start with the important people in your life. Back then, it was your folks; more recently it was Karen, then your daughter. When someone who you feel you should be able to trust leaves you to the wolves (Sparky, Karen's relatives, your brother), you become overwhelmed with grief and guilt, and you relive the pain of being abandoned all over again.

"It will surely take some time and work, but I think you'll surprise yourself. Just keep working on observing and sharing, okay?"

"If all that's true," Sam asks, "why do I still feel like I got a hand dealt from the bottom of the deck?"

Laura sucks in a deep breath and lets it out slowly. "Your life could have been different, but it still has been perfect. By that, I mean, as we talked about in our first session, some say from *up there* you chose your parents, your situation to be born into. You volunteered. Look at it that way, if you can. Even carrying this burden, look at all the good that's come from and through you."

Sam cries quietly into his hands once again.

"Would you say it's been worth it?"

Sam nods. "Yeah. Yeah."

"You can learn to choose now," Laura says, "but it's going to be hard work."

Sam smiles to himself.

"What is it?"

"I once wrote in my journal: *If it wasn't for the wine, T-bone steak, and sex, God would have a pretty hard time talking anyone into coming down here.* Two outta three ain't bad, huh?"

Laura smiles.

"One more thing," she adds. "For many who've lived through childhood sexual abuse, it's helpful to eventually confront their abuser, if possible."

"Oh yeah." Sam wrings his hands. "He's very alive. Maybe fifteen years later, after I was married and living closer to the city, he moved into his grandparents house, and has since then, more or less, become a pillar of the community. Saw the son of a bitch at a funeral down there in my hometown two years ago. After the service, he acted like I was invisible, but he knew who I was because I was with Jill. I caught him looking at us a couple of times. And then he'd turn away real quick."

"Confronting him is not a decision you have to make right now. You don't have to go there; it's only an option. We'll talk about it another time. It's your call when and how you deal with Sparky, personally, or if at all. The important thing is that you're over the hump now. You've taken the biggest step. Congratulations! You just graduated from being a solitary victim to taking your first steps down the path of a survivor, where there's plenty of help and support if you want it."

"I'm not so sure I want to go there," Sam confides. "Karen's gone. Now Sally's gone. I'm alone and, gettin' my head screwed on straight or otherwise, I am likely gonna stay alone."

Laura asks, "What about little Sammy? He's still here. He's still in pain from it. Only you can help him to heal. And your healing, your survival from the tragedy is his gift to you. Waddya say?"

"I dunno. I've been fucked up a long time. It's a way of life. Right now I'm shakin' just from talking 'bout it." Sam stares at his hands. "Life's not too bad…when I'm not thinking about *it*…"

"Believe it or not, your life just got better. Care to let me walk this path with you again next week, Sam? Sammy?"

He stands slowly, his head hanging and his moist eyes staring at the floor. "Do you really think I can change? That I can break that pattern of broken trust? That I can be happy, stay happy…like a normal person?"

"What's Little Sammy saying?"

"He's saying, *Keep talkin', Sam. It's time to call a spade a spade.*"

"What do you mean by that?" Laura asks sympathetically, her hands folded.

Sam squints out the window. "Sure, I could confront Sparky and get my revenge. But I don't know if I can forgive my parents."

He glances at the clock on the wall. "That's a whole other session on the couch, I think."

"I don't need details," Laura says. "For now, just give me an idea what you're thinking."

"My first big disappointment, disillusionment with them and life in general. My first grade teacher recommended I skip second grade and go right to third. But they wouldn't allow it. My tenth grade geometry teacher gave me a fifty point penalty for chewing gum in class. She was a friend of theirs and they sided with her—over me forgettin' to spit out my gum after lunch!

"I got an F that quarter and it cost me graduating with Honors. Otherwise I would have gotten an A. Dad took away my driver's license for six months of my senior year for gettin' a speeding ticket, only ten miles per hour over. When I went to court, the judge told Dad he would've given me a suspended sentence because it was my first offense and every kid deserves at least one break.

"That's enough…" Sam waves his hand as if pushing the tough memories to the side. "By then, my personal motto was already *FTW (Fuck the World) and where's the keg party this weekend?*"

"What is Sammy feeling about that stuff?" Laura asks.

"He says," Sam offers, smiling while wiping his eyes with his shirt sleeve, *I'm in if you're in.* And he wants to take Deja and have a campfire this evening…and roast venison sausage…and make s'mores…and sip homemade wild grape wine…and put Elvis on. He wants to help me figure out a way to make peace with my dad, and confront Sparky. He's thinkin', in person with both of them will do the job he needs, but let's think about it when we go swimmin' in the river with Deja after our picnic."

"You should've seen my girl yesterday, Sam!" Pop says into the phone. "Wait a sec, the water works seem to have come on."

"She likes the trailer, huh? You pulled it off and she didn't have a clue?"

"Sally said to make sure to tell you thanks. So, thanks."

"Well," Sam answers off-handedly, "it was just a job, ya know. Sam for hire."

With a sudden urge to unburden himself, he asks, "Pop, can you keep a secret?"

He then describes his boyhood experiences with Sparky, in full and painful detail. It's easier said over the relative safety of the phone line.

"Goodness, my boy. Somehow, by the grace of God, you survived and turned your ordeal into a special kinda love, especially for kids. Sadly, that's not always the case. Thanks for sharin'. This has to be so difficult. I'm here for ya…anytime day or night."

"And thank you," Sam says quietly. He hears Pop sniffling again.

Pop never knew for sure, but he thought his wife's brother Alan, who lived with Emma's parents, did something horrible to his boys. His wife's mom was watching them. He went to pick up the boys after work. They were about six and eight, both in the shower on full blast, screaming and sobbing—ice cold and naked. She was standing there with a leather belt smacking it into the palm of her hand so they didn't dare try to escape.

She shrieked that they'd been telling terrible lies about Alan. Lies so unspeakable she wasn't gonna repeat them. Pop rushed past his mother-in-law, shut off the water and got the boys dressed and warmed up.

He and Emma never left them over there again. Neither little boy would tell what made their grandma do that to them. In fact, they said she was right—they had lied. What they didn't tell Pop and Emma was, she'd told them if they ever breathed a word of their lies, nobody would believe them and they'd go straight to hell. *That* the boys believed.

The terrible family secret. Little boys turned into troubled youth. Troubled youth turned into…Bill and Robert.

He'd never said to them, "I'm here for ya…" That would've meant he acknowledged that there was, indeed, a terrible family secret.

CHAPTER 14

PLEASE FORGIVE ME

Bill takes the day off work Friday so he can shop for the items Sally wants for her new trailer. Dishes and glasses, silverware, bedding, food…anything and everything a camping trailer could ever need.

She comes home from work to find Bill in her trailer putting those things away, and rewards him with kisses.

Also as a surprise, Bill had bought some large bags of wood shavings for the horse compartment. He'd never before spent a nickel on Sally's horses. He'd even moved both horses into barn stalls, with fresh straw on the floors, fresh hay in the feed bags, and fresh water in the pails.

Besides that, he gives Sally a mushy card for her birthday, the first time since they were married he'd ever even acknowledged it. Bill's five days early with the card. It matters none to Sally that the card is so early; she's just grateful he remembered at all.

Bill and Sally are up early together Saturday morning, topping off the water tank and lighting the hot water heater. He tosses two hay bales into the truck bed, and sets a five-gallon bucket of oats in the tack room.

It's a two-day show. Bill apologizes he can't make it and that he won't be able to bring Pop over like they'd planned. He says he has to get back to Grand Forks by noon because somebody got sick and he has to man the trade show booth until at least eleven that evening.

They make a few calls, deciding that Pop will go with Sally to Detroit Lakes, and Maureen will bring him back to her place later.

Bill goes to fetch Dakota. Sally smiles when she hears him talking softly to her prize mare.

Suddenly Dakota hollers and rears, raising a hell of a ruckus so Bill can't lead her out into the barn alley. Sally runs to help. She knows he isn't particularly comfortable with horses, even with a pussycat like Dakota. But she appreciates his efforts at any rate.

Bill turns his attention to Sparky in the next stall, who leads out obediently.

Sally and Bill kiss goodbye. He wishes her good luck and slaps her on the butt.

Dakota's way off her game today. On the first run, she pulls up at the first barrel. Sally has to crank her hard to get Dakota to circle it. Already out of the money with that error, Sally just lopes her mare through the rest of the run.

Huddled around the camcorder, Sally and her girlfriends review the poor performance several times, seeking a clue as to what might be happening. Everything was fine until Dakota had to put the brakes on and bend.

Sally pulls off Dakota's saddle, then heads over to the other side of the arena to give a friend's horse a massage under the shoulder blade.

With Dakota tied to the trailer after that run, Pop can see she isn't touching her hay. Instead of standing relaxed, like she always does, she fidgets. Pop's instincts tell him something isn't right. He uses his walker to shuffle back and watches her intently from a yard away. She uses a hind leg to paw at her belly, then hunches up, her belly sucked in. Pop approaches alongside and runs his hand over the horse's flank. Dakota sucks her belly in further and arches her back. The mare tries to lie down, but can't because the rope is tied short. Pop slaps her butt hard to keep her from putting her weight on the rope.

"Oh shit!" Pop exclaims loudly to anyone within earshot.

"What is it?" asks a young girl riding by.

"Go get Sally, quick! Her horse is colicking!"

The word "colic" at a horse show spreads like an Oklahoma wildfire. The girl finds Sally and gives up her horse to her, who gallops the horse back, sliding to a halt. Someone else grabs the reins as she runs to Dakota. Folks are streaming over to the trailer.

"ANYBODY GOT ANY BUTE?" Sally hollers. "Anybody know if there's a VET on the grounds?" She keeps slapping at Dakota to stay upright.

"Get her walkin'!" Pop yells.

Frantically, Sally tugs at the rope and unties her mare, her fingers flustered and fumbling. She ponies Dakota behind a borrowed horse at a fast walk. Her ailing mare resists, Dakota's nose pointed straight ahead from the pressure on the rope. Other riders follow close behind, bumping her, urging the sick mare to move and stay upright.

They stop at another trailer, when a woman comes running out with a big syringe of bute. Others whip Dakota lightly to keep her from dropping to the ground. The shot of bute in her neck muscles takes only seconds to work. The mare's head droops, her ears go flaccid, her eyes glazed to emptiness. The horse shudders with her whole body, her legs go rubbery and she looks as if she's going to flop over.

A crowd gathers around Dakota, and with their shoulders and hands hold her up until the initial blast-like effects of the bute wear off.

"A VET!" Sally demands frantically. "Anybody know if there's a goddamn vet on the grounds?!!"

The man on the loudspeaker blares, "Sally, he's comin' around the end of the arena!"

When the vet finally arrives, he administers Dakota oil in both ends. "Now, we wait."

Between Sally and her girlfriends, they pony the sick mare for two hours, waiting for her to relieve herself. But the twisted gut isn't giving in.

"This isn't working!" Pop says. "Sally, call Sam! I know about what he can do, from Maureen. If you don't call him, I will!"

She immediately starts dialing. "Sam…Sam…" Sally weeps into her phone. "Dakota's dyin'. Colic. Nothin's workin'…"

"Detroit Lakes?" Sam asks. "Keep 'er moving. I'm on my way. Let's see if we can get her back here to my place. Call Maureen to meet us there. Wait a minute—she just pulled in."

Maureen, in her work as a nurse practitioner, is used to driving the country roads in the hills at breakneck speeds. She has yet to be late for a baby's arrival. She hasn't missed anybody dying either, assuming they were still alive when she got the call.

"What're you gettin'?" Maureen asks as they speed down the gravel road.

Sam's eyes are closed, visualizing Dakota. This is another of his gifts—intuiting where problems are. He's helped Maureen a dozen times on tough cases.

"It's on Dakota's left side, just in front of her flank. It's not colic either. I don't know what it is. An infection of some sort." He gets a flash of Dakota rearing in the stall back at the farm. "Ask Sally what happened in the stall at home."

Maureen dials her number. "Tell the vet to give Dakota penicillin. Sam says get enough for us to bring home for a bunch more mega-doses."

"What good would that do?" Sally demands in frustration.

"Don't argue with me! Just do it, goddamn it! Tell the vet to give her the biggest dose he dares. And what happened in Dakota's stall at home? Sam says he thinks something happened there."

Sally replies, "Well…nothing much. Bill went to fetch her for me, but she was fussin' and wouldn't come outta the stall with him. What are you talkin' about? How would Sam know anything about that?"

"Dear, you don't know everything about this man…"

When Maureen and Sam pull into the lot, Sally's walking Dakota on foot. The horse is calm—in an eerie way, like a person on morphine waiting for a painless death. Apparently the antibiotic is having some positive effect.

"I'll ride with 'er in the back," Sam says. "Have somebody else take Sparky. I'm gonna need the room."

"Pop and I'll be right behind," Maureen assures him, "in case she goes down or hurts you. We need a signal if you need to stop."

Sam suggests, "A rope hangin' out the back. If I pull it in, we got trouble."

Sally loads Dakota. She hooks a long lead rope to a ring in the front of the horse stall, and before shutting Sam and Dakota in, runs the rope out the right rear window.

"We're on our way!" Sally yells out the truck window. "Hang on."

She dials up her husband as she drives. In her haste, she mistakenly calls his apartment number. By the fourth ring she realizes Bill is at the trade show, and he'll have his cell phone with him. Just as she's about to end the call, a woman answers.

"Hullo?" She sounds drunk. "You get a new phone, honey? You almost here, Bill? Speak to me! Damn shitty cell service! Well, just in case you can hear me…I might start without ya, but don't worry, I won't finish without you!"

Sally disconnects. Her gut tightens. If she weren't driving hell-bent to Sam's place, she'd probably pull over and wretch.

She calls Bill's cell.

"You know you ain't s'posed to call me when I'm workin'," Bill snaps. "Make it quick!"

"I'm sorry. But Dakota's sicker 'n hell. She probably won't make it."

"So, waddya want me to do about it? She's your damn horse and your damn problem!"

"Well, I don't know. But Sam thinks somethin' might have happened in her stall. Did you see anything strange? She get into anything?"

"No! Fuckin' horse just didn't want to be led out. What's that damn Sam got to do with this anyway? Listen, I gotta get back to work. People standing around the booth wantin' to talk to me…"

In the background, Sally hears traffic noise, a car honking. Bill is apparently not inside the ice arena.

Not long after they leave the fairgrounds, Sam finds a hot spot on Dakota's flank. He holds his hands on it the entire thirty-minute trip to his place. Dakota's bowels finally move during the ride. If it was colic, that would've been a good sign. But it's runny and smells putrid, and that's a bad sign.

Dakota's weak and wobbly as Sally backs her out of the trailer at Sam's place. When Dakota reaches for the ground with her second hind foot, she stumbles and falls onto her butt, her front legs still in the trailer. The sick horse thrashes her head in intense pain. She can't get up by herself, nor can she roll out of the trailer.

"Get her outta there! Quick!" Pop hollers. "She'll suffocate like that!"

Sally, Sam, and Maureen scramble right over Dakota into the trailer. The three of them push on the mare's neck with all their might. One front hoof flails once, but then goes limp. Dakota's head slumps sideways onto the trailer floor. They can't budge her. Dakota's gulping air and grunting, her eyes rolling back in her head.

"A rope! A rope!" Pop hollers. "Around her neck—anywhere—doesn't matter at this point! Sam, your truck! Back it up here!"

Sam sprints to his truck. The women have knotted three lead ropes together and tied one end around Dakota's neck by the time he backs near the horse.

Pop instructs frantically, "A couple of wraps around the hitch! Don't tie the rope, just wrap it around the ball a couple or three times and you two hang on to it!"

Sam eases the truck forward. Dakota's eyes bulge and roll back in her head from being choked. The wraps begin to slip, so both women dig their heels into the driveway. One excruciating inch at a time, Dakota's head is pulled toward the edge of the trailer floor, and finally her head crashes clumsily to the ground.

"Let the rope loose!" Pop yells to Maureen and Sally, but they already had, and were stumbling over each other around behind Dakota to her head.

Dakota lies there, flat on her side. Her chest moves slowly with labored breaths, her eyes once again rolled back. The women are frozen.

Pop scrambles to the horse, while the other three stand with mouths agape. He begins hammering Dakota on the ribs with his walker, lifting it over his head and slamming it down. "Get up, goddamn it!" On the second try, Pop can barely pull it off Dakota.

"Pop!" Sally screams. "It's too late! Don't hurt yourself!"

She grabs him around the waist from behind, but he finds some strength and pushes her away.

"Kick 'er in the ass!" he orders Sally and Maureen. "You!" Pop points at Sam, "take over for me!"

Suddenly, Pop stumbles backward five or six steps, then keels over onto the gravel driveway. The three of them rush to him and drop to his side. His eyes are shut, but he's breathing. Beads of sweat are on his forehead and upper lip. He is deathly pale.

Pop's eyes blink open a slit. Then they grow wider, as if he's seeing the proverbial light and dead relatives coming to get him. A shit-eating grin spreads across his face, and the three bystanders really think he's leaving them. He lifts an arm and points behind them. Instinctively, they turn their heads to see where Pop is pointing. It's Dakota, standing next to the trailer.

"You crazy old son of a gun…" Sally mutters.

Sam and Maureen help Pop to the house. Sally walks Dakota slowly around the yard. The mare is still pawing at her belly. Once Pop is settled on Sam's couch, he comes outside to help Sally lead Dakota into the first barn stall, one he has partially framed up.

Maureen isn't far behind. "Waddya think, Sam?"

Sam runs his hands over Dakota's flanks. "The infection's spreading. I'll shoot her up with penicillin every couple hours. I'll just do my thing, see if it helps."

Maureen says, "I'd like to stay and help, but I think I better take Pop to the emergency room. He threw up, might have a concussion."

"Oh no…okay. Sally, you better go, too. Take my truck. Wait…first, can ya get me a few beers, jug of water, whatever's in the fridge to munch on? Oh yeah, coupla sage sprigs, on the shelf…and the abalone shell…the lighter…my eagle feather. I'm just gonna watch her for a few minutes…see if she'll tell me what she wants. Hurry. You better get Pop to Detroit Lakes…and I need that triple candle…and bring me the whip."

Sam's already going someplace. He doesn't seem to notice when they bring the items he requested and leave them on the stall ledge two feet behind him. He's standing with his back to the door, hands folded, head down. Sally starts to say something, but Maureen puts her finger to her lips.

Sam knows well the rules of spiritual healing. There are two ways to go about it. There's the plan based on complete faith, where the healer simply assists in expediting God's will. It's simple. He'll be an un-judging conduit who has no stake other than directing and focusing the Universe's limitless energy and love, to assist in either a healing or a transition, whatever His mysterious plan is.

Or Sam can attempt to direct the result himself, to heal the afflicted toward his personal desired end. To pay the ultimate price by giving his life force to Dakota, if that's what it takes.

He still loves Sally dearly. He'll do anything for her, even at his own expense, except enable her to be hurt more by Bill. And by being her ready friend, that's exactly what he's done, given her the time to find a sliver of hope in their hopeless situation. The least he can do is give her Dakota back, if he can.

Sam strips the dried leaves and flower buds from the sage stalk. He presses them into a ball, and lights them underneath with a match. Soon the yellow flame goes out, leaving behind glowing orange embers that will burn their way through, aided by a light fanning with the eagle feather.

He prays in a whisper as he wafts sage smoke over himself three times. "Dear God, help me to be the example of your infinite love, to use the eyes and heart of the Universe in all I do, and do the right thing for this horse."

He wafts smoke all over and around Dakota and the stall. The mare doesn't seem to notice. Her head still droops. She stands with her right front foot out, and her back legs splayed, to keep from falling over. She's too weak to paw at her belly anymore.

Sam offers the mare water; she takes none. He gives her another dose of penicillin in the neck; she doesn't even flinch. He places his hand on Dakota's flank. The hot spot has doubled, to about the size of a saucer. Strangely, there's a fire-hot pinpoint in the middle of the hot spot. It leaves a red mark on his palm, like a burn the size of a grape seed.

Sam falls into a routine. He holds his hands over the hot spot for ten or fifteen minutes, until the pain from the fire-hot pinpoint is too much for him. When he holds his hands off the mare's body an inch, the pinpoint still burns him. And even if he leans against the stall wall ten feet away, and thinks about the hot spot, the pinpoint burns that exact spot of his palm. His hand blisters.

"What the hell is this?" he asks, holding that palm toward the barn ceiling, toward the heavens.

He walks the ailing mare in slow circles in the stall. Sam rings out Dakota's energy field an inch above her hide, like you'd hand-squeeze water out of a cloth, from her head, down her front legs, along her torso, down her back legs, and out the tip of her tail.

A swig of beer. A bite of venison sausage. About four repetitions an hour.

Sam notices it's dark. How long has it been? He gives Dakota another giant shot of penicillin. She continues to fade, leaning against the stall wall, her head hanging with her nose in the straw. Her breaths are so shallow, the stalks of straw by her nostrils barely move. He knows if the mare crumples to the stall floor, it's over.

"Screw you, God! I'll do this myself!"

He pushes so hard on the hot spot, Dakota jumps sideways and bangs her head into the stall wall.

"So much for your goddamn infinite love!" Sam shouts. "You're gonna let this wonderful horse die, aren't you?"

He keeps pushing harder. Dakota bellows in pain, her first utterance since they began.

"Hey! Remember the night I came home from the Stone Creek muni? Drunk, pissed-off at you? This fuckin' hand you dealt me!"

Sam pushes harder on the mare's flank. She shies and kicks out sideways, catching him in the shin with her left rear horseshoe, ripping his pants, gouging loose a patch of skin the size of a silver dollar.

"Did you pay any attention to the twenty-three acre 'FUCK YOU GOD!' it took me half the night to trample out in the snow when it was twenty below zero?"

"Go ahead! Have her take out my other leg! Try again, motherfucker! You chickenshit, God!"

Sam pushes even harder on Dakota's hot spot. His hand burns where the pinpoint is, as if he's been poked with a red-hot welding rod.

He holds his hand aloft. "Is that all ya got?"

A stream of warm blood runs down his wrist toward his elbow. He quickly glances at his hand. There's a four-inch metal shaft, like an ice pick, buried in his palm all the way to the bone.

Sam squints and realizes immediately it's a busted-off needle from a hypodermic syringe.

With his other fist, he grabs hold and pulls it out. The pain is excruciating.

"You son of a bitch!"

He passes out from the pain, crumpling onto the floor of the stall.

Sally has resigned herself to losing Dakota. She stays at the hospital with Pop until the doctors are sure he's stable. It's two a.m. when she returns to Sam's place. The headlights of his truck shine in an arc as she turns into his driveway.

Suddenly, there's Dakota, standing right in front of the truck. Sally slams on the brakes, sending gravel flying. The mare bolts off the driveway, kicking her hind legs into the air, the lead rope trailing from the halter between her legs.

She bails out and hollers for Dakota. The horse obediently trots up to her and nickers. Thank God she's okay, but something isn't right. She runs with Dakota to the gate, unhooks the lead rope, and lets her into the pasture with Roy and Elvis. The only sources of light are a faint glow from the house, and a flickering candle in the barn.

"Sam! Sam!" Sally runs into the barn alley. "Oh Jesus! Sam, are you in here?"

He lies motionless in the straw, his right hand and arm covered with blood. His left pant leg and shoe are also soaked in dark red. She drops to the stall floor, fearing the worst. Frantically, she shakes him while muttering his name over and over.

Slowly, Sam opens his eyes. He rolls onto his back. Sally holds his shoulders and bends forward to embrace him gently.

He whispers, "Somebody tried to kill your horse… with this."

His hand opens to reveal the needle, which falls to the straw. Sally recognizes it from the syringes Bill used to vaccinate the cattle with. She feels the blood draining from her head but turns her full attention to Sam.

She whispers, "You did it. It's ok, Dakota's fine now. Let's get you into the house…"

Sam can't put much weight on the leg Dakota kicked. Sally drapes his bad arm over her shoulder. It bloodies her fancy western shirt, but she doesn't care. She blows out the candle sitting on the ledge and they inch their way through the dark alley of the barn and into the yard.

A coyote howls from the distant hills. Two more join in closer. And another just up the hill from the house. It's a dead-still night, so the air is heavy and sound carries seemingly from horizon to horizon. The chorus progresses—at least ten coyotes in all. Elvis, Roy, and Dakota whinny and blow nervously from the pasture. Sally can hear the thunder of their hooves as they run.

"Your fan club?" she asks. "Come on, cowboy, let's get you cleaned up and into bed…"

She helps him limp to the kitchen. The only light comes from around the corner in the bathroom. Fearing the overhead light would be too much for his overtaxed senses, she lights the two taper candles on the kitchen table. Sam winces as she helps him settle into a chair. He slumps heavily against the back and closes his eyes in pain. She begins running one side of the kitchen sink full of warm water.

Suddenly Sam stumbles to his feet, sways, and shouts, "Pop! How's Pop? Shit, I forgot about him!"

His legs immediately buckle and he slumps back toward the chair. Sally catches him and helps him ease onto the seat.

"Just a concussion. Shouldn't be a big deal. A couple days in bed."

Sally chuckles. "But he did admit about the pot when they found the one-hitter in his bag instead of his meds. The doctor was mad. Made Pop promise to go back on his regular meds."

Sam manages a weak smile and shakes his head.

She swings the faucet to the other sink and begins running cold water into it.

"Maureen got beeped to deliver a baby. I'll call her in the mornin' to take a look at you. You're gonna need antibiotics for the puncture in your hand. Got any?"

He points with a shaky hand to the cabinet beside the sink.

She gingerly unlaces and pulls off Sam's boots, then his socks which she drops into the cold water. She brings him a glass of water and a pill. He takes a long drink.

He fidgets with a shirt button.

"Let me get that…"

When she leans close, he can smell her hair. He closes his eyes and inhales deeply.

"What is it?" Sally asks.

"Nothin'..."

She helps him off with his shirt, then tosses that into the sink as well.

"We need to soak those pants, too."

"Naw, I'll just throw 'em away."

"Well, either way, I have to get at that leg and clean it up."

Sam undoes his belt, stands, and pushes his jeans down to his knees. He sits back down, stifling a moan. Carefully, Sally inches the bloody garment off his legs.

Ever so gently, she sponges and dabs at his hand and arm with warm, soapy water. He cringes and sucks in a quick breath when she touches the wound. Still, it's a strange but wonderful feeling to have Sally hold his hand. She's absorbed in her work, being careful not to hurt him again.

She finally asks, "Where'd that needle come from? How did it get stuck in your hand?"

"It was inside Dakota. I didn't know it was in there. She was dyin', I was pissed-off. Pushed on her as hard as I could...might've even been tryin' to put her out of her misery. I heard of folks stickin' a needle in the gut and pulling it out to kill a horse so as to not get caught. This needle probably wasn't s'posed to break off..."

"Who...who would do that to my mare?" Sally asks as her gut tightens and her head begins to go light.

Sam has his suspicions but decides now is not the time. Maybe there will never be a time. "It coulda been anybody...somebody jealous of your horse."

"And now this leg," Sally warns as she concentrates on Sam's wound. She dabs at it carefully with a wash cloth, moistening the dried blood.

She covers his wounds with antibiotic salve. There's a roll of gauze in the medicine cupboard. Carefully, she bandages his leg and hand.

When she finishes, she stands facing Sam. Without a word, she begins to slowly unbutton her blouse. His face is questioning. She points to the blood stain on her shirt.

Sally whispers, "Sam, you gotta forgive me. But I want to be with you tonight. I want you to hold me. I want you to make love with me. But I won't ever be back. I just can't…please forgive me."

Shyly, she smiles a small fraction of that incredible smile through a trickle of tears down each cheek. She kisses him lightly on his forehead.

She reaches the bottom button of her blouse. "Better get this soaking right away."

He watches her slowly undress in front of him, down to her bra and panties. He has always found her womanly attributes incredibly desirable, but somehow he can't take his eyes off her face.

She leads him by the hand to his bed, where they both undress the rest of the way. The three-pack of condoms is right in the nightstand, where Sam had put it five years ago. But first, they hold each other, skin against skin… and simply breathe together.

Finally, as if he might break, she straddles him. With him inside her, rocking back and forth gently, she leans down, cradling his face with her hands, her tears falling onto his cheeks. And she remembers, but doesn't speak, what Sam said that day on the river… how wonderful making love is with someone who just wants to be with you, who even just wants to look at you, who just wants to touch you, just because you are you…

Just before dawn, little Deja growls from her crate in the spare bedroom, waking Sally. While Sam still sleeps, she loads Dakota into her trailer, then comes back in to shower.

The jingling of the shower curtain rings awakens Sam. He listens, eyes closed, to the water gently splashing. It's been six years since he heard a woman in his bathroom.

He's surprised when Sally walks into the bedroom with only a towel wrapped around her, hair wet and flowing in ribbons onto her shoulders. She drops the towel confidently and slides under the covers next to him. As she snuggles against him, her head on his chest, again they can feel each other breathe.

Suddenly, she begins sobbing and slides out of bed. She picks up the bath towel and covers herself like she's embarrassed before turning slowly and walking out of the bedroom, her free hand wiping under her nose.

She heads for the horse trailer where she has some spare clothes. The trailer door is shut, but not latched. She thought she'd put spare socks and panties in the drawer, but there are only socks.

After changing, she returns to the bedroom and bends to kiss Sam on the forehead, pausing halfway to take in his peaceful form. A single tear falls from the corner of her eye onto Sam's cheek. His eyes flutter open and search her face. Without a word, Sally straightens, turns, and retreats quickly.

After Sam hears the front door close, he sits up on the edge of his bed and listens out the window as Sally's truck and trailer start to pull away. Her truck stops halfway down the driveway. He hopes she's having second thoughts, that she's coming back. Her truck idles for a couple of minutes and Dakota stomps and whinnies with impatience. Sam hears her truck door slam, and the truck and trailer crunch over the gravel out of his yard.

He closes his eyes. *I don't know whether I should get down on my knees and thank you that it's over...or mow a twenty-three acre* Fuck You, God *in the meadow...*

When Sam finally ventures out of his bedroom, he sees that Sally had made coffee. Next to the coffeemaker sits his favorite old mug. On the rim, Sally's lipstick imprint. Under the cup, a note.

> *Dearest Sam, I know this song, too.*
> *I will love you for a million years,*
> *but it didn't work out, and I have*
> *to say goodbye.*

Sam picks up the cup. He's tempted to inhale the sweet aroma of Sally's lipstick like he always did with Karen's, like he sometimes still does out of habit once in a while. He pauses and shakes his head. No, he doesn't want to be reminded of Sally, of anything about her—especially her lips.

His bandaged right hand trembles and burns as he grips the cup tightly. He grits his teeth, takes one final look at the mug, and fires it into the concrete block chimney behind the woodstove. It explodes into hundreds of jagged bits. At the sound of the crash, Deja yips from her crate in the spare bedroom, jolting Sam back to reality.

"Hang on, little girl! Gotta clean this up…"

After Sam sweeps up the broken shards, he opens the screen door for Deja and finds something on the seat of his old metal deck chair. It's a CD and another note from Sally written on the back of a used envelope.

> *This fell out of the trailer cupboard and hit me right on the head. I don't even remember putting it in there. But I swear I heard a little voice telling me I should give this to you.*

He fills a new cup with coffee. The CD's cover features a guardian angel embracing a sleeping child. He hits Play and settles in at his kitchen table to listen, staring out the window.

Elvis and Roy stand by their empty grain buckets; they twitch and stomp to keep the flies moving. Sam is late with their breakfast. Deja sits on her butt watching them intently, just out of reach of their noses.

A woman sings softly, accompanied by a keyboard. Her voice is rich, gentle and comforting, exactly like an angel's.

> *How could anyone ever tell you*
> *You were anything less than beautiful?*
> *How could anyone ever tell you*
> *You were less than whole?*

*How could anyone fail to notice
That your loving is a miracle?
How deeply you're connected to my soul.*

The song is simple and haunting as it adds in a recorder and vocal harmony, building to beautiful expression of unconditional love. Sam's head droops onto his arms and he weeps until the end of the song, and for several minutes after.

He tucks the CD away in his bottom dresser drawer, under clothes he never wears anymore, and decides to forget it's there.

He waits until his voice clears to call Maureen.

Within ten minutes, Maureen arrives with medical bag in tow. It takes nine gut-wrenching stitches to close the wound on Sam's shin. The Novocain doesn't work any better above his shin bone than it had on his noggin. He isn't in the mood for brandy. It's the price he should pay anyway, he tells himself, for getting mixed up with Sally.

Maureen gives him a tetanus shot. She tells Sam that Pop had another stroke, just a mild one thank goodness, and that he'll be staying in the hospital until they can dissolve the clots.

She can't help but notice the kitchen floor appears to have been recently swept. "You're turning into quite the little housekeeper, Sam," she teases.

"This damn hand," he lies as he holds it up a couple inches. "Dropped a coffee mug."

Maureen glances over at the wastebasket where she'd been discarding the gauze and wrappers and sees the hundreds of tiny pieces. Only the handle is still intact. "Oh no. Was it the one you've had since I've known you? As I recall, that was a pretty special cup."

"Not a big deal."

Following Maureen, he limps out onto the porch. "Sally and I said goodbye this mornin'. It's really over. I'm not angry, I'm just glad to know."

"You take care of yourself," Maureen orders. "If you get even a one-degree fever, get me on the horn immediately. You hear?"

"Yeah, yeah."

"Now get back inside. You should soak that hand right away."

As she shakes her finger, scolding him, Deja comes bounding from behind the house. She's growling at a rag she found, pawing at it and throwing it. They laugh at the puppy's antics.

Sam offers wryly, "To quote Dwight D. Eisenhower, *Things are more like they are today than they ever were.* Except now I got nine new stitches, a puppy, a coupla big ol' horses…and the rest of my life to…forget Sally. Dammit, it better not take that long."

ABOUT THE AUTHOR

I grew up just north of the Minneapolis city limits, when the north end of Anoka County was still *country* (and you could actually make it to Minneapolis in half an hour). There I hunted, swam, canoed, played ball and fished to my boyhood heart's content.

I stayed put for a while into adulthood, but upon approaching middle age, I realized the suburban sprawl had crept up and surrounded me. Home had become someplace claustrophobic. I joke that one Friday in 1984, I went "up north to the lake" and decided never to go back home. (Actually though, it was a planned move for our whole family.) I spent the next eleven years in west-central Minnesota–away from the big city traffic jams and with my beloved outdoors just steps away.

But the river of life beckoned. Twenty-one years and two divorces later, I looked around the next bend in the river, and found the quiet, friendly little burg of Nevis. It was smack-dab in the middle of northern Minnesota's beautiful rivers, lakes, forests, and hill country–the kind of place I'd always dreamed about living. I didn't realize it then, but I was finally home. For good. There's no better place on earth to live. And write.

Get the Rest of the Story
Watch for Book 2 of *Canoes in Winter* Coming Fall 2016

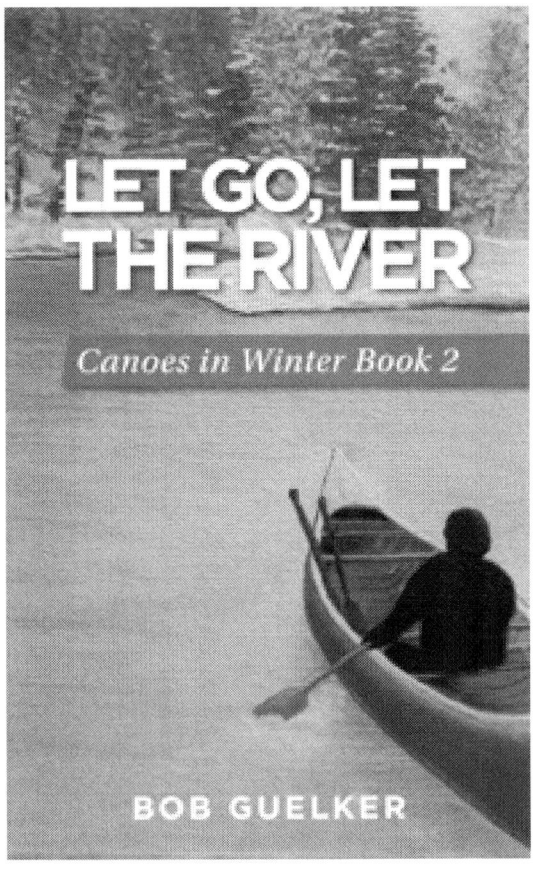